TO THE TYRANTS NEVER YIELD
NEVER YIELD
A Texas Civil War Sampler

TO THE TYRANTS NEVER YIELD

NEVER YIELD

A Texas Civil War Sampler

Kevin R. Young

Wordware Publishing, Inc.

 REGIONAL DIVISION

Library of Congress Cataloging-in-Publication Data

Young, Kevin R.
    To the tyrants never yield : a Texas Civil War sampler / Kevin R. Young.
      p.   cm.
    Includes bibliographical references.
    ISBN 1-55622-143-6
    1. Texas--History--Civil War, 1861-1865.   I. Title.
    E532.Y68   1991
    973.7'464--dc20   91-20143
                                             CIP

1506 Capital Avenue
Plano, Texas 75074

ISBN1-55622-143-6

10 9 8 7 6 5 4 3 2 1

9110

All inquiries for volume purchases of this book should be addressed to
Wordware Publishing, Inc., at the above address. Telephone inquiries
may be made by calling:

(214) 423-0090

Contents

DEDICATED TO
WILLIAM MARTIN CHASE
Whose passionate impatiences I know all too well
and
THE FOREST VIEW HIGH SCHOOL CLASS OF 1975
May our children never have to experience
what the class of 1860 did.

"Fiat Justitia Ruat Caelum"

Acknowledgments

Inasmuch as this work represents a period of writing, research, and study that has spanned over fifteen years of my life, there are numerous people spread out across most of the North and South who have had some bearing on this undertaking. In the writing and completion of this work, I would like to publicly recognize the following people, who, over those years, contributed directly and indirectly by thought, word, deed, and inspiration.

The staffs of Trinity University (San Antonio) Library; the Morris Library, Southern Illinois University at Carbondale; the Texas State Archives; the Eugene C. Barker Texas History Research Library at the University of Texas, Austin; the Gonzales (Texas) Public Library; the Goliad (Texas) Public Library; the United States Military Research Center, Carlie Barracks, Pennsylvania; the Archives of the United States Military Academy; the Alabama State Archives; the Mississippi State Library and Archives; the San Antonio Public Library, and the Daughters of the Republic of Texas Research Library, San Antonio.

Foremost, there is my family, and in particular, my mother, Myrtle Young-Clifton.

There are four individuals who have been more than instrumental in their help with this work. Gill Eastland of San Antonio and Michael Moore of Richmond, Texas, whose friendship, encouragement, and occasional use of their vast personal libraries were and are most appreciated; Wally Chariton, my publisher, without whose interest and prodding this book probably would have never been finished; and Dr. Stephen Hardin of Austin, whose critical eye and keen sense of history were always welcome.

In San Antonio, at the DRT Library, Sharon Crutchfield, former director, and her accomplice, the late Bernice Strong, former archivist, and Martha Utterback for their help in research and support; Dora Guerrea, director of Special Collections Department at the University of Texas (San Antonio) and Tom Shelton at the Institute of Texas Cultures.

In Austin, Larry Jones of the Confederate Calendar Works for his advice on period photographs; Jeff Hunt for his constant encouragement, his valuable research of Palmetto Ranch; Dr. Thomas Cutrer; Donnally Brice, Michael Green, and John Anderson at the Texas State Library and Archives; Ralph Elder at the Barker Research Center. In Gonzales, Dorcus Baumgartner; Danny Sessums of Lamar University (Port Arthur). In Dallas, Colonel (Ret) Ed Moore, USMC, for sharing information on his grandfather, General J. C. Moore; Robert "Hog" Jones of Corsicana. In Corpus Christi, Dan Kilgore; in McAllen, Jon P. Harrison; Vicki Betts of the library at the University of Texas (Tyler). In Goliad, Martha Mullenx of the *Texan Express*, who allowed some of these thoughts to jell in my weekly column from 1985-1987.

Outside of Texas, Lu Ann Parish of Corinth, Mississippi, for taking a Sunday afternoon to photograph Battery Robinette; Frank Thompson of East Berlin, Pennsylvania, for doing the same at Gettysburg; in Tennessee, Tim Burgess of White House, for sharing information of William Chase and Nancy Barnett at the Carter House, Franklin; Bill Gawltney of the National Park Service (Capitol Region) and his comrade Ted Alexander at Antietam National Battlefield; Elaine Owens of the Mississippi Department of Archives and History; Norwood Kerr at the Alabama Department of Archives and History; Jeff Long, who probably will not agree with most of this book, but who nevertheless encouraged me to pursue it; Lorraine and Jim Colwell; Marlyn Relles, Sue Rosenthberg-Lewis, Dean Hirshman, and Chuck Wilde, whose teaching (despite being in the North) during my formative years provided a lasting impression of what history and communication is all about.

I would like to recognize two groups of folks with whom I have spent the last fourteen years hobbying. Second Texas Infantry (reenactment) and the men and officers of the Texas Rifles and the 1st Confederate Brigade, past, present, and future.

And finally, but certainly not least, to Nanci, Kim, and of course, Christine Ann.

Introduction

On February 16, 1846, the government of the Republic of Texas ceased to exist. After nearly ten years of independence, the Lone Star Republic, by popular vote, surrendered its national sovereignty to that of the United States by act of annexation. The United States, in accepting Texas into its sacred union fold, added considerable southwestern territory to its borders. Within three years, the United States would triple its existing size and expand territorially to the shores of the Pacific, giving Americans, their culture, and their institutions, room to expand and grow. In surrendering their independence, Texians now gained the peace of mind of a strong federal government which would be able to protect its citizens from Mexican invasion and Indian raids. The people of Texas looked forward to continued growth under a system of government that they trusted (and most had been raised under) and which guaranteed their rights. They looked at this system of government with great trust. After all, these were the people who had rebelled against Mexico because its federal government had become a dictatorship and allowed centralists superior control over that of the states.

Something odd occurred as the Lone Star flag of Texas was lowered in somber ceremony at Austin that February day. The flag pole broke. It was as if the old Lone Star banner did not want to surrender itself to the new Stars and Stripes.

Nearly 15 years to the day later, the old Lone Star flag would once again be unfurled. It had taken that many years for the people of Texas to decide that being part of the United States was not in their best interests.

Annexation had been like a bad marriage. Its divorce was to be one of the messiest in history.

One of the participants of this saga, W. W. Heartsill of Marshall, wrote (perhaps with a little too much certainty) that, "In the after years, the man, woman, or child must be ignorant indeed, who has not learned that in November, 1860, Abraham Lincoln was elected president of the United States, and the people of the South construing this as an 'overt act' did in the following few months, put in motion the mammoth wheel of secession."[1] Heartsill and many of his fellows would be shocked to learn that less than 125 years after the event, many Southerners and Northerners are ignorant of not only the causes and effects of the struggle, but even who the participants were.

In September 1990, the Public Television Network launched its new season with a multihour documentary called "The Civil War." The brain child of writer/producer/director Ken Burns, the series received national attention and was acclaimed as a vehicle for the general public to at last learn something about the war. But the series seemed to create more issues than it answered. In the end, it was typical of how we have come to understand, or not to understand, this moment of our history.

For the novice venturing into the territory of the events of 1860-1865, a word of warning. Like all history, things are not as cut and dry as your junior high history teacher may have told you. Before I receive an avalanche of letters from junior high teachers, it is important to remember that in those formative educational years it is perhaps more practical to just stick with the routine and hope that a spark is triggered in some young mind to look further and deeper.

This is what happens to most of us. Something does trigger that spark and we do endeavor to look further and deeper into ourselves and our past. The past should never be disappointing — even if you find out your favorite historical hero didn't really utter his most famous words, or that he may have left his wife and child behind while he struck out for bigger pastures.

If you are lucky, you will perhaps find instead just how terribly human everyone was and, for that matter, is. In falling dust, when the marble man becomes but flesh and blood, you may latch onto a new brand of hero — the common person. After all, they are the stuff real history is made of.

In their lifetime, most Americans will have heard, at least once, about the Civil War. They will have probably observed the conflict

---

1   Heartsill, W. W., *Fourteen Hundred and 91 Days in the Confederate Army*, edited by Bell Irwin Wiley (Jackson, Tenessee: McCowat and Mercer Press, Inc., 1953), p. 1.

on their television via old films like *The Horse Soldiers* or made-for-television miniseries like "North and South" or the *Uncle Tom's Cabin* of modern mass communications, "Roots." They may have read a novel or even a real history book. As students, they may have taken a field trip to a museum where they gazed upon the artifacts and pictures. Perhaps their parents may have drug them off to something called a national park. They might even have taken some Sunday off to go see something called a reenactment where a bunch of folks dressed up like soldiers made mock war.

If they are lucky, they might, as a child, be fortunate enough to have a set of parents who, despite the pressures of twentieth century marriage, still endeavor to instill in them a sense of history. They might have the special breed of teacher that not only tells the bare facts but also encourages one to dig on and explore more than just the names and dates; to go to one of those national parks and stand in silence before a field and be able to imagine the sights and sounds of what terrors had unfolded; or to wander by the camps of something called a reenactment and look beyond the mock battle to see how Americans fought and survived for four years. One can imagine trying to keep warm in winter with only the clothes on your back, using only straw as your bedding, having only a worn blanket or two over you and some thin canvas to call home, and breaking your teeth on something called hardtack.

I have been fortunate, for all the above has happened to me. I not only know about the Civil War, I have come to understand it. My understanding of the people, places, and experiences of those four years continues to grow. I have also come to understand that knowing about something like the War Between the States is one issue. Putting it into historical context is another.

Historian James M. McPherson noted that "most of the things that we consider important in that era of American history — the fate of slavery, the structure of society in both North and South, the direction of the American economy, the destiny of competing nationalisms in North and South, the definition of freedom, the very survival of the United States — rested on the shoulders of those weary men in blue and gray."[2] McPherson and others have often made the dramatic point that the United States that we know

---

2   See Kennedy, Frances H., editor, *The Civil War Battlefield Guide*, (Boston: Houghton Mifflin Company, 1990), p. 6.

today did not start in 1776 with the Declaration of Independence or the writing of the Constitution or even the original formation of the Union. Instead, it emerged from the fire and blood of those four years when Johnny Reb and Billy Yankee slugged it out over such issues as different interpretations of the Constitution, the rights of states, property vs humanity, and such personal issues as defending one's home. The freedom that George Bush talked about in the Middle East is different from the concepts of freedom that both Jefferson Davis and Abraham Lincoln based their national policies on.

There is a lot written about the period. It is one of the most popular historical periods in print. There are literally tons of general histories — some good, some bad, a majority in the middle. There are some fantastically detailed histories of regiments, participants, and battles. There are published reminiscences and diaries which give us a look at the common person. Reading about the War Between the States is popular. We are drawn to the time when American fought American with a fascination unparalleled in popular historical studies. Magazines are devoted to it. An entire multimillion dollar semiprofessional sport/hobby has emerged from it. This was highlighted when over 12,000 living history reenactors gathered in 1988 to recreate the Battle of Gettysburg. In some areas it has taken on the form of a national religion. We have elevated "Old Abe" and "Mars Robert" as sectional saints. Over a five-night period, Americans tuned in a multihour documentary series on the Civil War presented on the Public Broadcasting System (the most watched single such program in the history of PBS). It was with some satisfaction and remembrance of several junior and high school science teachers that I note more people tuned in "The Civil War" than "Cosmos."

As producer/writer Ken Burns noted in his PBS series, we have tended to create our own images of this experience but have often been selective in our reality. Before 1861 only two American cities ever experienced total destruction at the hands of an invading army — Washington and Buffalo. After 1865 Atlanta, Columbia, Richmond, Chambersburg, Darien, and Lawrence (not to mention a good portion of rural Alabama, Georgia, and the Shenandoah Valley) could be added to the list. No foreign power did this. Americans wreaked these acts upon fellow Americans. In the name of the Union and the principal of one nation, we made war on each other. In a struggle that was designed to either preserve or break up the Union, another struggle emerged to dominate the experience — the rights of four million African-Americans. That struggle remains with us today.

People and governments sometimes attach different names to the same events. That is all well and good, in regards to matters of personal or official preferences, but can be somewhat confusing to people not so well informed when they venture into the realms of new learning. To start with, we should use the example of what name our national experience from 1860-1865 goes by. Most historians (and the North) prefer to call it the Civil War. This follows suit with their once popular usage of "the War of the Rebellion" during the latter part of the 19th century. Officially, the North considered the Southern secession as an act of rebellion. Thus, the War of the Rebellion, and now the Civil War. The South, of course, took and still takes exception to this, as they felt (and sometimes still feel) that secession was legal. So they prefer to call it the War for Southern Independence, or, since it was a conflict between the United States of America and the Confederate States of America, "the War Between the States." Some diehards also like to refer to it as "the War of the Northern Aggression." William P. Zuber, a veteran not only of the Arkansas and Missouri Campaigns, but of the 1836 Texas War for Independence, preferred to call it the "Confederate War" because the term was more brief and because it indicated that the Confederacy was really and justly an independent power. Today, the "Civil War" and "the War Between the States " are the two most popular, and still highly debated, terms used to describe the event.

Another example can be found in the names of the battles. The North preferred to name everything after the closest natural landmark, while the South selected the closest town or man-made landmark. So, depending on what side of the Mason-Dixon you hail from, you either called the first major battles Bull Run or Manassas; Wilson's Creek or Oak Hill; Shiloh or Pittsburgh Landing; Pea Ridge or Elkhorn Tavern; Antietam or Sharpsburg; Stones River or Murfreesboro; Fair Oaks or Seven Pines; Sabine Crossroads or Mansfield. On some battles both sides agreed — Gettysburg and Franklin are prime examples.

Several different names are also applied to the opposing forces. The United States troops can be Federals, the Union, and of course, Yankees (the rather descriptive term, "Damn Yankee" is traditionally applied after the Federals had gone through an area). Robert

E. Lee always referred to them as "those people." The Confeder-
ates can be Rebs, Rebels, Confederates, Secessionists, or "Secess."
Somewhere, the more pleasant, folksy names Johnny Reb and
Billy Yankee came about.

If the disagreement on preference of terms seems quaint, it does
clearly illustrate that we still debate the war with a vigor and
sometimes a vengeance. When Dr. Alan Orlins wrote in a letter to
Civil War Magazine that Robert E. Lee was our greatest traitor, a
storm of debate followed. The words "traitor" and "revered" were
redefined by readers. Issues of loyalty to state vs the federal
government were restated. One reader noted that if the federal
Constitution was violated by the act of secession, then the United
States was just as guilty as South Carolina when it admitted
Unionist western Virginia into the fold during the war as a
separate state. A Pennsylvania correspondent firmly stated that
"noble motives and high ideals cannot be used to rewrite history,
or the dictionary." In a wonderful example of modern revisionist
thinking, Dr. Orlins himself stated that "Robert E. Lee and his high
command were personally responsible for the futile deaths of
many thousands of Americans." The good doctor, in his American
patriotic pride, seemed to have failed to grasp one of the great
maxims of the war. We were not really a "united" states. Failing
to understand that, he went ahead to judge nineteenth century
people by his modern twentieth century standards.[3]

Laymen and professional historical writers have had a weary
road to travel. As the late PBS series illustrates, the winners are
allowed to write the critical essays. The epics of the war's history
and its causes have, therefore, been written by the likes of
Bruce Canton, Robert Penn Warren, Kenneth Stapp, and a host
of other Northerners. Southern historian Grady McWhiney complained that "a history written by Southerners that justified the
South's past and inspired Southerners to appreciate their heritage
was unacceptable to northern historians for two reasons. First,
it was incompatible with the so-called 'scientific history' taught
in German seminars and in the late nineteenth century being
popularized in the United States by northern professors. This
history stressed the evolution of New England institutions and

---

3   Dr. Alan Orlins to editor, *Civil War Magazine*, Vol. VIII, No. 6, (Nov-Dec,
     1990), p. 7.

how they contributed to the greatness of the United States."[4]
McWhiney further observed, "there was no place in such
'objective' history for either the bard or the poet upon whom Davis
[Jefferson Davis, former president of the Confederate States]
relied to celebrate southern values and heroes. Second, a history
of the South that revered Southerners and their values rather
than Northerners and their values would undermine all the Civil
War had decided. Northerners had no intention of allowing that
to happen. They believed that their victory over the South gave
them a mandate to write the nation's history, and they used that
authority to justify the North's victory. . . the accepted standard
of American history is written by New Englanders or their allies
and trainees to glorify northern ideals and heroes."[5]

McWhiney's concern may seem like sectionalized paranoia,
but a survey of the major scholarly works on the period does seem
to support his contention that our present interpretation of the
war comes from a decidedly Northern point of view. McWhiney,
who stands staunchly among those who support the interpretation of Southern Nationalism and cultural conflict, feels that
the Northern domination of Southern history has produced an
environment where studying the Southern point of view is
suicidal — "A Southerner, who is discriminated against in northern or in southern institutions because his ways and beliefs are
too southern, may well find that he has no home to go to in
academia."[6] In trying to come to terms with this, McWhiney
notes that:

> "Whole battalions of Northerners, and Southerners who
> thought like Northerners, invaded the field of southern
> history with a moral fervor and missionary zeal reminiscent
> of earlier self-righteous Northerners. They discovered
> much to deplore and little to defend in the region below the
> Potomac. Indeed, they seem as determined to impose their
> value system upon the past as the Radical Republicans and
> their carpetbagger allies were to impose an idealized value
> system upon the defeated Confederacy. Cleverly and effec-

---

4   McWhiney, Grady, "Historians as Southerners," *Continuity*, Volume 9 (1984),
     pp. 2-3.
5   McWhiney, "Historians as Southerners," p. 3.
6   McWhiney, "Historians as Southerners," p. 11.

tively, they ignored the hypocrisy and racial discrimination widely practiced in the North, characterized themselves as morally enlightened, and damned the sinful South as hopelessly deformed because it was and always had been full of white racists. Such tactics, with intellectuals again taking the lead, were essentially the same that antebellum Northerners had used to divert and to obscure the serious cultural conflict that existed between them and Southerners and to depict instead sectionalism as simply a struggle between good and evil — between freedom and slavery."[7]

Objectivity and the War Between the States seem not to dwell on common ground. McWhiney represents one aspect. An example of the other is the recent *Newsweek* coverage of the "Civil War" series. Instead of objectively reporting the facts, the writers chose to throw the gauntlet down at Southerners, particularly those who stood firm to the states' rights issues. Southern historians were used simply as reactionaries. The prerogative to play the good vs bad formula was evident with the less than subtle use of African-American historian Barbara Fields as a Northern commentator and the Memphis-based Shelby Foote as the Southerner. Both Fields and Foote had important points and interpretations to offer, yet these points may have been missed in the face of the public's gut reactions. The folks at *Newsweek* never went beyond the party line that the North had fought the war to end slavery and that the South had only fought to defend it. Anyone who even mentioned the issues of states' rights was labeled and thrown into "the lunatic fringe."[8]

As one can quickly ascertain, the war still continues long after the minie balls ceased to be fired. It is also apparent that even after 125 years, we, as a people, Southerner or Northerner, Celtic-American or African-American, academic or layman, have a very long way to go before we can come to grips with the years 1861-1865.

Texans looking to such histories for answers concerning the Lone Star State's role in the drama are often disappointed. Not only has the war come to us as one fought in the East, but as one waged by white Americans. The late PBS series is yet another

---

7   McWhiney, "Historians as Southerners," p. 7.
8   "Revisiting the Civil War," *Newsweek*, (October 8, 1990), p. 63.

example of this version of history. Little, if any, mention was given to the war in the West (other than the usual references to Vicksburg and Shiloh). Hardly any images of western troops were offered. Glorieta Pass and Sabine Pass were mentioned as if exotic locations (Sabine, by the way, was mispronounced by the narrator). To its credit, the series did strive to bring attention to the African-American participation, both as slave, abolitionist, freeman, and soldier. But what of the nearly 10,000 Hispanics who served on both sides during the conflict — separated not only by race and culture, but by economics and language?

The torchbearers who have striven to document Texas in the war include the late Harold Simpson of Hill College, who spent most of his adult life documenting Hood's Texas Brigade; Jerry Don Thompson of Laredo College, who adopted the story of the Tejanos and brought their legacy into focus; and Roy Sylvan Dunn, formerly of Texas Tech, who opened the door to understanding prewar sentiment as expressed by the Knights of the Golden Circle. There have been others who produced articles, pamphlets, and books on various subjects from Southern-Texan culture to regimental histories. In the future, Lamar University's Danny Sessums will document with exciting detail the saga of Granbury's Texas Brigade; Tom Cutrer, a much needed and well-deserved biography on General Ben McCulloch; and Jeff Hunt, a serious study of the battle of Palmetto Ranch.

Adding another volume to the histories of the War Between the States is like throwing a bucket of water on the Chicago fire. This project never started out as anything close to a general history — nor is it a detailed history of one particular event. I was approached by Wally Chariton to write a series of chapters representing some of my favorite moments of the War Between the States in relation to Texas. Thus, it became a sampling of the Texas-Confederate Experience from 1861-1865. These are histories that, in the course of ten years, I have been personally drawn to. Some are familiar, others are not. Most of the stories are confined to the boundaries of Texas. This is done to help folks understand that there was a great deal of activity inside the state during the war, particularly in the Rio Grande Valley. I have, however, elected to jump beyond the Sabine River on three occasions. This was done for dual reasons — first to highlight a particular Texas unit fighting beyond the Mississippi and second, to show three of the most particularly bloody experiences Texas troops faced.

While the name Hood's Texas Brigade is legendary and the name Antietam transcends beyond Maryland, few have heard of the 2nd Texas Infantry or its bloody charge at Corinth, Mississippi. And then there is Franklin, that little Tennessee community where John Hood murdered Granbury's Brigade and the Army of Tennessee.

It may have once been true what William Faulkner wrote that "at least once in his boyhood a Southerner dreamed of standing on the field at Gettysburg on the afternoon of July 3, 1863 — the hour before Pickett made his famous charge."[9] It grows doubtful how many boys or men (or girls for that matter) even know who Pickett was or what happened on that day. When some of us worked on the film *Glory* in 1989, we entertained noble thoughts that maybe young African-Americans might imagine with pride that they stood in the ranks with the 54th Massachusetts before Battery Wagner. It was perhaps wishful thinking, for the men of the 54th now form a battle line with their fellows, Yank and Reb, as we point fingers at them, challenging if they are proper role models for our youth.

One hundred and twenty-five years have passed since the last shots of the war were fired. As generations fade into generations, the image we have of these men fades and grows dimmer as our world becomes more complicated and automated. We who have seen Vietnam and question why our soldiers occupied and fought for Middle Eastern soil are less likely to understand why men and boys would stand in a line amidst shot and shell and make charges against fortified works. We who find offense in any image, cannot understand their devotion to the colors; flags that we today try to ban as racist. We who find cheer and joy in the separatist movements in Europe and the destruction of one nation's union annually give thanks that we crushed the same ideas in our own national experience. In our sophistication, we have become less likely to understand our ancestors' experience.

It is not within our power, mercifully, to make either heroes or villains out of them. While we may erect monuments of stone and bronze to their memories or deface their gravestones with graffiti, our reverence or our lack of reverence is only our measure. We may preserve or bulldoze their fields, but they alone have

---

9   Faulkner, William, *Intruder in the Dust*, (New York: Random House, 1948, Vintage Book Edition, 1972), p. 194-195.

hallowed the ground with their devotion to duty, their courage, and their personal honor. It is they, not we, who hold up their legacy. It is not their institutions or their political goals which they present to the future, but their courage.

Kevin R. Young
November 25, 1990
April 12, 1991
San Antonio de Bejar

Author's Note

Much of the original documentation of the War Between the States, including almost all of the official battle reports, was compiled and published in a series of government publications called *Official Record of the War of the Rebellion*. There are two separate series for military and naval branches. These are generally referred to as OR.

In accordance with naval usage, the article "the" is omitted before the name of ships.

"Other states have reputations to win, but the sons of the Alamo and San Jacinto have theirs to uphold."

Jefferson Davis

"... is there an American, we ask, who would not feel humiliated thus to see the glory of his country departing?"

Alamo Express
February 19, 1861

"I hope the day will never come when any of my children will be ashamed to own that I was a Confederate soldier."

A. R. Dandy
32nd Texas Cavalry

"Our flag is proudly floating, on the land and on the main,
Shout, Shout, the Battle Cry of Freedom!
Beneath it oft we've conquered and will conquer oft again
Shout, Shout, the Battle Cry of Freedom!
Our Dixie forever, She's never at a loss
Down with the Eagle, and up with the Cross!
We'll rally round the bonnie flag. We'll rally once again
Shout, Shout, the Battle Cry of Freedom!

Our gallant boys have marched to the rolling of the drums
Shout, Shout, the Battle Cry of Freedom!
Their motto is resistance, to the tyrants never yield
Shout, Shout, the Battle Cry of Freedom!"

Southern version, "Battle Cry of Freedom"

PART ONE

1860-1861

1860-1861

1860

July 8	Fires, blamed on Abolitionists, break out in various North Texas communities.
November 6	Abraham Lincoln is elected President.
December 20	South Carolina breaks from the Union by passing an ordinance of secession.

1861

January 9	Mississippi secedes from the Union.
January 11	Florida and Alabama leave the Union.
January 19	Georgia adopts articles of secession.
January 26	Louisiana leaves the Union.
January 28	**Texas Secession Convention meets in Austin.**
February 4	Ordinance of Secession passed in Austin.
February 7	Choctaw Indians ally themselves with the Confederate States.
February 8	Constitution of the Confederate States is adopted.
February 9	Jefferson Davis is elected President of the Confederate States.
February 16	**Texan volunteers under Ben McCulloch seize Federal property at San Antonio.**
February 18	General David Twiggs surrenders the U.S. Department of Texas at San Antonio.
February 28	Texas voters ratify the Secession Ordinance.
March 2	Texas officially assumes its independence from the United States and joins the Confederate States.
March 4	Abraham Lincoln is inaugurated as U.S. President.

April 13	Confederate forces fire on the Federal garrison inside Fort Sumter, Charleston Harbor, South Carolina.
April 15	Lincoln calls for 75,000 militia to crush the rebellion.
April 17	Jefferson Davis calls for 32,000 volunteers to protect the Confederate States.
April 25	**Colonel Earl Van Doren seizes the Federal troops trying to evacuate Texas from Indianola.**
May 6	Arkansas secedes from the Union.
May 9	**Van Doren captures Federal troops marching toward the coast at San Lucas Springs just west of San Antonio.**
May 20	North Carolina passes articles of secession.
June 24	Tennessee leaves the Union.
July 21	The first major battle of the war occurs at Manassas Junction, Virginia. The battle, named Bull Run, results in a Confederate victory.
August 10	The first major battle of the West takes place at Wilson's Creek near Oak Hill, Missouri. It is also the first major battle in which Texas troops take part. The Confederates win a major victory.
August 20	Missouri adopts articles of secession, but will exist with two state governments.

CHAPTER ONE

No Worshiper at the Shrine of the Union

The Gathering Storm
1860-1861

In November, 1860, the United States of America failed. The system of government which had been established after the Revolutionary War, designed to check and balance governmental power, suddenly became a threat to the populations of at least eleven states. Political parties no longer stood for individual platforms, but sectionalism. The Constitution, or the interpretation of the Constitution, became a source of violent confrontation. Within the next month, a nation of people who called themselves Americans would start the final step to sectional nationalism.

The combination of issues which were about to break the Union apart was compounded by the complexities of the human spirit. This is as true today as it was during that critical fall of 1860 as the nation prepared for the most emotional presidential election of its history. Two factions, both starting obscurely and far from mainstream thinking, had emerged out of the 1830s to become the driving opposing forces of this campaign. One was the abolitionist movement, whose goal was to stop and abolish forever the curse of slavery in the United States. The other was sectional nationalism which grew in equal strides as the abolitionist movement gained acceptability.

Americans had been debating slavery since 1776. Sections of the country had tried to exert their own political power since the first shots at Lexington and Concord. But the Constitution settled, by law, the issues of slavery and the Union. Yet, over the proceeding years, interpretations of the Constitution had disrupted this. Compromises over the expansion of slavery like the Missouri Compromise and the Kansas-Nebraska Act had come and gone, all with a lack of success or satisfaction for either side. Individual states had tried to assert their political liberties on several occasions (the New England states during the War of 1812 and South Carolina in 1832) with no great result. By the 1850s, the slave areas of the country had fallen into an argument of "states' rights" and the constitutionality of slavery while the abolitionists like William Seward declared that there was "a higher law than the Constitution."[1] The issue of "popular sovereignty" exploded in Kansas as the Society of Missourians for Mutual Protection openly battled the "immigrants" of the Massachusetts Emigrant Aide Company. Kansas bled over the issue of states' rights. As Page Smith observed, Kansas "deepened the Northern hatred of the South, intensified Southern paranoia, and, most important of all, made abolitionism and abolitionists respectable."[2]

As the radicals of both movements raised their voices, the individual population began to think of their neighbors in different terms. Not everyone in the northern states was a Yankee, nor were they abolitionists. Yet they all seemed to be. And so they were considered. And not everyone in the South was a slave-owning planter. Yet, they all seemed to be. And so they were. The concept of being different from other Americans became a reality by 1860. It became far more important to the individual than the actual reasons for the growing social and political strife. It brought

---

1 Smith, Page, *The Nation Comes of Age*, (New York: McGraw-Hill, 1981), p. 1163.
2 Smith, *The Nation Comes of Age*, p. 1105.

jealousy, hatred, paranoia, and mistrust on both sides. George Templeton Strong categorized Southerners as "a race of lazy, ignorant, coarse, sensual, swaggering, sordid, beggarly, barbarians, bullying white men & breeding little niggers for sale."[3] Southerners had equally less than kind things to say about Northerners.

Then it exploded. Extremists met in private and made daring plans of conquest and armed revolution. They received support from well-known merchants and social leaders. In the dead of night they actually stormed a United States arsenal, took hostages, and called for armed revolution against the United States. It would not be paranoid states' rights extremist Southerners who did this. The first act would fall on an abolitionist named John Brown. Supported by New England abolitionists, Brown and his followers would, in 1859, storm into the Virginia hamlet of Harpers Ferry. Seizing the Federal arsenal, Brown hoped to rally slaves to his cause.

Brown's raid failed. He was captured by U.S. Regulars, tried by the Commonwealth of Virginia, and hung for treason. The fiery abolitionist had wanted blood to cleanse the nation. He would have his wish.

Brown's raid sent a new fear into the hearts of the population of the South. They saw a man who had committed an open act of treason against the United States now being hailed as a hero by the Northern press. They stood witness to a man who had tried to start a slave insurrection in the South touted as a Moses by Northern admirers. The words of Ohio's Joshua Giddings rang in their ears, "I look forward to the day when there shall be a servile insurrection in the South, when the black man shall assert his freedom and wage a war of extermination against his master."[4] These events were chilling. Edmund Ruffin sent trophy weapons taken from Brown's men and sent them to the governors of the Southern States as "abiding and impressive evidence of the fanatical hatred borne by the dominant Northern party to the institutions and the people of the Southern States."[5] The idea of slave insurrection was something that all Southerners feared, as

---

3   Smith, *The Nation Comes of Age*, p. 1120.
4   Smith, *The Nation Comes of Age*, p. 1123.
5   Craven, Avery O., *Edmund Ruffin — Southerner*, (Baton Rouge: Louisiana State University Press, 1976), pp. 180-181.

much as people living on the frontier had a common fear of Indian raids. And the idea of slave insurrection being supported by Northerners was even more a dread, which helped create a bond between nonslaveholders and slave owners.

The democratic process started feeling the strain when the various political parties met to find candidates to represent their platforms. It quickly became apparent that this was not to be a simple matter. By the time it was over, the Democratic party had subdivided into three factions: Stephen Douglas leading the Northern Democratic party; John Bell as candidate representing the Constitutional Union party, which supported the preservation of the Union; and then U.S. Vice President John Breckinridge, supporting a solidly Southern Nationalist platform. Southern Nationalist William Lowndes Yancy drew applause when he told the convention nominating Breckinridge that "I am . . . no worshiper at the shrine of the Union. I am no Union shrieker. I meet great questions fairly, on their own merits . . . I am neither for the Union, nor against the Union . . . I urge, or oppose, measures upon the ground of their constitutionality and wisdom, or the reverse. When the government confessedly becomes a failure so far as the great rights of the equality of the States and of the people of the States are concerned, then its organization is but an instrument for the destruction of constitutional liberty; and, taking lessons from our ancestors, we should overthrow it."[6]

The Republican party, which was formed on an antislave platform in 1854, selected a Kentucky born, Illinois raised lawyer named Abraham Lincoln and saddled him with a platform which was abolitionist in its tone. The eighth plank of that platform stated, "the normal condition of all territory of the United States is that of freedom: that, as our republican fathers, when they had abolished slavery in all our national territory, ordained that 'no person shall be deprived of life, liberty, or property without due process of law,' it becomes our duty by legislation, whenever such legislation is necessary, to maintain this provision of the Constitution against all attempts to violate it; and we deny the authority of Congress, of a territorial legislature, or of any individuals, to give legal existence to slavery in any territory of the United States."[7] While Lincoln did not support slavery, he was not a

---

6   Lubbock, Francis Richard, *Six Decades in Texas*, edited by C. W. Raines (Austin: Ben C. Jones and Company, 1900), p. 291.

radical in his political thought. But his resolve was in keeping the union of states together.

The Southern Nationalists saw the Republicans as a major threat to the South. Lincoln did not even appear on the Southern ballot. The three-way split of the Democrats doomed the election more than the power of the abolitionists. The Republicans won the election because the South had divided itself.

Texian Elkanah Greer of Marshall summed up some of the feeling following Lincoln's election by saying, "a more consummate piece of folly could not be committed, than to wait for the North to inaugurate her withering, dishonoring, and diabolical policy. The overt act has been committed. Let the South speak out, or forever hold her peace."[8] Mary Maverick, pioneer of early Texas, wrote of her husband's views by saying, "Mr. Maverick had always been a Union man in sentiment, he loved the Union of States, and although he may have believed that we had the abstract right to withdraw from the Union, he thought the Union was sacred. At last he came to believe the quarrel was forced upon us, and that there was before us an 'irressible conflict' which we could not escape, no matter where we turned."[9]

The Mavericks were not alone. Before 1860 could finish, South Carolina had called for convention and taken the radical step. The Charleston *Mercury* proudly proclaimed, "The Union Is Dissolved!" One of the sacred principles of the Southern Nationalists was that a state could nullify its admission into the United States by act of public secession. South Carolina, which one native noted "was too small to be a republic and too large to be an insane asylum," did just that on December 20. Northern politicians were still debating the legality of secession when Alabama, followed by Mississippi, Georgia, and Florida, joined the secessionists. As President James Buchanan's term of office drew to an end, it was overtaken with the last vestiges of uncertainty which had plagued the country for the last few years.

By the time of Lincoln's inaugural, the Southern states, on February 4, 1861, had formed an alliance known as the Confederate States of America. A provisional government

---

7   Lubbock, *Six Decades in Texas*, p. 208.
8   Lubbock, *Six Decades in Texas*, p. 303.
9   Maverick, Mary, *Memories*, edited by Rena Maverick Green (Lincoln: University of Nebraska Press, 1989), p. 113.

had been formed, a constitution hammered out, and a president, Jefferson Davis, elected. Davis, like Lincoln, came from Kentucky but had been raised in Mississippi. A planter, lawyer, hero of the Mexican War (which Lincoln had opposed), congressman, and former U.S. Secretary of War, Jefferson Davis took the reins of power of a nation based on the principles of anticentralist government.

Other Southern states, including Texas, had joined the new fold by the time a stalemate had developed between the two nations. Lincoln more than resisted the reality of secession. He was prepared to use everything he had to stop it and keep the Union together. The focus of his resolve centered on a brick fort located on a rock island in the middle of Charleston Harbor, South Carolina, called Fort Sumter. Since Christmas, 1860, the Federal garrison stationed there had resisted firm, but nonviolent, pressure to surrender. Resolves on both sides were strong. Federal commander Robert Anderson was determined to obey his instructions to hold out (until ordered otherwise), while the Confederates were equally resolved to have this bastion of the Union placed under their control.

As the weeks dragged on, each side seemed hesitant to make the actual step from agitation to violence, although South Carolinian gunners had fired at a charter ship, *Star of the West*, which had been contracted by the Federal government to bring supplies to the fort. Despite considerable pressure, Davis' new Confederate government had restrained from actual bombardment of the fort. Anderson himself admitted that he would soon be starved out. But the longer the situation continued, the more the symbolism dramatically increased. Fort Sumter became a cherished bastion of the Union cause for the North, while it stood out as a final symbol of Yankee domination in a circling nest of secessionists.

In the end, it would be the Confederates who fired first. On April 12, 1861, the orders were given. At 4:30 A.M. a single round was fired from Captain George James' mortar battery. In the morning darkness, the shell sputtered an arched course and then exploded over the fortress.

Edmund Ruffin, secessionist who helped fire the first shot of the war and probably fired one of the last. *Courtesy of the Eugene C. Barker Research Center, University of Texas at Austin.*

Seconds later, one of the 8-inch columbiads on Morris Island was fired.[10] Pulling its lanyard was a crusty, die-hard Southern Nationalist named Edmund Ruffin. He had come from his native Virginia, which had yet to secede, to play an active part in this unfolding drama. The cause of states' rights and secession had become a religion to him. As he yanked the lanyard back, he had the satisfaction of firing the first hostile shot. It took on the nature of a personal message to the minions of the North. This Southerner would resist them whatever the cost.

The shell flew over the harbor and exploded into Sumter's parapet. It was followed by a dozen Confederate batteries adding their thunder to the unfolding storm. Two hours later, Major Anderson ordered Sumter's guns to fire back. The Federals would only last some thirty-four hours. Anderson surrendered on April 15 and the last Federal flag to fly over South Carolina was lowered.[11]

Edmund Ruffin and his fellows would be exuberant as they watched the Stars and Bars of the new Confederacy raised over the battered fortress. The United States' most costly war had begun.

Had events gone differently some 1500 miles to the west of Charleston Harbor, Edmund Ruffin might have been cheated out of firing the first shot. If one nervous Federal sentry, one over-zealous member of the Knights of the Golden Circle, or one Federal officer had questioned his superior's orders, the whole bloody affair could have well started on February 16, 1861, in San Antonio, Texas. The corner of Main Plaza and Soledad might well have become a national landmark, or the Alamo, already known as the "Shrine of Texas Liberty," might well have been also remembered as the "Starting Point of the War Between the States."

Antebellum Texas stood out as the only frontier state in the Southern block. Its population was new and, in many ways, clung to the traditions of their former homes. East Texas stood as probably the most traditional Southern region of the state since at least eighteen of the state's top 54 slave holders lived in the area just

---

10 A columbiad was a large-caliber cannon used for throwing solid shot or shells.

11 For a complete accounting on the crises at Charleston, see Swanberg, W. A., *First Blood — The Story of Ft. Sumter*, (New York: Charles Scribner and Sons, 1957). Some historians dispute that Ruffin actually fired the first shot.

south and west of Houston.[12] But voting Texans, which comprised every free male person 21 years of age who was a citizen of the United States or the Republic of Texas and had resided in the state one year, represented a diverse population, divided not only by lines of alliance and economics, but race. Only Indians who did not pay taxes, Africans, or the descendants of Africans could not vote. This left Anglo, Celtic, German, Hispanic and tax-paying Indians eligible to vote.

Texas was economically sound in the 1850s. After ten years of struggle during the Republic period, Texas had emerged from statehood with a new vitality. Slavery was widespread in Texas, although slaves were scarce and often expensive. In West Texas, with the strong Hispanic element, they were impractical. Tejanos neither needed nor could they afford the institution. The German population, who were to bear the brunt of the "pro-Union" accusations, considered slavery an economic threat to the prosperity of the working freeman.

Within the year, however, a series of events would rocket Texas' diverse population into the mainstream of Southern Nationalism. Texas' conversion would be sudden and swift.

---

12 Buenger, Walter L., *Secession and the Union in Texas,* (Austin: University of Texas Press, 1984), p. 12.

CHAPTER TWO

". . . well may the patriots tremble."

Secession
1861

The month before John Brown and his abolitionists made their raid on the U.S. Arsenal at Harpers Ferry, the folks in South Texas had a scare of their own. Juan N. Cortina, a sometime patriot, sometime rebel, sometime bandit, crossed over the Rio Grande and occupied the town of Brownsville. Cortina, who switched causes as easily as he did occupations, expressed a desire to force the government of Texas to guarantee the rights of Hispanics. Historians have questioned his actual motives, and in retrospect they are probably less important when compared with the real impact the raid had on Texan thinking.[1]

---

1 For further information on this incident see Ford, John S., *Rip Ford's Texas*, edited by Stephen B. Oates (Austin: University of Texas Press, 1963).

Cortina's incursion, combined with continuing Indian attacks in West and South Texas, reinforced a growing concern that the United States was not adequately protecting the Texas frontier. One of the reasons Texas had surrendered her national independence in 1845 was the promise of military protection along the frontier by the United States. Cortina's raid, which was followed by John Brown's attack in Virginia, gave Southern Nationalists in Texas a growing platform — the United States was not living up to its annexation agreement. Since U.S. Regulars had to be assisted by Texas Rangers in order to drive Cortina back across the Rio Grande River, the incident illustrated the federal government's failure to adequately defend the Texas borders. Cortina's expulsion also served to illustrate that Texans could and would be able to defend themselves.

By the summer of 1860, some of the concerns of frontier protection had died down. Unfortunately, that summer proved to be a rather hot and dry one, particularly in North Texas. In July a series of sudden fires broke out in North Texas. They were mysterious and rather destructive. The first of these occurred in Dallas on July 8. The Dallas fire was followed, within hours, by similar incidents in Denton, Milford, Pilot Point, and other locations. The Denton fire was particularly severe, destroying the west side of the town square. Before the ashes had cooled, the Southern Nationalist press had attached blame for the fires on Negro insurrection and the more radical element of the Methodist Episcopal church. The Methodist Episcopal church was singled out as a result of the antagonistic views against slavery which were expressed at its 1859 meeting near Bonham. One of the fires was actually connected with a slave insurrection conspiracy inspired by traveling preachers. As more fires broke out in August (including one that almost totally destroyed Henderson) plots were uncovered; there were hangings and a general uproar that the abolitionists were trying to start slave rebellion in North Texas.[2]

Once again, the storm broke and was just clearing when the 1860 election captured everyone's attention. Texas voters, given a

---

2   Sandbo, Anna Irene, "First Session of the Secession Convention of Texas," *Southwestern Historical Quarterly*, Volume 18. For a detailed look at the North Texas fires, see Ledbetter, Bill, "Slave Unrest and White Panic: The Impact of Black Republicanism in Antebellum Texas," *Texana*, Volume 10.

choice between Bell, Breckinridge, and Douglas, threw their votes toward the Southern Nationalists.

One secessionist was a young school teacher at Goliad's Aranama College. Twenty-five-year-old William Martin Chase had come to the historic South Texas community directly after graduation from the University of Georgia. He was probably not quite prepared for the dramatic difference in lifestyle which contrasted his boyhood home in Athens and the rough frontier cattle town. Goliad had changed little from the time of Texas' annexation. The majority of the Anglo-Celtic population (with the usual German mix) was centered in the "new" town on the north bank of the winding San Antonio River. The new stone courthouse stood in the center of the town square with a large live oak, remembered as "the Hanging Tree." The Hispanic population was clustered just south of the river in the "old" town of La Bahia. Here, in 1749, the Spanish had established a royal presidio (station for troops) and two Catholic missions. Around the rambling fort a cluster of jacales grew where once had been the third largest community in Texas. Raising cattle had been part of Goliad's economy since the days of the Spanish (the Mission Espiritu Santo once boasted the largest cattle ranch in Spanish Colonial Texas). The Anglo-Celtics had brought in cotton, corn, and the usual mix of livestock.

Civil strife was also part of Goliad's past. As one of Spain's chief military bases in Texas, Goliad seemed to attract every adventurer, freedom fighter, filibusterer, and self-promoter who marched into Texas. At least six different armies had occupied — or tried to occupy — the old La Bahia presidio from 1800-1845. One group of soldiers prematurely declared Texas independence there in 1835 only to be censored by the provisional government. They also raised what is touted as "the first flag of Texas independence." The most famous, or infamous, moment happened in 1836 when 320 Texian prisoners of war were captured and executed there during the Texas war for independence.

Chase arrived in Goliad in 1860. A college had been started in the ruins of the old Mission Espiritu Santo just south of town. The Georgian had the task of educating Goliad's aspiring youth. Often there was little difference between Chase and his students, as one letter home talks fondly about his attempts to decide which of the daughters of Colonel J. W. Patton to pursue.

Like most youths, Chase was soon getting caught up in the growing fever of secession. The Goliad community was clearly not universally in favor of secession, despite the fact that two prominent KGC members, Pryor and Albert Lea, lived there as did Southern Nationalist Hamilton Bee. Chase wrote home "the political excitement here is very great & immediately in this neighborhood, parlors are so equally divided and so fiercely opposed to each other, that neither the Union nor Secession flag could be hoisted. Every other town heard from in the state has run up the Lone Star flag, and Goliad stands alone in her disgraceful indecision."[3]

Chase may have been a little too critical of his neighbors, but in many respects he was right. Just down the San Antonio River, the citizens of Indianola held a mass meeting denouncing Lincoln and the Republicans. A public discussion which favored Southern Nationalism was held at the courthouse and was followed by a grand parade. Rather unique to the celebration was the use of 28 transparencies which were images painted on glass and lit by candles and lamps behind them. The citizens of Indianola visually connected the South, cotton, states' rights, and Texas history in one mass parade, as the transparencies proclaimed, "States' Rights," "Union Only With Honor," "Who is not for us is Against us," "the 2nd of March," "Crocketts and Bowies not all Dead," "Texas is Sovereign," "The Alamo," "Gonzales and Goliad, 1835," "21st of April, 1836," and "We are with South Carolina." The ladies of the community presented the organizers with a Lone Star flag which led the parade.[4]

Indianola was not alone. Way over in East Texas, the town of Marshall held a meeting denouncing the election of Lincoln as "a violation of the spirit of the Constitution, and should be resisted by the States." A lone star was hoisted here as the crowd was reminded that "the crisis is upon us and must be squarely met."[5]

Not all Texans shared in this view. Those who believed in the Union, including Austin lawyer George Paschal, former governor E. M. Pease, and San Antonio newspaper man James P. Newcomb,

---

3   Chase, William, December 20, 1860. Transcript copy of the letter is in the Goliad County Library.
4   *Indianola Courier*, November 24, 1860.
5   Lubbock, Francis Richard, *Six Decades in Texas*, edited by C. W. Raines (Austin: Ben C. Jones and Company, 1900), pp. 302-303.

Austin, Texas, at the time of the war. *Courtesy of Texas Department of Public Safety, Austin, Texas. From a copy in the Institute of Texan Cultures, San Antonio.*

formed the Union Club, dedicated to be against Lincoln but for the Union. They had fought the campaign for Bell's presidency and lost. Newcomb, whose *Alamo Express* became the voice of Unionism in South Texas, declared, "we do not consider the simple election of Lincoln to the presidency sufficient cause for the dissolution of the Union."[6] The Unionist cause was bolstered by the fact that Texas' most famous living hero, Sam Houston, was the governor and stood against secession. With the state legislature currently adjourned, Houston tried a delaying action to keep the growing secessionist tide at bay. He refused to call an extra session of the legislature.

Houston, whose political life spanned Texas history from her days as a Mexican colony, emerged from this period as the great hero of the Union. The overwhelming, oftentimes overbearing personality of the man secured his place in Texas and American history. He was a man who, when the rest of the country favored independence, fought for annexation to the United States. He helped deliver Texas her independence on the plains of San Jacinto and had signed the republic's declaration of independence, yet always considered himself an American and that Texas' destiny was forever tied to the United States. He was not likely to let his fellows forget his contributions to Texas. Once, he showed up at his successor's inauguration dressed as George Washington, thus illustrating he was the father of his country, and when later challenged by a sentry for a pass, he pointed towards the San Jacinto battlefield yelling, "San Jacinto is my pass."

Houston was one of those rare people who could — and often did — fall into a pigpen and come out smelling like a yellow rose. His popularity had risen and fallen only to rise again many times. But he would not be able to withstand the crises in the Union. He spoke for the Union and against secession. He lobbied for Texas, if she elected to leave the Union, to stay clear of an alliance with the rest of the South. He proposed that the southern states should meet and send representation to negotiate with the federal government. His ideas were more than unpopular. At a New Year's Day speech in Waco, the crowd turned so ugly that he had to leave town — in a hurry. When the federal government offered

6   *Alamo Express*, February 9, 1861.

troops to help him keep his office, Houston refused. His loyalties were divided.

Judge O. M. Roberts, along with William P. Rogers, led the efforts to force Houston to take action. In the end it was resolved that since a special convention of elected delegates had been called in 1845 to approve Texas' annexation, then it figured that a similar body could be called to take the Lone Star out. Houston again tried to stall, but in the end he called for the convention to meet in Austin.

The elected delegates came to the capital on January 28, 1861. The Unionists had only been able to elect a few of their men to the body. The rest, most of which were Southern born, were not the typical planter class. In truth, the Texas Secession Convention held prosperous farmers, lawyers, and small planters who dominated the economic, political, and social life of most of Texas. Some, however, were supporters of the Knights of the Golden Circle who saw their second great goal, the support of a Southern state leaving the union, about to unfold. One member of the convention, Edwin Waller, had been a member of the 1836 convention which had created the independent Texas republic.

On the same day, the resolution to declare Texas once again independent was made. It fell on John A. Wharton, whose family had been the staunchest supporters of the 1836 revolution, to introduce the resolution. Wharton would soon be helping to organize one of the more famous Texas cavalry regiments to serve the Confederate cause — Terry's Texas Rangers. Without debate, his resolution passed with a total of 152 delegates in favor and six opposed.

It was decided that a public vote would be held on February 23, and if the ordinance of secession was approved, Texas independence would be in effect on March 2 — the 25th anniversary of the first Texas republic. The ordinance was drafted, and on February 1, with Governor Houston in attendance, the delegates approved the document by a vote of 166 for and seven against. One of the seven was J. W. Throckmorton. It was to be his voice, not Houston's, who spoke for the Union. "In view of the responsibility, in the presence of God and my country — and unawed by the wild spirit of revolution around me, I vote no." His words were followed by boos and hisses from some of the delegates and observers, but Throckmorton was not unnerved. In a voice full of conviction and courage, his answer to the crowd echoed across the chamber, "When the rabble hiss, well may the patriots tremble."[7] Thomas P. Houghes of Williamson, William Johnson, Lem Williams, and George W. Wright of Lamar, Joshua Johnson of Titus, and A. P. Shufford of Wood joined Throckmorton in their voting.

The issue of secession was now up to the voters of Texas. Francis Lubbock, who would soon become wartime governor, noted "As an original question, secession, perhaps, would have failed to carry in Texas; but, the six leading cotton States having already resorted to an exercise of the right, banded themselves together in a new confederation, and formed a new government, Texas was apparently confronted with the alternatives of becoming a party to the new compact, remaining in the Union or resuming her sovereignty as a separate republic."[8]

In Goliad, William Chases' attempts to get the secession ball rolling were met by many obstacles. When word of Lincoln's election arrived, Southern Nationalists elected to raise a "southern flag." Some of the local belles went to work making the banner. Miss Virginia Billups was given the honor of presenting it to the community. However, the young lawyer who was appointed to accept the flag got cold feet. He went to work persuading Miss Billups to keep the flag at home and out of sight — displaying it in public might cause bloodshed. Chase and his fellows were not to be stopped. A few days later, they talked Miss Billups out of the flag and went to work trying to raise it in the town square. Before they could get it unfurled, a typical Texas "blue norther" howled down. The heavy rain postponed the glorious moment. In disgust, Chase and his fellows went to supper and finally got the flag up after dark by the light of a large bonfire.[9]

The public mood apparently got better a few weeks later. When word arrived of Georgia's secession there was much celebration. However, Chase had a sour taste in his mouth. He resigned from the college and headed home.[10]

---

7   Sandbo, Anna Irene, "The First Session of the Secession Convention of Texas," *Southwestern Historical Quarterly*, 18:191.
8   Lubbock, *Six Decades in Texas*, p. 305.
9   William Chase to mother, January 2, 1861. Transcript copy of the letter is in the Goliad County Library.
10 William Chase to mother, January 28, 1861. Transcript copy of the letter is in the Goliad County Library.

The Immortal Seven. These are the seven delegates who voted against Texas' secession. Top row, left to right: A. P. Shuford (Wood County), James W. Throckmorton (Collin County), Lemuel H. Williams (Lamar County), Joshua Johnson (Titus County). Bottom row, left to right: William H. Johnson (Lamar County), George W. Wright (Lamar County), and Thomas P. Hughes (Williamson County). *Courtesy of the DRT Library at the Alamo.*

On February 4, in one of its final actions, the Texas Secession Convention elected to send delegates to the new provisional Confederate States government at Montgomery, Alabama. Texas' rebirth as an independent republic had lasted less than one week.

Two days prior, the Convention met in secret session with its newly created Committee of Public Safety. One of the realities of secession was the simple fact that nearly one third of the United States Army was stationed in a string of forts across West Texas. The growing stalemate in Charleston Bay did not present a positive outlook concerning this issue. So the delegates instructed the committee to go to San Antonio (military headquarters for the Department of Texas) with the purpose of taking over all U.S. military property in Texas.

For a state with little, if any, militia or military forces, the concept was rather ambitious. But Texas had a couple of surprises which could work in its favor. One was a general named David Twiggs, the other was the Knights of the Golden Circle.

CHAPTER THREE

From Filibusterers to Secessionists

The Knights of the Golden Circle

It is remarkable that in today's general history of the secession movement, little is written about or even discussed concerning one of the principal organizations which helped take Texas out of the Union. The role of the secret organization known as the Knights of the Golden Circle has been one of the most overlooked and misunderstood aspects of the secessionist movement in Texas.

As an organization whose expressed goals were to establish and expand Southern institutions into Latin America and assist the cause of the South, the KGC is today looked at in the most unfavorable and critical terms. The very thought of an organization being formed to invade, conquer, and then redirect a people's national character is most uncomfortable to most Americans. The concept seems radical and most objectionable. Yet, the KGC was more than just a small radical fringe organization. It was, by the critical winter of 1860, a viable political force whose influence and power was not taken lightly. Unionist Charles Anderson, with his usual prejudice against Southerners, noted, "it was to this band of mostly mere villainous desperadoes that the success of rebellion in Texas was mainly due."[1]

There are two aspects of the KGC which both illustrate the radical mood swings of not only the antebellum South, but Texas as well. The KGC began as a by-product of the growth of Southern Nationalism in the 1850s. It was during this period, as the abolitionist forces in the North increased their political strength and limits on Southern expansion, that the advocates of the idea of Southern Nationalism began to express desires to increase the South's political power by increasing the size of the country with new lands. It was also a time in which serious talk about reopening the African slave trade was entertained. As the abolitionists increased their ranks with the central issue of slavery, the Southern Nationalists increased their defense of the institution. Like the laws of physics, so the debate grew. When the abolitionists talked limiting slavery, the Southern planters echoed increasing it.

One of the expansion theories concerned the idea of securing large sections of Latin America for Anglo-American development. For many, the concept of manifest destiny did not stop with the Mexican War and the winning of California. They looked southward. During this period, several plots and expeditions were organized by filibustering Americans (usually backed by some local support) to invade Latin American countries. The most famous of these were the Narciso Lopez Cuban Expedition, which failed, and the expeditions of William Walker, "the Grey-Eyed Man of Destiny."

In 1854 a Tennessee physician-turned-newspaper-editor named William Walker injected himself into a Nicaraguan civil war. Expounding the liberal cause, Walker soon became commander and chief of the army and, in 1856, president elect. The complex character of this small, thin man created a series of changes in his personal goals. One of the best examples of this was his sudden departure from his antislave viewpoints and his subsequent reestablishment of slavery in Nicaragua. Walker's policies succeeded not only in estranging him from the liberal cause, but

---

1   Anderson, Charles, *Texas Before and on the Eve of the Rebellion*, (Cincinnati: 1884, Privately published), p. 19.

uniting his enemies, both foreign and domestic. His attempt to nationalize the chief Atlantic/Pacific transportation route brought down the wrath of American capitalist Cornelius Vanderbilt. These forces would eventually destroy Walker's dream of an empire.

Despite his intentions and failures, William Walker became a hero to the American public, in particular to the South. He would later become a classic example of not only American arrogance towards Latin America, but of Southern racism towards Hispanic America and slavery. Oddly enough, Walker was not so much a product of the Southern mentality. When he lived in New Orleans, he did not support the institution of slavery. Walker was never an agent of the South or the Southern Expansionists. His first attempt at land grabbing, which occurred in Northern Mexico, was launched from California, as was his first attempt at filibustering in Nicaragua. His original followers were not Southerners. They represented a dramatic cross section of American society, including free blacks. His main supporter — until he crossed him — was a New Englander, Cornelius Vanderbilt. And the goal for Walker's filibustering in Nicaragua was not one based on Southern institutions or expansion. It was to secure for Vanderbilt the transportation route across Nicaragua to speed up travel between the east and west coasts of the United States. In short, expanding Southern culture and creating a southern empire were far from William Walker's mind when he lead his first band of "Immortals" into Nicaragua and set himself up as ruler.[2]

Those factors did not stop Southerners from embracing Walker's cause. Southern Nationalists, frustrated by the control on territorial expansion, saw Nicaragua as a base from which to independently expand the institution of slavery and to increase the power base of the South. As odd as it may seem to us today, Walker's dreams were encouraged publicly.

Texas, who shared its longest border with Mexico, was no exception. The Lone Star State soon became fertile ground for dreams of expansion in Latin American. However, it would be a failed Virginian doctor named George Bickley who would put the wheels into motion and create an actual organization whose goals

---

2   For additional information on the career of Walker see Carr, Albert Z., *The World and William Walker*, (New York: Harper & Row, 1963).

were "the expansion of Anglo-Americanism; to strengthen the South and thereby the whole scheme of American civilization."[3]

As is typical with most organizations, historians tend to judge the Knights of the Golden Circle through the personality of its founder, George Bickley. The result is a more than critical, contemptuous appraisal. It is painfully apparent that Bickley had a natural talent for organization and creating on paper, which tended to fall apart when put into actual practice. One can also gather, by looking at the organization's dues structure, that Bickley may have been behind all of this as a simple way of getting his hands on money. Yet, Bickley was no Adolph Hitler or Benito Mussolini. He didn't have the personality for it. Nor were the Knights fascists or Nazis. Bickley did not create ideas or philosophies or even national consciences — he simply tapped into them. People had been screaming Southern expansionism, Latin American intervention, and nationalism long before Bickley.

Yet, trying to get a handle on Bickley is often like trying to get a handle on his organization. There were claims that he was a graduate of or had at least attended West Point, and that he had received his medical training in London. Both claims have been disproved. He did end up in Cincinnati, helping to found a local historical society and a literary magazine. He held a professorship at the Eclectic Medical Institute, established something called the "Wayne Circle of the Brotherhood of the Union," and was a member of the Know-Nothing party during the 1856 elections. Bickley left the Medical Institute to work for the American Patent Company. After a year with this organization, the so-called doctor moved on to bigger and better things.[4]

It is rather interesting to note that in 1858 Bickley wrote the following words about slavery: "The institution is one altogether unenviable, every reasonable man in America will at once admit."[5] If this sounds strange, then consider that William Walker, the man who reintroduced slavery to Nicaragua, once was the editor

---

3   All of the doctrine for the KGC is taken from *Rules, Regulations & Principles of the KGC*, (New York: Benjamin Urner, 1859), and Pomfrey, J. W. *A True Disclosure and Exposition of the Knights of the Golden Circle*, (Cincinnati: Privately published, 1864). The latter contains all of the KGC secret signs, grips, and charges of the three degrees.
4   For more on Bickley, see Crenshaw, Ollinger, "The Knights of the Golden Circle: The Career of George Bickley," *American Historical Review*, Volume 47.
5   Crenshaw, "Knights of the Golden Circle," p. 25.

of an antislavery newspaper. Bickley, it seems, was just following character.

Soon after leaving Cincinnati and his abolitionist views behind, Bickley commenced working on the organization which would be soon known as the Knights of the Golden Circle. The organization expressed a desire to support "the protection of Constitutional Liberty, bequeathed us by our fathers, the opening of new markets, and furnishing new avenues for the sober and industrious laboring man."

The new markets and avenues, as previously mentioned, were in Latin America. Bickley's little organization was bent on becoming an empire — a golden circle of Southern states and territories with Havana, Cuba, as the center point. As Bickley continued to work on his plans, the KGC began to evolve and conform to the current political ideals. In original concept, the whole purpose of Latin American expansion was to give the nation as a whole something to divert its negative North vs South energy towards. This soon was joined by the idea that Southern expansion into Latin America would give the South an avenue of growth and help check the growing territorial limitations placed on it and Southern institutions by the abolitionists. That most definitely meant slavery.

The organizational chart for the Knights centered on a local club or castle. Members could join into three degrees: Military, Financial, and Political. Most of the members of the KGC would fall into the first degree, particularly in Texas. Members were asked if they believed the white man superior to the Negro; if the U.S. Constitution recognizes slave property; that the South had the right to demand protection from that kind, as well as other property; if people of one section of the country have the right to make war on the institutions of another; and if the abolitionist societies of the North were right and proper. The million dollar question was, that in case of conflict between North and South, which side would you stand up for.

Providing one answered correctly to these questions, you took an oath where you vowed to defend constitutional rights; to spare, in time of war, old men, women, children, the sick and disabled; that you would oppose the admission of any negro, abolitionist, confirmed drunkard, convict, felon, or low and vicious character; and that you would obey the laws of the United States provided that they were consistent with the spirit and letter of the Constitution as interpreted by the Supreme Court.

Bickley's organizational skills went beyond the rites and secret signs stages. The KGC published tracts which established official guidelines and maxims for military and government, including a civil and morality code. Bickley borrowed from everyone from Thomas Jefferson to Davy Crockett. But when all was said and done, the KGC stood squarely on two goals. The first was the expansion of Southern institutions into Latin America with Mexico as the first field of operation. The second was to be ready and organized to offer the KGC services to any Southern states to repel a Northern army. Bickley was at least clever enough to realize that if the idea of diverting negative energies into Latin American conquest failed, then channeling them into nationalist feeling would serve as a substitute.

Bickley had only been at work less than a year on the Latin American concept when the growing secessionist crisis commenced. As his own inadequacies became apparent and the shift of national attention turned, he would soon find himself outpaced by his Texas members.

It is difficult to say when the Texas KGC got started, but by January 1860, its leadership was well in place. Elkanah Bracken Greer, a prominent Marshall, Texas lawyer and a veteran of the Mississippi Rifles of the Mexican War, issued a broadside identifying himself as the "commander-in-chief and President of the Texas Board of War." The broadside called on other KGC members to join Texas and prepare for the conquest of Mexico.[6]

Greer would emerge as one of the leading KGC organizers in Texas. The ardent states' rights advocate would soon write Governor Sam Houston, volunteering to provide a "regiment of Mounted Volunteers" which were apparently already organized and ready to march.[7] Houston had openly supported the idea of placing Mexico under the American flag. His reasons, typically complex in true Houston form, centered on helping to divert attention from the growing national crises and would help to gain him national attention. The old "hero of San Jacinto" may not have

6   Greer, Jack Thorndyke, *Leaves From A Family Album*, edited by James Judge Greer (Waco: Texian Press, 1975), p. 34.
7   Greer to Sam Houston, February 20, 1860. Governor's Letters, Texas State Library.

supported the KGC concepts of slavery expansion or disunion, but he certainly had no objections to using the organization to help further his own personal ambitions.

Houston apparently was unwilling to use state funds to back the plans, but he did lobby Washington for appropriations, which never came. This did not stop KGC activities. Two South Texas Knights, Albert Lea and his brother, Pryor, of Goliad, went so far as to approach the new commander of the U.S. Army Department of Texas with their plans. A quirk of fate was that the new commander was Colonel Robert E. Lee, who as Albert Lea informed Houston, "would not touch any thing that he would consider vulgar filibustering." Lea added, that "under sanction the Govt. might be more than willing to aid you to pacificate Mexico."[8]

In the end, neither Colonel Lee nor Sam Houston would pursue the plan of Mexican invasion. A reported large group of armed Knights had assembled around Gonzales with plans of advancing southward. Houston, on March 21, ordered them to disband. A second group was later reported to be forming in Encinal County that October, but it never materialized.

The great leader Bickley was in New Orleans during all of this activity, trying to keep the organization — and his leadership — intact with dissatisfied members. The result was a general convention of the KGC in Raleigh, North Carolina. The grand meeting, held between May 7-11, 1860, succeeded in keeping both the organization and Bickley together. It also took the organization out of the realm of a secret society and into public light. The convention issued forth a public document in which its goals and philosophy were outlined.

The Texas KGC was growing, despite national organizational problems. Sam Lockridge, one of William Walker's former filibusterers noted that "some of the finest men in our country are in the association of the KGC and they are forming under or upon a different basis in Texas and other states and may yet succeed in their objects."[9] Lockridge wasn't far off the mark. As the fall and election of 1860 came, the Texas KGC not only grew, but shifted

---

8   Albert Lea to Sam Houston, February 24, 1860, Governor's Letters, Texas State Library.
9   Dunn, Roy Sylvan, "The KGC In Texas, 1860-1861," *Southwestern Historical Quarterly*, 70:552. To date, Dunn's study of the KGC is one of the most complete appraisals of the organization and it's impact on secessionist Texas.

gears. Its members quickly grasped the second charter of the organization — to make themselves ready for secession.

Bickley, with the Raleigh compromises behind him, arrived in the main theater of operations to find the ideas of Mexican invasion put aside. He quickly realized that the Texas castles were moving on the secessionist path. Not to be outpaced, he switched his own rhetoric and joined the bandwagon. Setting foot in Texas on October 10, Bickley established his headquarters in San Antonio but threw most of his efforts into East Texas.

One of his first stops was Houston. His October 31 speech at the courthouse square was well received — at least by the *Houston Telegraph*. That paper noted, "The day may come when the Lone Star flag will again court the free breezes of heaven; a civil war may be forced upon us . . . Therefore we bid the K's. G. C. God speed."[10] Of course, the editor of the Houston paper, E. H. Cushing, was a strong Southern Nationalist who had supported William Walker. Yet, general support and acceptance of the KGC was growing by leaps and bounds.

Bickley reported on November 3 that castles had been established in Austin, La Grange, Brenham, Chappell Hill, Houston, Navasota, and Huntsville. By the 12th, Rusk had joined the pack (Marshall, with Greer and Sam Richardson, had long been a KGC community — San Antonio, as headquarters, also could be counted). Four days later, Booneville, Independence, Caldwell, and Owensville were added to the list. A second San Antonio castle as well as one in Bastrop soon came about. As 1860 drew to a close, Columbus, Alleyton, Eagle Lake, and Gonzales had established castles. David Jones reported to the *Houston Telegraph* that the ladies of Owensville were "making the Lone Star flag, and on Saturday it will wave over the Court House." He further noted that the town "was enlivened by squad drills, conducted by our fellow townsman, Lieutenant E. W. Herndon, and the blue cockade with the Lone Star in the centre, glistening upon the caps of the mustermen."[11]

From the weeks before Lincoln's election until the time of the Texas Secession Convention, KGC activity reached a fever pitch.

---

10 *Houston Telegraph*, November 14, 1860, quoted in Dunn, "The KGC in Texas," p. 555.
11 Hicks, Jimmie, "Some Letters Concerning the Knights of the Golden Circle in Texas, 1860-1861." *Southwestern Historical Quarterly*, 75:84.

Roy Sylvan Dunn estimates that there were at least thirty-two castles established in twenty-seven counties. By the time it was over, an interesting cross section of men emerged to assume active roles in the Texas KGC and the secession movement. Alfred M. Hobby of Refugio; Pryor Lea of Goliad; Thomas Lubbock, John Littleton, and John Wilcox of San Antonio; and Philip Luckett were all KGC members and representatives in the secession convention. George Chilton can be added to this list for he was soon to be elected Texas commander of the organization. Professor H. A. Tatum of Columbus, George Chappell of Chappell Hill, George W. Harris of Austin, Thomas Gammage of Rusk, J. Wright of Seguin, and Gonzales Sheriff A. D. Harris were all listed as organizers of local KGC castles.[12] The San Antonio castle listed members such as John M. Carolan, former mayor and district clerk; Albert Wood; George Cupples; and J. A. G. Navarro, the illegitimate son of Tejano patriot, Jose Antonio Navarro, signer of the Texas Declaration of Independence.[13]

Many contemporaries, including Caroline Darrow, wife of a military clerk in San Antonio; Robert Anderson; and James Newcomb clearly cite the KGC in Texas as one of the chief forces which brought Texas out of the Union and, more importantly, helped secure Federal property and troops in Texas. Historian Walter Buenger is less convinced, joining Anna Ira Sandbo in saying that "the most that one can safely say is that probably the order encouraged secession and the extension of slavery and that it was a factor of some importance at the time." Buenger goes on to add, "no amount of neat mathematical wizardry or circumstantial evidence justifies a stronger statement."[14] Roy Sylvan Dunn is more certain, stating that "it brought together men who desired adventure, fame, and fortune. It appealed to those who feared the influx of foreigners and the spread of Roman Catholicism. It offered a weapon to Southerners who resented the unrelenting, ofttimes abusive efforts of the abolitionists."[15]

Today, we may not like the idea of what the KGC stood for. Many people may not like anything about the organization. Yet,

---

12 Dunn, "The KGC in Texas," p. 556.
13 By-laws of the San Antonio Castle, KGC, June 15, 1861, Texas State Archives.
14 Buenger, Walter L., *Secession and the Union in Texas*, (Austin: University of Texas Press, 1984), p. 157.
15 Dunn, "The KGC in Texas," p. 543.

in looking at the secession crisis which gripped Texas, we should come to understand that despite its repellent nature and philosophy, the Knights of the Golden Circle represented more than an organization. It was a centralized force where Southerners and Texans, feeling themselves being pushed and losing control, could find unity and purpose. Expansionists, filibusterers, glory seekers, Southern Nationalists, states' righters, secessionists, or just worried people, all could find something in the KGC to embrace. At the very least, if a man did not join the KGC castles, he could and did tolerate them.

The Unionists of the period may have given the Knights too much credit in saying that they swayed the popular vote. But one thing is certain, by the time the Texas Secession Convention was meeting, the Knights of the Golden Circle were not only organized, but were ready to move. "Hurrah for the independent Texas," a Dallas paper editorialized. "Hurrah for the noble band of K's G C who in the hour of need, prooved [sic] themselves so prompt in striking for the rights of the South! Hurrah for Texas and the Southern Confederacy."[16]

---

16 *Dallas Herald,* February 27, 1861, quoted in Dunn, "The KGC in Texas," p. 568.

CHAPTER FOUR

"Has it come so soon to this?"

Confrontation in San Antonio
1861

The great Secession drama now drifted away from Austin and to San Antonio, headquarters of the Military Department of Texas. Historically, San Antonio has been involved in every military movement which took place in Texas since it was founded by the Spanish in 1718. The original purpose of the settlement was that of an urban military outpost, from which the Spanish could help govern the vast territories between the Rio Nueces and the Sabine. The combination of political and military control subsequently made the growing village a magnet for anyone wishing to control Texas. Mexican insurrectionists in 1813, Spanish Royalists, Mexican soldiers, and Texian revolutionaries had all, at one time or another, occupied the city. With the possible exception of Goliad, San Antonio, by the fall of 1860, was one of the most fought over cities in the Southwest.

When the Republic of Texas joined the Union, San Antonio once again played host to an invading army. This time, their arrival was most welcome. A single company of U.S. Dragoons arrived in October, 1845, establishing the United States Military Post of San Antonio. Some eight months later, when war between Mexico and the United States was in full swing, the Army of the Center under General John Wool arrived. The Americans used the town and its surrounding missions as a base of operations from which to commence their march against Mexico. By the time the Mexican War was concluded, the United States military was firmly entrenched. The establishment of a string of frontier forts in Central and West Texas called for the permanent use of San Antonio as not only a departmental headquarters, but a quartermaster's depot as well.

By the fall of 1860, the Department of Texas boasted some 37 companies of U.S. Regulars. Some 22 of these companies were located on the Rio Grande. The headquarters in San Antonio was guarded by one company each of the 8th and 1st Infantry. There were probably close to 3,000 men stationed in the series of forts and outposts from Brownsville to Fort Bliss.

The Army liked San Antonio and certainly the merchants of San Antonio enjoyed the Army. Because of the positive interaction, the town enjoyed a great prosperity during the 1850s. Oddly enough, the Army never really came to grips with the fact that San Antonio was home. This was evident by the lack of any permanent buildings for military use. Worrying that the frontier expansion might necessitate moving the departmental headquarters, the Army never bothered to secure any property on which to build. Headquarters was in a rented two-story building at St. Mary's and present-day Houston Street owned by the Vance brothers; the ordnance department was located just down the street at the corner of Soledad; the soldiers were billeted in several different locations. The quartermaster had established himself in the ruins of the Alamo.

The occupation of the Alamo caused problems between the Army, the city, and the Catholic church. All three claimed legal title to the property, although the Republic of Texas had recognized the church's right to the property. The Army, however, did not consider the old mission a church, but rather a fort since it was used for that purpose after 1803. The annexation treaty between Texas and the United States turned all military property over to the United States. The city also claimed the property and, for a while, the Army was having to pay rent to both church and state. In the end, the church won.[1]

In 1849 the quartermaster, Edwin Burr Babbitt, suggested tearing down the existing structures and building permanent ones. The Army turned the idea down, and Babbitt went to work roofing the old chapel. The result was the addition of the now familiar Alamo "hump." The old convent or barracks had already been repaired and altered in 1847 for use as offices, while the south barracks were used for forage.[2]

The secession crisis in San Antonio caused great concern. It is nearly impossible to get an objective view of what transpired between the time of Lincoln's election and May 1861, inasmuch as the participants left accounts which are far from impartial. Considering the emotional undertones of most of their histories, it is really a wonder that the war didn't commence in the streets of San Antonio.

The cast of characters was most impressive, however. On the Union side we have Charles Anderson, the brother of Colonel Robert Anderson; James P. Newcomb, editor of the *Alamo Express*; Caroline Baldwin Darrow, wife of an Army clerk; C. A. Waite, colonel of the 1st U.S. Infantry. On the Secessionist side we have John Wilcox, former Mississippi congressman; Ben McCulloch, the famous Texas Ranger; Sam Maverick, signer of the 1836 Texas Declaration of Independence; and a whole bunch of Knights of the Golden Circle. In the middle is one David Twiggs, commanding officer of the 8th Infantry and by December 1860, commander of the Department of Texas.

Special mention should be made of James Newcomb, editor of the *Alamo Express*. As the Lincoln election drew nearer, the editor's bias was plainly apparent as he commenced directing most of his copy against the Secessionists and, in particular, the Knights of the

---

1 Records of the Office of the Quartermaster General (RG92); Consolidated Correspondence File 1794-1915 files on the Alamo, Edwin B. Babbitt and San Antonio; Records of the Office of Chief of Engineer (RG77), National Archives.

2 Young, Kevin R., "Major Babbitt and the Alamo Hump," *Military Images*, Number 6 (July-August, 1984).

Golden Circle. One of the great tragedies of time is that very few copies of the rival newspaper, the *San Antonio Herald*, survive from the period. That paper was decidedly in favor of secession and apparently had a running editorial battle with Newcomb. Unfortunately, the debate today is one-sided, and we have only Newcomb's often sarcastic Unionist viewpoint from which to judge some of the pro-Southern activities in San Antonio.

The Unionists in San Antonio were already more than concerned that the Knights of the Golden Circle were stirring up secession when news of the Lincoln election arrived. The next day a call was made for all of the supporters of John Breckinridge and his Southern Nationalist platform to gather on Alamo Plaza on the evening of November 24. The Unionists saw this as a direct move by the Knights to build the secession fever.

Charles Anderson, who was in town on business, happened into the store of a fellow Unionist when all of this talk of public meetings was transpiring. He was quickly persuaded to represent the Union point of view at the upcoming meeting. Anderson termed it the most "cut and dried affair ever known amongst the shams of politics."[3] Irregardless, the Kentuckian resolved to speak his piece.

An Episcopal reverend started the affair off with "a most eloquent speech calling upon all who were men to stand up for their sacred rights, and to defend their cherished institutions from the intolerable arrogance of the Northerners."[4] His rousing talk was followed with cries of "down with the Yankees; to hell with the Abolitionists!" and an equal number of pistol shots. John Wilcox followed next. Since he was a leader of the local Knights, Wilcox's speech followed party lines. The next speaker was a lawyer from Buffalo, New York, who had embraced the South and her causes. Anderson was far from impressed with him.

After three decidedly pro-Southern speakers, Anderson rose. The crowd was in no mood to listen to Unionist talk. At one point, Anderson himself lost control and became angry about a supposed insult from Wilcox. Considering that the Knights were in the majority and were also armed, the possibility of bloodshed

3 Anderson, Charles, *Texas, Before and on the Eve of the Rebellion*, (Cincinnati: Privately published, 1884), p. 15.
4 Williams, E. W., *With the Border Ruffians*, (New York: E. P. Duntton Company, 1907), p. 159.

was imminent, but cooler heads — remarkably on the Southern side — prevailed and calmed Anderson down. R. H. Williams was one of the observers, who, fearing an outbreak of civil war then and there, quickly exited the plaza. There was some more shooting in the air, however, no one was killed or wounded that night.

Anderson later claimed that his Unionist brother ended the evening by hiring a band and marching around town playing every patriotic song they could think of. While Anderson claimed that the secession rally was a "flat failure," it is doubtful that the Unionists attempts to disrupt the affair were successful.[5]

Clearly, the deteriorating situation called for someone of a strong character and convictions to be able to evaluate and react. Unfortunately for the Unionists, none of these character criteria were to be met.

Colonel Robert E. Lee of the 2nd Cavalry had been placed in temporary command of the Department of Texas in the fall of 1860. Events might have taken a dramatic turn had Lee remained in command, for his character as an officer had already been well established. However, Lee's position ended when the old commander, Major General David Twiggs, was recalled from sick leave. This was the start of a chain of events which still are clouded by intrigue and secrecy.

Twiggs was a Southerner from Georgia, thus sharing Lee's Southern heritage, but apparently did not hold the strong resolve the honor bound Virginian had based his life on. The general had been an officer in the 8th Infantry since the War of 1812. He had won honors during the Mexican War and by 1861 was one of four major generals in the United States Army. As J. J. Bowmen noted, Twiggs' entire career "was one highlighted with caution and self-preservation."[6] The now aging general had removed himself from the active list in 1858, retiring to New Orleans. Now, on the eve of the crisis, he was back assuming command of the Department of Texas on November 27, 1860. Immediately, rumors circulated that Twiggs had been brought in by the Secessionists to ensure the neutralization of the Federal forces.

As early as December 27, the Georgian was writing his superiors on what course to take if Texas did secede. He followed his

---

5   Anderson, *Texas Eve of Rebellion*, p. 17.
6   Bowden, J. J., *The Exodus of Federal Forces From Texas, 1861*, (Austin: Eakin Press, 1986), p. 2.

initial request with letters on January 8 and 15 but received no response. The growing crisis was making hard demands on Twiggs. His personal views were well stated when he informed his superiors that, "As soon as Georgia has separated from the Union, I must, of course, follow her." To Adjutant General Samuel Cooper he wrote, "I will never fire on American citizens."[7]

A few days after Twiggs arrived in San Antonio, word arrived that Ranger Colonel John Baylor was organizing a great "buffalo hunt." Rumors immediately circulated that Baylor's real purpose was to move against San Antonio and take, by force if necessary, the Federal property there. Twiggs had already resigned himself to the certainty that the Texans would attempt to confiscate all the military stores. A letter from Sam Houston did not improve things — the wily governor suggested that Twiggs surrender all of the Federal property to him, as governor of the state, and thus prevent it from being taken by any type of mob. As it turned out, Baylor's "buffalo hunt" did not initially threaten San Antonio. But it did serve to heighten anxieties on both sides. Twiggs continued to wait on instructions from Washington, while the Secession Convention convened in Austin. He was still waiting when the ordinance taking Texas out of the Union was passed.

The Committee of Public Safety, consisting of Sam Maverick, Judge Thomas Devine, and Philip Luckett (the fourth member was absent) had received their charter to enter into negotiations with Twiggs concerning the situation. The instructions were clear. They were to "demand, receive, and receipt for all military, medical, commissary, and ordnance store, arms, munitions of war, and public money," under Twiggs' control.[8] However, before they arrived in San Antonio they had taken precautions. Texas Ranger Ben McCulloch, on February 3, was commissioned a colonel of the cavalry and was ordered to remain near his brother's home in Seguin. He was also ordered to prepare a sufficient force and keep it ready to move against San Antonio if needed. With their backup plans instituted, the three commissioners arrived in San Antonio and, on February 6, commenced negotiations with Twiggs.

The result of their first meeting was a general understanding that upon Texas' secession, Twiggs would surrender all Federal property. However, the general refused to surrender any of his

---

7   OR, Series 1, Part 1, p. 581.
8   OR, pp. 511-512.

General David Twiggs. *Courtesy of the DRT Library at the Alamo.*

command or weapons. Twiggs further noted that if and when the time came to march his men out of Texas he would do so via the Indian Territory. When pressed for a written statement to this effect, Twiggs declined, stating that he would effectively surrender the public property and evacuate his command commencing on March 2.

The meeting was far from calming. The commissioners felt that Twiggs was stalling for time. They informed their committee chair in Austin that "we must obtain possession of that which now belongs to Texas of right by force, or such a display of force as will compel a compliance with our demands."

The aging general was now caught between a tide of forces. He was personally against the idea of secession, yet had resolved to resign if his native state left the Union; he did not want to shed any blood, yet was unwilling to disarm and surrender his men. Twiggs was also determined to transfer all public property to the State of Texas upon its secession from the Union. However, he did not consider the actions of the Convention legal and would not consider Texas' secession a definite fact until after the public vote and acceptance.

Editor Newcomb at the *Alamo Express* did not help matters much. His paper ran a statement on February 6 that Twiggs was in league with the Knights of the Golden Circle and was conspiring to hand Texas over to the secessionists. Caroline Darrow was more than convinced; she claimed to have accidentally overheard a conversation between Twiggs and a "prominent Southern lady" which indicated that the general was about ready to "betray his trust."[9] Anderson, who also blamed Twiggs, noted that "he was assuredly unfit for any important business, and ought to have been retired for life."[10]

Twiggs now appointed his own committee to meet with the commissioners. His choices were Major D. H. Vinton (quartermaster), Major S. Macklin (paymaster), and Captain R. H. K. Whiteley (ordnance department). They met daily with Maverick, Devine, and Luckett, but things reached an impasse on February 15. The problems arose when the Federal officers refused to consider handing over any funds in their care to the secessionists

---

9   Darrow, Caroline, "Recollections of the Twiggs Surrender," *Battles and Leaders of the Civil War,* 1:34.

10 Anderson, *Texas Eve of Rebellion,* p. 23.

or to discuss details on the withdrawal of the Federal forces. Then they let the cat out of the bag. Twiggs had been replaced by Colonel Waite of the 1st Infantry, who was currently on his way to San Antonio.

Even if Twiggs was stalling, he was nevertheless a Southerner. Waite was definitely not; he was a very staunch Unionist. This created an impossible situation. If the commissioners waited until March 2 to receive the property, it was probable that Waite would already be in command.

With the Convention about to adjourn, the commissioners received final instructions which gave them "large discretion." The Federal property in San Antonio and Texas must be secured, but not as to dishonor the U.S. Army. The instructions concluded that the Convention was "relying upon your wisdom and prudence." McCulloch and his command were ordered to San Antonio.

In Seguin, under a stand of live oaks near Walnut Springs, McCulloch and his brother organized their forces. The fact that the local KGC companies were already prepared to march didn't hurt matters. When the force rode out, the local college brass band accompanied them to the city limits, adding a martial sound to the formation. They arrived at Salado Creek, some five miles east of San Antonio, and there awaited their fellows.

At least nine companies of volunteers would answer the call. Besides the Seguin men in a Captain Martin's company, additional citizens would arrive from Gonzales, Lockhart, and Dewitt County. The backbone of the force was the already organized Knights of the Golden Circle castles, which included the Pleasanton, New Braunfels, Castroville, and Seguin castles.

San Antonio itself would supply at least two groups in the demonstration. One of the companies all ready to go was the Alamo City Guards under William Edgar. Formed in 1859 as a militia company, its ties with the Knights were more than close. With them were the Alamo Rifles, also a militia company with strong KGC ties. John Wilcox and John Carolina were leading officers in the company.

The collection of volunteers and Knights was far from military in appearance. Some had coats, but most were in shirt-sleeves. The weather was cold. This resulted in some of them wrapping old shawls and extra saddle blankets over their shoulders. The armament was equally as diverse. McCulloch had had his officers sew a red-flannel stripe on their shoulders.

Under the cover of darkness, the mounted men moved into San Antonio, quickly occupying the streets and plazas. McCulloch intended to have his men in position before the sun came up, thus surrounding all of the Federal property before anyone could react. The Guadalupe and Caldwell County men, 100 in total, took positions around the arsenal with Lt. Tribble of the KGC in command. The editors of the Lockhart newspaper were with this group.[11]

Caroline Darrow was asleep in her room at the Read House when she was awakened in the predawn by some Negroes screaming, "We're all going to be killed!"[12] The fiery female Unionist took her revolver and peered out into Main Plaza. She could see a group of mounted men, proceeding orderly, entering the area. Before them was the Lone Star flag.

Some eighty men were delegated the responsibility of taking positions on the flat roofs of some houses overlooking the Alamo. E. H. Williams was one of these men. He would remember standing with loaded rifle for nearly four hours, expecting every moment that hostilities would commence. The sun rose to reveal the United States flag being hauled down over the Alamo and a "Lone Star flag" raised in its place. The Texans went wild with hurrahs and cheers.[13]

Just what flag was hoisted over the historic Alamo is subject for debate, although it is more than likely that it was either a Texas state flag or the Alamo City Guards flag. That flag, made by some San Antonio ladies, was a traditional "Bonnie Blue flag" with the white star on a light blue field. Besides bearing the name "Alamo City Guards" it carried the motto, "Fiat Justitia Ruat Coelum" [sic] (Though the Heavens Fall, Let Justice Be Done).[14]

Owing to his orders, the officer of the day Captain John H. King, First Infantry, had instructed the guards at the Alamo not to load their muskets or to resist an armed force attempting to seize

---

11 *Seguin Southern Confederacy*, February 22, 1861.
12 Darrow, "Recollections," p. 34.
13 Williams, *Border Ruffians*, p. 163.
14 Connor, J. E., *The Centennial Record of the San Antonio's Army Service Forces Depot, 1845-1945*, (San Antonio: Privately published, 1945), p. 46.

the public property. Upon the arrival of McCulloch's men, the guard was retired.

The men in the plaza were lavished with coffee and refreshments. Someone distributed blankets and additional clothing, which improved the improvised army's appearance. Two Secessionist woman had dressed in male attire, complete with pistols in their belts, to join the men.[15] Most, if not all, of the Federal officers were caught at different locations. Major Larkin Smith received word at 3:45 A.M. that a large force of armed men was entering the city. Smith headed over to the 8th Infantry's quarters, formed Company A, and ordered them to remain indoors. With his troops accounted for, the major elected to visit the headquarters and see what was developing.

Some 80 of McCulloch's men surrounded the building but apparently did not disrupt traffic, as Smith now returned to his quarters. At Main Plaza, Smith encountered Ben McCulloch himself, who was in the process of directing a party of his men up the stairs of the ordnance building. Smith informed the Texan that there were soldiers inside. McCulloch proceeded to tell the Federal officer that his forces were in commanding positions and would take possession of all the public property. If the Federals remained secure, they would not be molested. McCulloch further illustrated the futility of the Federal's position by stating that a force on the east side of the river had already cut off the Federals.

Lieutenant Colonel Hoffman was notified in the early morning that there was excitement in town. He quickly headed for his office. Next door was the quarters for Company I of the 1st Infantry, and Hoffman overheard one of its corporals report to the officer of the day that, with the appearance of the large armed force, he had withdrawn his guard from the Alamo. The building being used as an arsenal was already in possession of the Texans, who were now thronging the streets around both the infantry quarters and the commissary department. Remarkably, things actually remained pretty quiet.

Hoffman returned to his quarters around sunrise only to have a note addressed to the commander of the department delivered. Realizing there had been a misunderstanding, Hoffman directed the note to A. A. G. Nichols.[16]

---

15 Darrow, "Recollections," p. 35.
16 OR, pp. 517-518.

Ben McCulloch.   *Courtesy of the Eugene C. Barker Research Center, University of Texas at Austin.*

The bullet (top) which killed Ben McCulloch at Elkhorn Tavern, March 2, 1862. The buttons (bottom) are from the coat he was wearing when he was shot. *Courtesy of the Eugene C. Barker Research Center, University of Texas at Austin.*

Twiggs himself was in transit, en route to headquarters, when he was stopped in Main Plaza. He was taken over to the nearby Plaza House Hotel and there received a brief statement from the Committee of Public Safety: "You are hereby required, in the name and by the authority of the People of the State of Texas, in Convention assembled, to deliver up all military posts and public property held by or under your control."[17]

Twiggs surrendered, telling the commissioners that he "gave up everything."[18] Without firing a single shot, McCulloch and his men had secured every building occupied by the Federals, and the commissioners had obtained the total surrender of the entire United States Army in Texas.

The next day, fearing the possibility of retraction since the answer had been verbal, the commissioners addressed Twiggs as "to avoid even the possibility of a collision between the Federal troops and the force acting on behalf of the State of Texas — a collision which all reflecting persons desire to avoid, and the consequences of which no man can predict — we again demand the surrender up to the undersigned of all the posts and public property held by you, or under your control, in this department."[19]

The Georgian quickly complied, directing "the positions held by the Federal troops to be turned over to the authorized agents of the State of Texas, provided the troops retain their arms and clothing, camp and garrison equipage, quartermaster's store, subsistence, medical, hospital store, and such means of transportation of every kind as may be necessary for an efficient and orderly movement of the troops from Texas, prepared for attack or defense against aggression from any source."[20]

The commissioners responded, accepting Twiggs' terms and agreeing that the troops should leave Texas by the coast, with the provision that when they arrived at the point of embarkation, they agreed to deliver up all means of transportation and artillery.[21]

The surrender of the artillery became somewhat of a last minute hitch. Twiggs considered the surrendering of any of his light artillery batteries "a lasting disgrace upon the arms of the

---

17 OR, p. 513.
18 OR, p. 513.
19 OR, p. 514.
20 OR, p. 514.
21 OR, p. 514.

United States." The commissioners agreed to allow the two batteries of light artillery, in addition to the infantry and cavalry's small arms to be retained.

The issues now decided, Twiggs issued General Order No. 5 in which he ordered the post evacuated and the men of the garrisons to march to the coast with their arms and light artillery.[22] The Committee of Public Safety also issued a general circular reinforcing the agreement and adding that "there shall be no infraction of this agreement on the part of the people of the State. It is their wish, on the contrary, that every facility shall be afforded the troops. They are our friends. They have heretofore afforded to our people all the protection in their power and we owe them every consideration."[23]

Remarkably, no one was shot or killed. Colonel Hoffman had apparently ordered his men not to load their muskets but then rescinded the order. The fact that McCulloch's men never tried to physically disarm any of the Federal troops probably prevented any armed clash. The only casualties that occurred were on the Texan side, and they were caused by someone dropping a shotgun on Main Plaza, wounding several men and a couple of the horses.

Hoffman and Smith were allowed to march their respective commands to San Pedro Springs, where they would camp until such times as transportation to the coast could be arranged. Newcomb, with his usual Unionist zeal, reported that they "marched out with colors flying and band playing the national airs, and the old bullet-riddled and war-stained banner of the 8th Regiment floating in the breeze." He added that "people cheered the troops all along the streets." To the newspaper editor, the entire scene represented "the reality of all the sham, farce and incipient tragedy" of the surrender, noting, "our citizens feel humiliated and sorrowful, and there are few men who can trust their eyes in their neighbors face. And is there an American, we ask, who would not feel humiliated thus to see the glory of his country departing?"[24]

Into this atmosphere soon arrived two Federal officers; Carlos A. Waite, the new commanding officer of the Department of Texas, and Colonel Robert E. Lee, the former commander. Lee was on his

---

22   OR, p. 515.
23   OR, p. 516.
24   *Alamo Express*, February 19, 1861.

Artistic renditions of the Twiggs surrender done for *Harper's Weekly*, March 23, 1861. *Courtesy of the DRT Library at the Alamo.*

The surrender of General Twiggs. This photograph was taken from the south side of Main Plaza looking towards the Plaza House Hotel. John Carolan's auction house is to the left. *Courtesy of the DRT Library at the Alamo.*

way to Washington, D.C., at the orders of General Winfield Scott, and had little idea of just what he was getting into. It was about two in the afternoon when his coach arrived from his command at Fort Mason. He found Main Plaza still full of McCulloch's men. The Virginian dismounted and proceeded to walk toward his lodgings at the Read House, where Caroline Darrow was waiting to greet him.

Looking back at the Texans in the plaza, Lee asked, "Who are those men?" Darrow informed him that they were attached to Colonel McCulloch and that Twiggs had surrendered. "I shall never forget his look of astonishment, and with his lips trembling and his eyes full of tears, he exclaimed, 'Has it come so soon to this?'"[25]

For the honor bound Virginian, the realization of what was transpiring was more than sobering. Mrs. Darrow, whose room was below his at the Read House, could hear him pace all night long. When Captain Reuben Potter ran into him, he was still distressed. "When I get to Virginia," he said, "I think the world will have one soldier less. I shall resign and go to planting corn."[26]

He made a similar statement to Robert Anderson, remarking, "If Virginia stands by the old Union, so will I. But if she secedes, then I will still follow my native State with my sword and, if need be, with my life." Anderson knew that Lee was opposed to secession and felt it unconstitutional. "I know," Lee told him, "you think and feel very differently, but I can't help it. These are my principles, and I must follow them."[27]

Apparently, some effort was made to entice Lee to resign his commission while in San Antonio. He refused, electing to continue on to Washington. Some problems developed concerning his personal baggage when the Confederates insisted that there was no room in the transportation cabin for the trunks. Lee deposited his trunks at the Vance House and arranged with Charles Anderson to have them shipped to him. There is some doubt as to whether or not the trunks were ever forwarded.

---

25 Darrow, "Recollections," p. 36.
26 Darrow, "Recollections," p. 36.
27 Anderson, *Texas Eve of Destruction*, p. 32.

Lee was not the only person to have transportation problems. Some of the Seguin volunteers had left their horses at the Salado and had to pay a dollar to ride the stage to get back.[28]

After a week, Robert E. Lee left San Antonio for the East and his destiny. Before the Virginian lay an offer to command the United States Army. True to his word, Lee resigned his commission when Virginia left the Union. He did not become a farmer. The seeds Lee planted were to grow into the Army of Northern Virginia.

Colonel Waite, the new Federal commander, arrived from Camp Verde in the middle of the afternoon and he also found McCulloch's men everywhere — and his entire command surrendered. The colonel quickly evaluated his alternatives. The prospects were not good. With his command spread out across the frontier, it was apparently not practical to concentrate any type of force to resist. Waite was compelled to comply with Twiggs' agreement. On the 19th, he formally relieved Twiggs of his command.

On March 1, a two-week-old order arrived from Washington informing Waite that "in the events of the secession of the State of Texas, the General-in-Chief directs that you will, without unnecessary delay, put in march for Fort Leavenworth the entire military force of your department."[29] Waite informed Washington on March 13 that he had already established a camp at Green Lake, twenty miles from Indianola, and was instructing his various commands to concentrate at the spot. Green Lake offered the best water in the coastal bend plus plenty of grazing for horses and mules. It was the perfect spot to organize the evacuation of the Federal troops from Texas.[30]

In the meantime, the historic March 2 date had come. The San Antonio Unionists struck again at Carolan's Auction Room by taking the flag; they also defaced a KGC flag over Braden's Grocery and, in an effort to haul down the Alamo City Guards flag over the Alamo, caught the flag up on the pole. It hung at half-mast for the rest of the day, despite every effort to free it.[31]

---

28 *Seguin Southern Confederacy*, February 22, 1861.
29 OR, p. 589.
30 OR, p. 534.
31 *Alamo Express*, March 4, 1861.

David Twiggs, who had departed for New Orleans, was stricken from the United States Army on March 1, 1861. Just how involved he was in any plot by Secessionists is still not clear. Anderson, Darrow, and the other Unionists felt him entirely to blame. J. Bowden, in his history of the affair, found Twiggs innocent, stating that "time has shown these accusations to have been false" and that Twiggs was being blamed by "the stunned and disappointed populace of the North."[32]

---

32 Bowden, *Exodus of Federal Forces*, p. 119.

CHAPTER FIVE

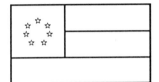

"No further hope of our escape"

Confrontation at San Lucas Springs

Jefferson Davis had barely begun his term as president of the new Confederate States when General Braxton Bragg, the new commander at New Orleans, dispatched him an urgent letter regarding the status of the U.S. troops evacuating Texas. Inasmuch as it was still three weeks before hostilities would commence in South Carolina, Davis, via his new Secretary of War, advised Bragg that "the question submitted for consideration is not altogether free from difficulty."

The letter went on to state a policy of "good faith" — that if a formal capitulation or a formal agreement had been reached either "in the surrender or abandonment of the forts, that they should have peaceful exit through the territories of the Government." However, should any of these troops try to "posses or occupy any of the forts, arsenals, or other property of this Government within these States," Bragg was authorized to hold them at once.[1]

Federal troops were still encamped and embarking homeward from Indianola in April when, on the 17th, word of Fort Sumter arrived. The Seguin Southern Confederacy was announcing the war had begun two days later. The commencement of hostilities and the call for volunteers by Lincoln naturally changed any arrangements or policy enacted by Texan officials or the Confederate government. Orders were immediately sent for the interception and prevention of movement of any Federal troops remaining in Texas.

Matters now took a serious turn. With Federal troops still evacuating from Indianola and additional forces still on the march from the western forts, a sizable number of Federal soldiers were still active and under arms in Texas. If the Confederates now considered any previous agreements void and hostilities active, then it was highly possible that the Federal commanders might also have similar thoughts. If that was the case, then the reality of fighting was very apparent.

Earl Van Doren, a colorful Mississippian and former officer in the 2nd Cavalry was dispatched to Galveston to help organize Confederate response to the problem. His actions over the next few weeks would demonstrate just how quickly the Confederates could react to a problem even with an infant government just in place. Arriving on April 16, Van Doren was informed that a large force of Federal troops were encamped at Green Lake between Victoria and Indianola. This force included elements of the 1st and 8th Infantry from Forts Chadbourne, Lancaster, and Ringgold Barracks, plus the two regimental staffs. Major Caleb C. Sibley was in command of the encampment.

In addition, the regimental staff of the 8th Infantry, plus its band, was still encamped outside of San Antonio. The officers of the departmental headquarters were still in San Antonio and at least two other forces were still on the march: that of Captain Arthur Lee from Fort Stockton, and the combined garrisons of Forts Bliss, Quitman, and Davis.

Van Doren quickly formulated plans to systematically cut off any possible escape routes and isolate each of the forces. Since

---

1   L. P. Walker, Secretary of War, to Major-General Braxton Bragg, Commanding New Orleans, February 25, 1861, OR, Series 1, Volume 1, p. 35.

Sibley's force at Green Lake was better organized and also had arranged transportation at Indianola, the Confederate commander elected to handle this group first.

General Earl Van Doren. This photograph was taken when he was still an officer in the Federal army. *Courtesy of the Department of Archives and History, Archives and Library Division, State of Mississippi.*

With 125 men from Galveston, Van Doren set sail aboard the steamer *Matagorda* for Passo Cavallo at the mouth of Indianola Bay. There he found *Star of the West* at anchor and chartered to transport the Federals to New York. Fearing that his slower, smaller vessel was no match for *Star of the West*, Van Doren continued on to Saluria where he found *General Rusk*. This vessel had also been employed as a transport. A plan soon developed. Van Doren took over *General Rusk*, transferred his men aboard, and set out for *Star of the West*. At just after sundown, *General Rusk* approached *Star of the West*, whose crew called out for identification. Van Doren responded that they were Federal soldiers. The trick worked. *General Rusk* pulled up alongside *Star of the West*; Van Doren's men boarded and seized the vessel. Sibley's force was now stuck inland.

Sibley, meanwhile, had contracted two other schooners to help transport his men. While he worked at this with renewed effort, Van Doren had returned to Galveston, secured two more vessels, and made a call for volunteers. This time he had artillery from his boats, which were lined with cotton bales for protection. The fleet sailed for Indianola while Van Doren rallied his volunteer infantry at Victoria. This time, volunteers and Knights of the Golden Circle companies came to his aid from all over the coastal bend.

Sibley had brought his command to Indianola where, failing to find *Star of the West*, he reluctantly moved his force back. On April 21, he chartered *Horace* and *Urbana*. Delays occurred as *Urbana* had not yet unloaded her cargo. On the 23rd, Sibley was able to commence his retreat. Then the weather turned against him. It became apparent the heavily loaded *Urbana* would not be able to withstand the rough seas. So Sibley once again was forced to delay as he dispatched a small detachment under Captain Bowman to secure the services of a vessel reported off Port Lavaca. Bowman and his men never returned.

On the morning of the 25th, Sibley looked out in disgust to see three schooners blocking the bay. He noted the cotton bales and the artillery. Van Doren's fleet had arrived. "There being no further hope of our escape," he wrote, "I was obliged to accede to the requirements of Colonel Van Doren and surrendered my command as prisoners of war."[2]

---

2   OR, Series 2, Volume 1, pp. 49-50.

General C. C. Sibley. *Courtesy of Massachusetts Commandery, Military Order of the Loyal Legion and the U.S. Army History Institute.*

Bowman and his men had been captured near Powderhorn. They, too, surrendered. On the 25th Sibley and Van Doren entered into an agreement:

"It is stipulated and agreed to that the United States troops, officers, and men, shall become prisoners of war, with the privilege of giving their paroles of honor if officers, and their oaths if soldiers, not to bear arms or exercise any of the functions of their office, under their commissions or enlistments, against the Confederate States of America, unless an exchange of prisoners shall be made, or until released by the authority of the President of the Confederate States. The arms and equipments of the men, and all the public property in the possession of the company commanders, to be given up to an agent, appointed for the purpose, on board the transport which shall be employed to convey those who may desire it to the United States; private property to be unmolested.

"It is further stipulated and agreed to, that all the officers and men who shall give their paroles and oaths, as above stated, shall be allowed to pass unmolested through the Confederate States of America, by the way of Galveston and up the Mississippi River to any point they may see fit to go within the limits of the United States of America, or by any other route they may see fit to take."[3]

On the 30th, Sibley's command, now on three vessels, was allowed to proceed on to New York. They arrived on May 31 and June 1. Round one had gone to Van Doren.

Things did not go quite as smoothly in San Antonio. Van Doren dispatched Strickland Maclin, his inspector general, to secure the Federal personnel there as prisoners of war. Maclin turned to the Knights of the Golden Circle for help, enlisting both the Alamo City Guards and the Alamo Rifles.

One of the first problems to arise was that the garrison from Fort Stockton, which had been encamped just north of San Antonio, had moved before the Alamo City Guards could intercept them. The Guards' acting commander, James Duff, had to quickly assemble his command in Main Plaza in order to set a trap. Lieutenant Edward H. Read (who was acting commander) came marching in with Company "C," 1st Infantry, not suspecting a thing. The trap was sprung before the Federals could react. The

---

3   OR, p. 50.

lieutenant demanded an audience with his superior, Colonel Waite. Duff obliged but all the Federal commander could do was advise Read to surrender. There was simply no other alternative.

While Read and Waite were talking, Colonel Hoffman came marching in with his headquarters company. Duff surrounded them in the same manner. Within a matter of a few hours, all of the Federal infantry in San Antonio had literally marched into the Confederates' hands.

Now it was Captain John Allen Wilcox's turn. With his KGC Alamo Rifles as backup, the ardent Secessionist was dispatched to inform Colonel Waite that he and his officers were under arrest as prisoners of war. Wilcox went alone to their quarters and found both Federal officers less than ready to comply. Waite launched into the captain with a tirade about authority, about "unwarranted" acts of "usurpation" and violations of the modes and customs of civilized warfare, and "a gross outrage upon individual rights." Waite refused to recognize Wilcox, Maclin, or the Confederate States. As a matter of fact, he added the only authority he would respond to was one of "a force greater than I can overcome."

Wilcox took his leave and within a few minutes returned with "a force greater" — some 36 Texas infantry armed with rifles and sabre bayonets. Waite again protested "this gross and unwarranted act of usurpation" and "violation of my personal rights." J. T. Sprague, who was present, informed Wilcox that he agreed fully with every word uttered by Colonel Waite. In the end, the two protesting Federals agreed to accompany Wilcox to the ordnance office.

Upon arrival here they found their fellow officers present, also already under arrest and under guard. Waite was fuming when Major Maclin arrived. His mood probably did not improve when he came face to face with the new Confederate inspector general who, up until March 1, had been the paymaster for the department. The Confederate was also in a no-nonsense, business mood. Former friendships and comrades-in-arms relationships aside, he informed Waite that he and his fellow officers were under arrest as prisoners of war by the power of the president of the Confederate States. Waite, who apparently was not thrilled by having a "traitor" dictate terms to him, replied that he didn't recognize such an authority. He followed by pointing out that he and his fellows had done nothing to deserve this; that they had kept their agreement with the Texas commissioners in February and that they should be allowed to leave the state unmolested.

Maclin was in no mood for this. He informed Waite that he had his orders and that protests were useless. The debate continued for a few moments. At last Waite pushed Maclin by stating that only "the presence of a force requires me to listen to such measures, much more than obey them. Had I the means, it would be quite different." The gauntlet was thrown, but Maclin refused to pick it up. He simply acknowledged the courage of Waite and his officers.

Now Waite and Maclin locked horns on the subject of paroles. Waite had serious objections to even considering signing the documents which would take him from a prisoner of war, a status he really did not accept, to a paroled prisoner. The two argued over the wording of the documents, and the time allowed the officers to decide. Waite then insisted that he be allowed to have one of his officers remain behind in charge of the enlistment. Maclin refused, saying that the Confederates would take care of the prisoners and that he had no desire to permit any of their officers to remain and have contact with them — particularly Waite himself. Waite exploded. "It is your wish," he told Maclin, "to corrupt them and to force them into your service." Maclin fired back that he found Waite's language offensive. The Yankee major responded, "The facts, sir, are doubtless offensive!"[4]

Waite asked for permission to send his official report to his superiors with a paroled officer. In the end, Maclin allowed each of the Federal officers 24 hours to consider the subject of their paroles. On the 24th, the Federal officers elected to accept the paroles rather than "be subjected to the rabble, to crowds of indisciplined troops regardless of authority or control." At least with the paroles they would be allowed to leave Texas. Under protest, the paroles were signed. The documents stated that the signer would not take up arms against the Confederate States and that no communication would be entered in with the authorities of the United States unless the signer was officially exchanged.[5]

The paroles signed, Waite officially dismissed his officers. All except Lieutenant Hartz left with their families shortly thereafter.

---

4   Sprague, J. T., *The Treachery in Texas*, (New York: Press of the Rebellion Record, 1862), pp. 137-139.
5   Sprague, *Treachery in Texas*, p. 139.

A few days later, Hartz, with Sergeant-Major Joseph K. Wilson and Corporal John C. Hesse of the 8th Infantry, happened to be inside the regimental headquarters when they noticed that the regiment's flags, which had been carried in the Mexican War, were still there. Hartz quickly proposed that the trio do something to insure the flags would be saved. Hesse took one of the flags and wrapped it around his body, concealing it with his shirt and tunic. He then proceeded to walk out of the office, past a large guard of Confederates, with the concealed flag. As soon as they were safely in Hartz's quarters, Hesse divested himself of the banner and placed it in one of the lieutenant's trunks. The Confederates never suspected a thing, and the flag was returned to Washington, D.C. when the trio arrived there on May 26.

After the great Locomotive Chase in 1862 (when Federal raiders stole a Confederate train and attempted to disrupt the railroad lines in Northern Georgia), the United States Army adopted the Congressional Medal of Honor for meritorious service. Hesse, by then a clerk in the adjutant-general's office, petitioned Colonel E. D. Townsend, assistant adjutant-general, for the medal. "Under the circumstances, I think that I am entitled to award them to enlisted men who have done acts similar to mine," he wrote. "I have performed one of the highest duties of a soldier, having saved the colors of my regiment, and it will always be a happy day for me if I can see my regiment marching with their colors flying, and can say, 'That color I have carried on my body, and have rescued it from the hands of the rebels.'"[6] Despite Hesse's modesty, he was awarded the Medal of Honor on September 10, 1864.

The one last group of Federals still wandering around Texas was the command of Lieutenant Colonel Isaac Reeve. This force consisted of six companies of the 8th Infantry, representing the garrisons of Fort Bliss, Fort Quitman, and Fort Davis, a total of 320 men (including ten officers, two stewards, and twelve musicians).[7] Reeve had received General Twiggs' orders to evacuate his post and proceed to the coast for transportation, but owing to the remoteness of his command at Fort Bliss, he took longer in preparation and travel than his fellow officers.

---

6   Hesse, OR, Series 1, Part 1, p. 567. Hesse's medal was later revoked.
7   Reeve, May 12, 1861, OR, pp. 567-568.

On May 2, Reeve and his command arrived at Fort Clark (Brackettville) to find its Confederate garrison reinforced and ready for action. Reeve quickly calmed the fears of the post commander, who was certain the Federals had every intention of attacking, by assuring him that he had no desire to break the treaty. Reeve's own uncertainty was heightened when he was informed from a stage passenger that Waite and the other Federal officers in San Antonio had been made prisoners of war. The Federal commander, nevertheless, proceeded on with his command, arriving at Uvalde on May 5.

It was now becoming apparent that something was up with the Confederates. Reeve weighed his options. Returning to New Mexico was impractical, since he only had five day's rations left and most of the transportation had become worn. The presence of 200 Confederates at Fort Clark to his rear also entered into his decision not to attempt a return. The only option was a run to the Rio Grande, which Reeve quickly discounted, owing to Twiggs' treaty and the possibility of international complications of taking 200 U.S. Regulars into a foreign country.

So Reeve continued marching east. The news grew more gloomy with each mile. Word of the *Star of the West* incident arrived. The Federals still pressed on to Castroville, arriving at the Medina on the eighth. Here Reeve purchased supplies and camped, only to learn that a large force of Confederates, with artillery, was advancing from San Antonio towards his position. To avoid surprise and to be in possession of plenty of water, Reeve ordered a march at midnight, heading to Lioncito Creek some six miles to the east. Finding no Confederates there, he pushed on. Lieutenant Z. R. Bliss suggested that Reeve halt his command at a good water hole known as San Lucas Springs.

The springs were against a high hill, and the site contained corrals, houses, and a well in the yard. The elevation was "a commanding position" known as Adam's Hill. Here, just after sunrise on the ninth, Reeve elected to stop and make preparations for defense.[8]

Around 9 A.M., two riders bearing a white flag were sighted. They approached the Federals and identified themselves as representatives of Colonel Earl Van Doren of the Confederate army.

---

8   Reeve, May 12, 1861, OR, p. 570.

Colonel I. V. D. Reeve. *Courtesy of Massachusetts Commandery, Military Order of the Loyal Legion and the U.S. Army History Institute.*

Their message was simple — surrender unconditionally to Van Doren's overwhelming force. Reeve was not impressed. So far, the only Confederates he had seen were these two officers, and until a superior force presented itself or one of his officers could inspect such a command, he refused any surrender demands. The officers departed and soon afterwards, the "overwhelming force" made its appearance.

Van Doren, who still maintained his "desire to arrest and disarm"[9] the Federals without violence, had assembled a mixed command of cavalry, infantry, and artillery. The cavalry was placed under Henry McCulloch (the toughened Ranger veteran and brother of Ben McCulloch), while James Duff held command of the infantry. The Alamo City Guards under Edgar were there, serving as artillery. So were the Alamo Rifles under John Wilcox and Eugeno Navarro.

The Mississippi colonel sent word to Reeve. If the "display of force was not sufficient" he could "send an officer to examine it."[10] Reeve replied that it wasn't, so he dispatched Lieutenant Bliss to take a long, careful look at it.

Bliss, with Van Doren's permission, rode within 30 yards of the Confederate lines, which lay a half mile in front of the hill, occupying the low ground, blocking the road, and partially obscured by the high brush. Bliss got close enough to ascertain that the cavalry were armed with rifles and revolvers, the infantry with muskets and revolvers, and that there were four pieces of artillery. The total strength of the Confederates was estimated at between 1200 and 1500.

The Federal lieutenant was now impressed. So was Reeve. The road to the coast was blocked, he was outnumbered five to one, short on provisions, and had no hope of reinforcements. In short, Van Doren held all the cards. "I deemed that stubborn resistance and consequent bloodshed and sacrifice of life would be inexcusable and criminal, and I therefore surrendered."[11] Round three went to Van Doren.

The Confederate commander immediately allowed Reeve to march unmolested to San Antonio. A camp was established where the Confederates took all arms and equipment. Reeve noted that

---

9   Van Doren, May 10, 1861, OR, p. 572.
10   Reeve, OR, p. 570.
11   Reeve, OR, p. 570.

his men were well treated, "with generosity and delicacy" adding that as "harrowed and wounded as our feelings are, we have not had to bear personal contumely and insult."[12]

Colonel Van Doren was proud to inform General Cooper at Montgomery that he had captured the last of Twiggs' soldiers without firing a shot, adding that "the troops under my command . . . conducted themselves throughout the expedition [with] cheerful obedience to orders." He added that, "The discipline was maintained in their camp, where judges, lawyers, mechanics, and laborers could be seen walking post as sentinels on the same rounds, all willing to do duty in a good cause, and at the close there was the delicacy of brave men, of soldiers, which checked everything like exultation over an unfortunate enemy who a stern necessity had caused us to disarm. It was gratifying to me, as it is a pleasure to me to report to you, that the whole expedition passed off without one unpleasant incident."[13]

Reeve was equally pleased with his men. "With the exception of some five or six," he wrote, "they remained faithful to their Government and refused all offers and inducements to join the Confederate service." He added, "They have been as well if not much better treated than is the usual fate of prisoners of war. Their peril consists of the fact that they are retained as hostages against the rigorous treatment of any prisoners who may fall into the power of the United States."[14] However, Mrs. Darrow stated that she found the soldiers almost destitute and "cursing the man who had placed them in this position."[15]

On June 1 word arrived at San Antonio that Reeve's oldest daughter had died. Despite the fact that approval of parole had yet to arrive from Montgomery, Van Doren allowed Reeve the opportunity to return home to care for his family.

As to be expected, Newcomb at the *Alamo Express* used the incident to take yet another hit at the Confederates. His paper ran the headline "Brilliant Expedition" reminding his readers that the Federals were bound by treaty not to resist, therefore contributing greatly to the outcome of Van Doren's "Glorious

---

12 Reeve, OR, p. 570.
13 Van Doren, OR, p. 572.
14 Reeve, OR, p. 571.
15 Darrow, Caroline, "Recollections of the Twiggs Surrender," *Battles and Leaders of the Civil War*, 1:37.

Battle." He further stated that he had run the editorial "taking it for granted that this is a free country still, and that there is liberty of the press."[16]

The fearless editor really did take things for granted. He had been taking every opportunity to insult the secession movement since before the Lincoln election, and his uncompromising stand did not make him any admirers from the Confederate ranks. The Medina River (Castroville) KGC ran a notice in the *San Antonio Herald* that Newcomb had used the *Alamo Express* columns "for the purpose of injuring the KGC, an order devoted to the protection of southern interests and preservation of southern institutions."[17]

The night that Newcomb blasted Van Doren and his men on the San Lucas Springs affair, an unknown party (who the Unionists claimed were actually Knights) broke into Newcomb's office, destroyed the press, and fired the building. The editor was not injured in the destructive raid but, fearing for his life, fled to Castroville. The *Seguin Southern Confederacy* noted, "We are astonished that the good people of San Antonio allowed that abolition sheet to live as long as it has. If we get clear of a few more in the same way, Texas will be free of incendiary newspapers. Won't Mr. Newcomb see the error of his way now?"[18] Newcomb soon exited Texas for California as did his fellow Unionist, Charles Anderson.

At least six of the Federal officers who had been under Twiggs' command resigned their commissions to join the Confederate States army. Two or more of the officers captured at San Lucas Springs were also to follow the Stars and Bars. From Texas outposts future Confederate leaders like Edmund Kirby Smith, Fitzhugh Lee, John Bell Hood, and, of course, Robert E. Lee would take their leaves of the United States Army. Others would remain with the Union. Once evacuated, some of the officers who remained with the Union went on to win honors at Perryville, Cold Harbor, Ceder Mountain, Chickamauga, Culpepper, Murfreesboro, and Gettysburg. Two of them, Abraham Arnold and Z. Bliss, would win the Medal of Honor. Apparently, some

---

16 *Alamo Express*, May 13, 1861.
17 *Alamo Express*, February 25, 1861.
18 *Seguin Southern Confederacy*, May 17, 1861. Quoted in Dunn, Roy Sylvan, "The KGC In Texas, 1860-1861," *Southwestern Historical Quarterly*, 70:570.

members of the 2nd Cavalry got their licks in before leaving Texas. Passing through Goliad, the enlisted men took the opportunity to tear down the Secession flag which William Chase and his fellows had labored so hard to raise. With Chase gone (and apparently anyone else who cared) the Federal troopers tore the flag into ribbons and then proceeded to decorate their mules with the streamers.[19]

For now, the Federal army was gone from Texas. Before the summer was out Texans would fight their first battles in Missouri at Wilson's Creek, while to the east in Virginia (and just outside of Washington, D.C.), two overconfident armies would clash near Manassas Junction. Both of the battles would be Confederate victories. They would serve to illustrate that this war was not to be a quick one, and it would be a bloody family affair.

---

19 Simpson, Harold B., *Cry Comanche—The Second U.S. Cavalry in Texas, 1855-1861*, (Hillsboro, Texas: Hill Junior College Press, 1979), p. 165.

CHAPTER SIX

"A soldier for this war"

Texans Go to War

Following the surrender of Fort Sumter, Lincoln issued a call for volunteers to crush what he termed "a rebellion." The Southern Confederacy was just as swift to issue a proclamation for military mobilization. When that call for volunteers was issued, Texans quickly rallied. In the course of the three years between Manassas and Appomattox, Texas was to supply 28 regiments of cavalry, 4 battalions of cavalry (many of these were dismounted and fought as infantry), 22 regiments of infantry, 5 infantry battalions, and 16 artillery batteries to the Confederate army. This figure does not include various state and home guard units organized to help protect the frontier.[1]

---

1   See Wright, Marcus J., *Texas in the War, 1861 - 1865,* edited by Harold Simpson (Hillsboro, Texas: Hill Junior College Press, 1965).

The companies, when formed, usually represented a community or county. In some cases, companies were formed in one town or county by men from a neighboring county or community. A case in point is the Hardeeman Rifles, which was formed in Gonzales. A look at its original muster role will confirm that while half the company did come from that historic community, the rest were from Prairie Lea, in neighboring Caldwell County. The Hardeeman Rifles went on to become Company "A," 4th Texas Infantry in Hood's Brigade.

The individualistic nature of the companies produced an interesting assortment of "nicknames." Apparently, guarding something was real important, for there were a rash of Guard units. There were, respectively, the Alamo City Guards; Anderson County Guards; Bayland Guards, which became part of the 2nd Texas Infantry; Davis Guards, who would successfully stop the Federals at Sabine Pass; Galveston City Guards; Harrisburg Guards; Indianola Guards, who, with the Van Horn Guards, would defend Port Lavaca from Federal invasion; the Marshall Guards; the Monumental Guards; Orange County Coast Guards; Sherman Guards; and the Wharton Guards.

If they weren't proud of guarding something, then they were of carrying rifles. There were the Woodville Rifles, the Walker Mounted Rifles, the Texas Mounted Riflemen, the Starr Rifles, the Lampasas Rifles, the Lone Star Rifles, the Marion Rifles, the Galveston Rifles, the Gillespie Rifles, the Houston Turner Rifles, and the Independent Rifles.

Texas, being famous for the exploits of the Texas Rangers during the Mexican War, suddenly produced an entire crop of new "Rangers." Brazoria, Caldwell County, and Graham all had "Rangers" to which were added such units as the Herbet Rangers, the Lone Star Rangers, the McCulloch Rangers, Sabine Rangers, the Titus Rangers, and the South Kansas-Texas Rangers. There were also the Mounted Rangers and the Partisan Rangers, and even the Ladies Rangers. The entire 8th Texas Cavalry was known throughout the war as Terry's Texas Rangers. Despite the title, none of these units were real Texas Ranger organizations.

When the men who formed Company "C" of the 5th Texas Infantry got together, they apparently all enjoyed a day's worth of sport, for they became the Leon Hunters. Captain Orlando C. Phelps' men enjoyed the revolutionary spirit, for they became known as the Brazoria County Minute Men. Captain Perry's command from Richmond were called the Fort Bend Scouts while one die-hard Texas unit was known briefly as the Sons of the South.

There were at least 25 field armies organized by the Confederate States. Basically, by mid-1862 there were two major Confederate armies; the Army of Northern Virginia, commanded by Lee; and the Army of Tennessee, who in the course of its history would have five commanding generals. The Army of Northern Virginia, as its name suggests, basically served east of the Appalachians, while the Army of Tennessee served in the "heartland" between the Appalachians and the Mississippi River. As Richard McMurry points out in his book, *Two Great Rebel Armies*, the Army of Northern Virginia fought its battles in and around Virginia, except when Lee tried to invade Maryland and Pennsylvania, while the Army of Tennessee fought from Columbus-Belmont on the Mississippi across Kentucky and Tennessee, into Georgia, back to Tennessee, and ended its days in North Carolina. There was also an Army of Mississippi whose soldiers fought at Corinth, Champion's Hill, and Vicksburg.[2]

Texans served in all three of these armies and in some of the smaller commands. The famous Texas Brigade, associated with John Bell Hood, served in the Army of Northern Virginia; Granbury's Texas Brigade served in the Army of Tennessee as did the famous 8th Texas Cavalry (Terry's Texas Rangers). The 2nd Texas Infantry fought in the Army of Mississippi. Of these armies, the most written about is the Army of Northern Virginia. After all, Robert E. Lee commanded it, and it did fight at Antietam and Gettysburg. The Army of Tennessee, which suffered a series of setbacks and change of commanders, is less well known to the general public. Other than Vicksburg, the Army of Mississippi is practically forgotten. In the great desire to look eastward, many Texans have failed to notice those who fought along the Rio Grande and the Gulf Coast.

On the local scene, Texas was a military department, independent at first, but later consolidated into something called the Trans-Mississippi District in January 1862. That became the Trans-Mississippi Department in May of 1862, which administered

---

2 For a comparison of the major armies of the Confederate States, see McMurry, Richard M., *Two Great Rebel Armies*, (Charlotte: University of North Carolina Press, 1989).

Louisiana, Arkansas, and Texas. There were several submilitary departments created to better administer various regions.

Soldiers in the Confederate army were paid although sometimes it was a long spell between pay periods. A private soldier in the infantry or artillery received eleven dollars per month while his mounted counterpart in the cavalry received twelve. An infantry or artillery captain was paid $130 a month while his cavalry equal received an additional ten dollars. Confederate brigadier-generals like Hamilton Bee or John Moore received $301 per month and Robert E. Lee's pay was $500. Union army soldiers received about the same scale but payments were a lot more regular. Black troops were paid less.

The men who volunteered were a cross section of Texan society and ethnic groups. Most of them represented the very best Texas had to offer; others were less desirable. By 1862 both the Union and the Confederacy were turning to conscription to help fill the depleting ranks. The draft was resented in both North and South. Traditionally, Texan officers were not pleased with the idea of having conscripts in their companies and regiments. In the North, actual draft riots broke out and a particularly nasty one occurred in New York City during the critical summer of 1863. But on the whole, Texans volunteered for military service.

A sampling of the men who participated serves as an illustration: Postal clerk Tom Edgar of Galveston was "A Union man and voted for Douglas" but as a "states' rights Democrat" supported Texas' "justified" secession to serve in the 26th Texas Cavalry.[3] Elizah Petty was just the opposite. "Upon the election of Lincoln," he wrote, "I took the stump for Secession — spoke, electioneered, legged wire, worked and voted for Secession. Attended the Texas Convention and lobbied for it and when Texas over the opposition of Governor Houston and his satelites [sic] went out of the Union on the 2 of March 1861 I rejoiced and shouted."[4] Petty would later write home that he was "a soldier for this war determined to be a free man or a dead man."[5] He lived up to his boast, being killed on April 6, 1864, at the battle of Pleasant Hill, Louisiana.

---

3   Yeary, Mamie, compiler, *Reminiscences of the Boys in Gray, 1861-1865*, (McGregor, Texas, 1912), Reprint, (Dayton: Morningside House, 1986), p. 208.
4   Petty, Elijah P., *Journey To Pleasant Hill*, edited by Norman D. Brown (San Antonio: Institute of Texan Cultures, 1982), p. xi.
5   Petty, *Journey To Pleasant Hill*, p. xxi.

William P. Zuber, who, at the age of sixteen, cried because he was left behind prior to the battle of San Jacinto, wanted to volunteer but, being "embarrassed with debt," could not leave home without ruining his family. He worked to clear his financial situation and enlisted in 1862.[6] John Wood Henderson served on the Texas frontier fighting Indians until the 1864 Missouri campaign.[7] Fritz Witte, of Prussia, enlisted at Washington County to serve in Waul's Texas Legion, only to be captured and sent to St. Louis where he escaped in February 1864 and proudly "never took the oath of allegiance" to the United States after the war.[8] W. C. Robenson enlisted wearing a distinctive wildcat skin coat and earned the nickname "Wild Cat" from his comrades in the 5th Texas Partisan Rangers.[9] G. W. Wilson of Company "D," 6th Texas Cavalry, gave up his last white shirt to bury a boy who had died from illness in camp.[10] Thomas Elliotte Bollings, of Columbus, joined the famous Terry's Texas Rangers only to be wounded after firing his first shot at Shiloh (the Yankee bullet hit his wrist, went up his arm and into his side, struck a rib and came out near the spine). Despite his disability, Bollings remained in the army until the end of the war.[11] E. W. Krause left his position as a music teacher at a Waco female college and, after he "reluctantly told a lovely music class of sweet and patriotic Southern girls goodbye," went on to become the leader of Waul's Legion band.[12] L. Ballou enlisted in Company "A" of Alfred Hobby's 8th Texas Infantry with dreams of going east to fight Yankees and instead remained guarding the Texas coast, only to miss his chance at the battle of Galveston because he was sick with the measles.[13] Henry Landes enlisted in 1862 at Chappell Hill to fight in only one battle at Galveston.[14]

Others like William Dellis served in Sibley's Brigade in New Mexico and Louisiana; he "was never wounded, captured nor

---

6 Zuber, William P., *My Eighty Years In Texas,* edited by Janis Boyle Mayfield (Austin: University of Texas Press, 1971), p. 133.
7 Yeary, *Reminiscences,* pp. 818-819.
8 Yeary, *Reminiscences,* p. 813.
9 Yeary, *Reminiscences,* p. 649.
10 Yeary, *Reminiscences,* pp. 806-807.
11 Yeary, *Reminiscences,* p. 64.
12 Yeary, *Reminiscences,* p. 411.
13 Yeary, *Reminiscences,* p. 53.
14 Yeary, *Reminiscences,* p. 419.

promoted."[15] Captain Miles Dillard of the 7th Texas Infantry also made it through the war unwounded but recalled, "at the battle of Murfreesboro had my horse killed and a ball passed through my whiskers (he was later to serve as lieutenant-colonel of the regiment).[16] J. B. Faulkner, a preacher from Collin County, wasn't so lucky; he was slightly wounded in the shoulder at Shiloh and in the head at Chickamauga, but "was never captured, but had to fight hard and run fast many times to prevent it."[17]

Their belief in their cause was their courage, even in the worst of conditions. J. D. Shaw, who enlisted in Company "C," 10th Texas Infantry, recalled of his service, "I simply did the best I could, getting into the struggle as early as possible and remaining to the close."[18] C. B. Wilson, who fought in the New Mexico and Louisiana campaigns with the 4th Texas Mounted Volunteers proudly wrote, "I am one of the Confederates who know we were right, and have nothing to take back."[19] M. W. Deaver, who helped secure Federal property in the Indian Territory and reenlisted in the 11th Texas Cavalry, was "just a common, ragged, plain private soldier all through the war. Frequently hungry; scared lots of times . . . ."[20] A. R. Danchy, a private in Company "C," 32nd Texas Cavalry, who was standing a few yards away from General Tom Green when an artillery shell killed him at Blair's Landing, noted, "I hope the day will never come when any of my children will be ashamed to own that I was a Confederate soldier."[21]

Many years after the war, Mamie Yeary of the Pearl Witt Chapter 569, United Daughters of the Confederacy, McGregor, Texas, took on a project to help preserve these personal records of the many volunteers to serve. She canvassed all of the Confederate veterans she could find still alive in Texas for their stories. The result was the lengthy volume, *Reminiscences of the Boys in Gray*, published in 1912. While it is true, as Robert Krick pointed out in the 1986 reprint of the volume, that many of the veterans "experienced memory lapses late in life," Miss Yeary's

---

15 Yeary, *Reminiscences*, p. 183.
16 Yeary, *Reminiscences*, p. 187.
17 Yeary, *Reminiscences*, p. 221.
18 Yeary, *Reminiscences*, pp. 680-681.
19 Yeary, *Reminiscences*, pp. 804-805.
20 Yeary, *Reminiscences*, p. 181.
21 Yeary, *Reminiscences*, pp. 171-172.

work is a remarkable biographical testimony to the experiences of these men.

Loyalty was a strong word in 1860. The secession crisis and call to arms tested the definition of that word for many. Marylanders threw stones at Federal troops passing through Baltimore; southern Illinois residents marched south to join the Confederate army; and Texans actually joined the Union army. At least two regiments of Federal cavalry were raised from former Texas residents who, in their support for the Union, fled the Lone Star State. In the fall of 1862, Edmund J. Davis organized the 1st Texas U.S. Cavalry in New Orleans. The 2nd Texas U.S. Cavalry was formed in December 1863, at Brownsville under the command of John L. Haynes.

Both Davis and Haynes were Southerners and had been soldiers in the Mexican War. They were not German, and both were highly successful businessmen and politicians before the war. I stress this point only because it has become acceptable to try to stereotype the Unionists in Texas as being of German blood and middle class. By the time both regiments were formed, the Union army could boast around 1,037 Texans serving in these two regiments.[22] The majority of the 2nd Texas were Hispanics. This should not be interpreted as illustrating that Texan Hispanics were against the Confederacy, for an equal number fought in Confederate units and served in the Home Guard.[23] The two regiments served in South Texas and in the Red River campaign.

The placement of the Unionist regiments on Texas soil was a direct slap in the face of the Confederates, who, by midwar were regarding such folks as nothing less than traitors. Even worse was having these folks recruit in Texas. Davis himself found out just how unpopular this activity was when he was sent to Matamoros to recruit Texas Unionists in exile.

Prior to his arrival in Matamoros, a raiding party had slipped north over the Rio Grande, robbed a supply train, and killed a local judge. Confederate General Hamilton Bee, who was in com-

---

22 Smyrl, Frank. H., "Texans in the Union Army," *Southwestern Historical Quarterly*, Volume 75.

23 See Thompson, Jerry Don, *Mexican Texans In the Union Army*, Southwest Studies Series, Number 78, (El Paso: University of Texas El Paso Press, 1986), and Thompson, Jerry Don, *Vaqueros in Blue and Gray*, (Austin: Presidial Press, 1987).

mand of the region, was enraged. He was certain that the raiding party had been part of the 1st Texas U.S. and wanted the Mexican government to arrest and extradite the murderers to him. This request was refused. Bee was still fuming when Davis arrived in March 1863.

The result was a raid against Davis' camp at the port of Bagdad. Major George Chilton of Tyler — the same George Chilton who was a more than active member of the Knights of the Golden Circle — was given command of the unauthorized expedition. The raid, which occurred on March 15, was a rousing success. Davis was taken prisoner inside his own tent with his wife in attendance. W. W. Montgomery, Davis' aide, was overpowered after he knifed two of the Texans, and three more of the Unionists were taken prisoner.

As the prisoners were being transported back to Brownsville, a current of ill feelings toward Montgomery was beginning to surface. No one is really certain who instigated the talk, nor do they agree on who gave the order to take Montgomery over to a nearby thicket where he was hanged.

The results of the raid were, to some extent, far reaching. The Mexican government protested the invasion of its soil. That resulted in the release of Davis and the three other survivors, who were returned to Mexico. General Bee, when asked to account for his involvement in the affair, noted that the raid had occurred without his consent or knowledge and was a violation of orders. However, "it will be a consolation that the indignity cast upon us by the authorities of the United States has been avenged by the gallant sons of Texas."[24] Montgomery became a hero to the Unionists who later reburied him in the public square at Fort Brown, and his lynching would be a source of investigation during and after the war.[25]

One of the more famous and often cited examples of Unionist sentiment is the story behind the "Treue der Union" monument located in Comfort, Texas. It represents a lasting tribute to a determined band of Hill Country Unionists who not only elected to exit Texas, but got themselves killed in trying to do so.

---

24 Hamilton Bee to Major A. G. Dickinson, OR, Series 1, Volume 15, p. 1017.

25 For an excellent study of this incident and its ramifications on those involved see, Betts, Vicki, "Private and Amateur Hangings: The Lynching of W. W. Montgomery, March 15, 1863," *Southwestern Historical Quarterly*, Volume 87.

Texans in blue — officers of the 1st Texas U.S. Cavalry in a photograph taken at New Orleans. *Courtesy of the estate of Emmie Brauback Mauermann, from the Institute of Texan Cultures in San Antonio.*

In May 1862, before the Texas Union regiments were formed, Confederate officials became alarmed at what they considered pro-Union activities in the counties of the Texas Hill Country. The local population there, a good majority of which was German, had formed a Union League, which, according to their side of the story, was organized to helped defend the region from possible Indian raids and bandit attacks. The Confederates considered such an organization as being a direct threat to the internal security of the state. Both sides had already established very fixed, negative viewpoints on each other when, on May 31, Captain James Duff arrived in the Fredericksburg area. Duff had orders from the Confederate high command to declare marshal law and insure that all inhabitants swear allegiance to the Confederate States.

In all fairness to the Unionists, Duff was not exactly the best choice for this job. One of his own men described him "as cowardly, cold-blooded a murderer as I had ever met" and "a scheming rascal." Since the man who made this observation, E. W. Williams, had once ridden in the Kansas-Missouri fights, he spoke with some aspect of expertise.[26] Apparently, Duff bullied and threatened his way around and probably overstepped his authority on more than one occasion. Williams recalled that Duff had made it fairly certain that he wanted no prisoners brought into camp. "The majority of the men, especially those who were Southern born, were utterly opposed to such deeds."[27] Williams himself resolved that he would do all in his power to stop such deeds from occurring.

While Duff was doing everything to soil the name of the Confederate States, a band of Unionists under Fritz Tegener gathered some 18 miles west of Kerrville. They elected to leave the state as soon as possible. Out of the 80 men who came to the meeting, only 61 actually followed through. The route was to be overland, towards the Rio Grande and Mexico. When Duff got wind of it, he dispatched a force of his Partisan Rangers to intercept the Unionists.

---

26 Williams, E. W., *With the Border Ruffians*, (New York: E. P. Duntton Company, 1907), p. 230.
27 Williams, R. H. and Sansom, John W., *The Massacre on the Nueces River*, (Grand Prairie, Texas: Frontier Times Publishing House, no date), p. 8.

Burial of victims from the Nueces Massacre. Services held in Comfort, Texas, in 1866. *Courtesy of the Institute of Texan Cultures, San Antonio.*

The Unionists had already begun their trek when the Con-federates commenced their pursuit. In all fairness to the Confederates, the Unionists certainly made following them an easy affair. Absolutely no precautions were taken, no attempts made to cover up trails or former campsites. This may be inter-preted that the Unionists felt that, since they had elected to leave the state, no one would actually follow them. However, they did have the foresight to be well armed, at least with civilian weapons.

On August 9 the Confederates caught up with the Unionists on the west fork of the Nueces River about twenty miles north of Fort Clark (Brackettville). After capturing and killing two of the Unionists, the Confederates formed for attack, which occurred sometime between one in the morning and daybreak. The attack, when it came, was sudden and devastating. By the time it was over, some thirty of the Unionists were dead and twenty-four were wounded. Tegener himself was wounded but made good his escape.

The Confederates had suffered only two killed and eighteen wounded, including their commanding officer, Lieutenant C. D. McRae. Williams busied himself with helping to treat the wounded Unionists. One of them had fallen into a campfire and had to be pulled out. He died a few minutes later.

Later that afternoon, Lieutenant John Luck (a friend of Duff's) elected to enforce the unwritten law. He had the Unionist wounded moved from where Williams had left them. The old border ruffian had just returned from getting the wounded fresh water when he heard gunshots. Fearing the camp was under attack, Williams raced for his gun but was stopped by one of his comrades. "You needn't be in a hurry, it's all done; they shot the poor devils, and finished them off."[28]

Even to a hardened veteran like Williams it was inconceivable. He sought out Lieutenant Luck and proceeded to denounce "the bloody deed in as strong language as I could use, telling the perpetrator, to his face, what he was, and what every decent, honorable man would think of him as long as he lived." For a few seconds, it appeared that Luck would pull his pistol, but several of Williams friends arrived to back him up. The lieutenant had to

---

28 Williams, *Border Ruffians*, p. 19.

be satisfied with merely assigning Williams "the most awful day's work I ever did in my life."[29]

McRae, in his official report of the battle, merely noted that, "They offered the most determined resistance and fought with desperation, asking no quarter whatever; hence I have no prisoners to report."[30] The battle and subsequent massacre at the Nueces became a Unionist legend in Texas following the war. On August 10, 1865, the remains of those killed in the attack and those later executed were returned to Comfort and buried with full honors. A white limestone monument was erected over the burial spot, inscribed in German. "Treue der Union" — "True to the Union."

It should be noted that the divided loyalties in Texas were not isolated to this region, nor were the lynchings and the killings. One aspect of a civil war is its terrible tendency to become impassioned and brutal. Texan Unionists, who were a minority, received occasional tastes of that lesson as did former Confederates during the Reconstruction period that followed.

---

29 Williams, *Border Ruffians*, p. 19.
30 McRae, August 18, 1862, OR, Series 1, Volume 9, p. 615.

CHAPTER SEVEN

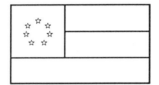

"Hurrah for the Bonnie Blue Flag"

A Look at the Flags of the Confederate States

One of the most popular songs to emerge from the Southern side of the War Between the States was a lively, brassy patriotic number which celebrated secession and Southern rights. Written by New Orleans musician Harry McCarthy, the song was known as "The Bonnie Blue Flag." While "Dixie" gave the South its musical soul, "Bonnie Blue Flag" gave it a national anthem. When the Federals occupied New Orleans, they arrested the writer and fined anyone who sang or hummed the tune $25.00.

The song's title comes from the popular design hoisted by some Southern states during the secession crises to show their independence. Traditionally, the flag is a blue banner with a single white star in the center. As the song illustrates, when more Southern states leave the Union and join the Confederate fold, the stars on the Bonnie Blue Flag increase. By the end, eleven stars were celebrated.

The use of the single star in the secession flag was nothing new for Texians. Flags with a solitary star had been a staple of Texas history. James Long in his ill-fated invasion of Spanish Texas in 1819 carried a banner with stripes and a single star; two separate single-star flags showed up at the Texian camp in Gonzales after the firing of the first shot of the 1835-1836 revolution from Mexico. One of these was the famous "Come and Take It" flag and the other, an elongated tricolor designed and stitched by Sarah Dodson. Other flags bearing lone stars quickly showed up on the battlefields of Texas. The Texian government adopted no less than three official Lone Star flags for their national ensign. The last of these, which became official in 1839, still remains as the state flag.

Texans in 1861 were just as proud of that flag as they are today. Some hurt feelings quickly developed when Louisiana adopted a lone star flag soon after its secession. Some of this debate erupted on the floor of the Texas Secession Convention, particularly when Colonel C. G. Forshey of the Texas Military Institute (Fayette County) composed a letter protesting Louisiana's use of the design. It was eventually dropped, particularly after it was pointed out that Liberia and Chile also used the design.[1]

Confederate officials understood the importance of a national emblem, and once the Confederate provisional government met, it quickly set about the task of coming up with a proper flag for the new nation. After several similar designs were submitted, the Confederate government adopted a style on March 4, 1861. The pattern consisted of three horizontal bars of equal width, red-white-red respectively, with a blue union in the corner. The union was to contain seven 5-pointed stars arranged in a circle. A German artist named Nicula Marschall has been given the credit for the actual design. There were to be variations, the most popular being the addition of a star in the center of the circle. Many a hometown military unit was presented a flag like this with the additions of company names or mottos.

This design was known as "The Stars and Bars." One of the immediate problems which developed with the design was that at a distance, it resembled the United States flag. However, it

---

1   See *Journal of the Secession Convention*, p. 103-106.

would not be until May 1, 1863, that the Confederate Congress changed the design.

A series of different flags developed for regiments in the field. These were known as battle flags. At the start of the conflict, various units appeared in the field with a host of distinctive flags, often made by the female population of their home town. In some cases, these were state flags adopted for military use. The 4th Texas Infantry carried a lone star flag made by Senator John Wigfall's wife from her wedding dress. The 1st and 2nd Texas Infantries each carried Texas State flags and both were lost in battle. Confederate officials again became concerned about the variations, and various commanding officers implemented designs to help standardize flags in their armies. William J. Hardee adopted a rather unique design for his Arkansas troops in mid-1861. It consisted of a blue flag with a white dot in the center and with a white border. General Simon Buckner claimed to have designed this flag which found use in the Army of Tennessee. General Pat Cleburne's Brigade retained the design after 1863, and the appearance of this flag let everyone know that "Old Pat's" men were on the field. Granbury's Texans fought under these flags in Atlanta and at Franklin.

The most popular battle flag design was developed by General Beauregard and Joseph E. Johnston in September 1861. It consisted of a 4 x 4 flag for infantry, 3 x 3 for artillery, and a 2.5 x 2.5 for the cavalry. The design was a bright red field with a blue St. Andrew's Cross, in which 12 or 13 five-pointed white stars were arranged. The Army of Mississippi adopted this flag in March 1862. Like everything else, variations existed, including six-pointed stars and a flag rectangular in shape. That flag became the standard for the Army of Northern Virginia. It is the design which most people recognize as the "Rebel" flag today, although it never existed as a national color.

Elements of the battle flag were, however, retained when the Stars and Bars were replaced in 1863. The new design consisted of a white color with the battle flag St. Andrew's Cross in the union. Known as the 2nd National or the "Stainless Banner," it too had immediate problems. From a distance, it looked too much like a flag of surrender. On March 4, 1865, with less than a month left of the war, the Confederate government again changed the design by adding a red stripe at the end of the flag to help break up the

The flag of the 5th Texas in the Army of Northern Virginia pattern. *Courtesy of the Texas State Archives, Austin.*

The first national flag of the Confederacy. *Courtesy of the Texas State Archives, Austin.*

The battle flag of the Confederacy. *Courtesy of the Texas State Archives, Austin.*

The second national "stainless banner" of the Confederacy. *Courtesy of the Texas State Archives, Austin.*

white. Because of the lateness of this design's adaptation, it saw very little use.[2]

Texas units used all of the above, depending on their location. When Hobby's men defended Corpus Christi from attack, they fought under a "Stars and Bars;" when the 2nd Texas withstood the Federals at Vicksburg, a 2nd National flew over their lunette; Terry's Texas Rangers fought the entire war with a flag unique only to them; the 3rd Texas carried the Army of Northern Virginia battle flag. When Rip Ford's men fought the last battle of the war in South Texas, they did so under a rectangular battle flag.

Most of the flags which were captured by the Federals during the war were returned to the various states. Others, were not. The 14th and 15th Texas Cavalry, which fought in the Army of Tennessee as infantry, had the unfortunate occurrence of having their flag captured by some Iowan troops during the Atlanta campaign. The flag ended up at the War Department, which loaned it for exhibition at the new cyclorama battle display in Atlanta during the 1880s. Some caring person, realizing where the flag should really be, had the foresight to "unloan" the banner and dispatch it to Texas. The flag, an excellent example of the Hardee battle flag, has been preserved in the collection of the Texas State Archives. At least ten other Texas Confederate flags reside in that institution's care. One of the original Terry's Texas Ranger flags on display at the United Daughters of the Confederacy Museum in Austin was stolen a few years ago.

---

2   For a discussion on Confederate battle flags, see Madus, Howard M. and Needham, Robert D., *The Battle Flags of the Confederate Army of Tennessee*, (Milwaukee, Wisconsin: Milwaukee Public Museum, 1976).

PART TWO
1862

1862

February 12-16   Confederates win at Fort Donelson, Tennessee.

February 21   The battle of Val Verde, New Mexico.

March 6   The battle of Elkhorn Tavern (Pea Ridge). Ben McCulloch is killed in the fighting which results in a Union victory.

March 9   The ironclads U.S.S. *Monitor* and C.S.S. *Virginia* battle off Hampton Roads, Virginia.

March 28   The battle of Glorietta Pass (Pigeon's Ranch), New Mexico.

April 6-7   **The battle of Shiloh. Albert Sidney Johnston is killed on the first day when the 2nd Texas Infantry sees its first combat.**

April 25   New Orleans falls to the Federals.

May 9   Battle of Farmington, Mississippi.

June 25-July 1   The Seven Days Battle in Virginia.

June 27   The battle of Gaines Mill, Virginia.

August 16-18   **Corpus Christi, Texas bombarded by Federals.**

September 17   The battle at Antietam.

September 19   The battle of Iuka, Mississippi.

September 22   Lincoln issues the Emancipation Proclamation.

October 3-4   The battle of Corinth, Mississippi.

October 8   The battle at Perryville, Kentucky.

October 31   **The battle of Port Lavaca, Texas.**

December 7   Confederates win at Prairie Grove, Arkansas.

December 31   The battle at Stone's River (Murfreesboro), Tennessee.

CHAPTER EIGHT

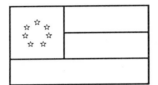

"Texas weeps over her noblest son."

The Reburial of Albert Sidney Johnston

The reality of war came for many Texans near a Tennessee church called Shiloh. The Federals, under the command of U. S. Grant, had swung down out of southern Illinois, blasted their way into Kentucky, captured the important Confederate strongholds of Fort Henry and Donelson, and had pressed into southern Tennessee. Grant, who was slowly winning a name for himself as an aggressive general, now threatened the important Confederate railroad terminal at Corinth, Mississippi. He paused his army just north of the state line, near Pittsburgh Landing on the Tennessee River. Here, the Confederate army caught Grant by surprise, slamming into the unsuspecting Federal camps on the morning of April 6, 1862. By the time the day was over, such names as "Bloody Pond," "Hornet's Nest," and "Peach Orchard" would be forever etched into the minds of a nation. The two-day battle of Shiloh would illustrate that the war in the west was going to be hard, bloody, and bitter.

Tragedy was to strike the Confederate army early in the first day of fighting. Albert Sidney Johnston, the Confederates' commanding officer, was struck by a minie ball which entered the back of his right leg, just below the knee. In its destructive path, the lead projectile tore the popliteal artery. Within 15 minutes, Johnston was dead.

The Confederacy had lost one of its most experienced generals in the west. Jefferson Davis lauded, "My long and close friendship with this departed chieftain and patriot forbids me to trust myself in giving vent to the feelings which this intelligence has evoked. Without doing injustice to the living, it may safely be said that our loss is irreparable."[1] Historians have long debated if Johnston's death at Shiloh had any negative effect on the outcome of the battle or the western campaign. Others have cast doubts on his abilities as a tactician. But Johnston's early death at Shiloh made him an early, revered martyr for the Southern cause. It would be an image that would cause controversy for many years after Johnston's death.

Johnston was barely cold when his staff covered his remains with a blanket and transported the fallen leader to Shiloh Church. The curious were told a Colonel Jackson of Texas had been killed and these were his remains. By the next day, it was apparent to his men that Johnston himself was dead. As the Confederates prepared to fight on the second day, Johnston was moved to Corinth, Mississippi. Here the body was prepared and sent by rail to New Orleans.

The Crescent City was chosen probably because of its easy transportation links to Texas. Johnston had always considered himself a Texan and therefore it was assumed that his family would eventually want his remains sent there. In the meantime, Mayor J. T. Monroe offered his family tomb at St. Louis Cemetery as a temporary repository. After two days of lying in state, Johnston was laid to rest in the Monroe tomb on April 11. In time some Texas soldier had written on the crypt, "Texas weeps over her noblest son."[2]

---

1   Johnston, William Preston, *The Life of Albert Sidney Johnston*, (New York: D. Appleton and Co., 1880), p. 88.
2   Johnston, *The Life of A. S. Johnston*, p. 689.

Johnston's temporary rest lasted almost five years. Within weeks after the funeral, New Orleans itself fell to the Federals. Under Union General Benjamin Butler's infamous control, New Orleans became the hostage city of the South. Johnston's grave became a popular symbol of Southern independence.

In 1866 the Texas Legislature passed a resolution to move Johnston's remains from New Orleans to Austin with the purpose of interring them in the State Cemetery. Since 1854 Texas had maintained a cemetery for its notables, although before the Civil War, only a few had actually ever been buried in the facility. Johnston naturally filled all the requirements for burial in a state plot. "The worth of Albert Sidney Johnston is to the people of Texas, to their children, and their children's children a possession and an inheritance forever," wrote fellow veteran Ashbel Smith.[3]

Texans needed no reminder of the great public servant Johnston had been to them. A native of Kentucky, Johnston had been studying at Transylvania College when he suddenly decided to follow a military career and sought admission to the United States Military Academy. He emerged from that institution in 1826 and remained an officer in the regulars until 1834, when his wife's failing health demanded more of him. When she died the following year, Johnston looked for something else to occupy his troubled life — he found it in the cause of Texas independence. Arriving after the victory at San Jacinto, Johnston met with Sam Houston and was quickly advised of the unstable situation which had developed between the government and the volunteer army in the field.

Houston's wounding at San Jacinto had left Thomas Rusk, ad interim Secretary of War, as head of the army. In July M. B. Lamar was appointed head of the army, but the volunteers encamped near Victoria refused to accept him. As a matter of fact, they had actually voted Rusk out of command and had put in his place Felix Huston, a newly arrived "volunteer" from Mississippi. Most of the army was currently made up of men of Huston's brand — newly arrived adventurers looking for some fame and fortune after the colonists had already established independence.

---

3 Ashbel Smith to Texas House and Senate, 1866. See Johnston, *The Life of A. S. Johnston*, p. 698. Smith had served under Johnston at Shiloh and had been a lifelong friend of the general since the days of the Texian Republic.

But it was a shaky independence, and with the first real government elections about to be held, stability was a necessity. So it
was as Albert Sidney Johnston arrived in the camp of the Texas
army. His first days with Texas troops were spent as a private.
Eventually, he was appointed adjutant general of the army, a
position which reminded him no doubt of the days he had spent
in the Black Hawk War. By February 1837, the government of
President Sam Houston had appointed Johnston the senior
Brigadier General of the Army. It was everyone's hope that the
professional soldier would bring discipline to the unruly volunteers now encamped on the Lavaca River.

Everyone, that is, except Felix Huston. The Mississippi fire-
brand considered the placement of Johnston as his senior a blow
to his pride and honor. After what appeared to be a first night's
cordial dinner, Huston issued a challenge sighting that "in assuming the command under an appointment connected with the
attempt to ruin my reputation, and inflict stigma on my character,
of course [Johnston] stands in an attitude of opposition to myself."
The new brigadier was between a rock and a hard place. Common
sense dictated he refuse, but the nature of the volunteers dictated
that he must accept.

The duelists would exchange a total of at least six shots before
Huston would hit Johnston in the right hip. Despite the fact that
Huston had won the actual duel, it was Johnston who prevailed.
For after all was said and done, Huston promised to obey the
orders of his superiors, the volunteers were impressed with
Johnston's grit, and the army of Texas began to take shape. The hip
wound would cause Johnston some pain for the rest of his life, but
it set a career into motion. By the time Texas had became a state
and the Mexican war was concluded, Albert Sidney Johnston had
served as commander of the Texas army, secretary of war under
President Lamar and commander of the 1st Texas Volunteer
Infantry.

During the Mexican conflict, Johnston won himself a place on
the staff of General Zachary Taylor. After the capture of Monterrey,
Johnston found himself obligated to accompany a fellow officer
to the headquarters of the Mexican commanding officer to receive
copies of the yet unsigned armistice. Johnston was not in uniform.
His own tunic had shrunk after an accidental dunking in the sea
earlier and so he was dressed in what can best be described as
typical "Texian" clothing.

The Mexican soldiers did not particularly like the hated "Devil Texans," so Johnston's attire excited the Mexican troops as the duo rode toward the headquarters. Eventually, a Mexican officer appeared who turned out to be an adjutant general. Johnston reasoned that it was best to keep the officer with them. So he and his comrade actually blocked the Mexican's path and then demanded he accompany them to his general. The plan worked, and they rode safely to the headquarters.

Johnston's fellow officer never forgot the incident. He stated that Johnston's move "exhibited that quick perception and decision which characterize the military genius." Because the fellow officer was none other than Jefferson Davis, the incident was to have lasting results.

When, after the war, Johnston reaccepted a commission in the U.S. Army, his old friendships were to pay off. Eventually, when the new 2nd Cavalry was created in 1855, Johnston was appointed its colonel. It was no small matter. But inasmuch as Jefferson Davis was then secretary of war, the appointment seemed natural. Johnston was more than delighted — for the 2nd Cavalry was posted in Texas.

By the time the secession crises was breaking out, Johnston himself was still a Federal officer, this time stationed in California. He had been absent from Texas for some time, yet never considered himself anything less than a citizen of that state. A duly professional soldier emerged in the fateful spring of 1861. Johnston the Federal officer vowed to protect Federal property under his control and care while Johnston the Texian waited for news from home to determine what course he would take. In the end, Johnston passed all Federal property safely over to his replacement before he headed east to offer his services to Texas.

The trip was a remarkable personal exodus. Fearing to land in "Northern" ports, Johnston elected to go overland. From Los Angeles, he crossed the Gila Desert and traveled through harsh southern New Mexico before finally arriving at the Rio Grande. Once he was safe in Texas, he moved on, electing to proceed directly to Richmond and present himself to Jefferson Davis.

From that meeting, Johnston received command of all Confederate troops from the Alleghenies to the western Indian Territories. Arriving in Nashville, Johnston quickly made an inspection of his northernmost bastion — Columbus, Kentucky — and then settled in at Bowling Green. His critics, both now and then, claim that he became so involved in planning ways to defend the area that he failed to appreciate the needs of his other commands. When the Yankees under Grant came down the Cumberland and took Forts Henry and Donelson on the Tennessee, all of Johnston's plans to protect Kentucky and Tennessee fell apart. The Confederate command was quickly pulled together at last and removed to Corinth, Mississippi. From there, Johnston planned to make a strike against the invading Yankees.

That strike came on April 6, 1862, just north of the Mississippi line near Pittsburgh Landing on the Tennessee River. The Confederates (and the world) remember the place from the name of the little church which was nearby — Shiloh.

While his critics remember a man who was insular in his thinking, too trusting, and influenced by amities with his subordinates, in particular A. P. Beauregard, the lasting impressions of Johnston come from those final hours. The impressions include an elated general who realized he had caught his enemy completely off guard and a commander who rebuffed an officer for looting a Federal camp and then, picking up a tin cup, remarked that it would be his only booty.

There was also the sight of Johnston helping reform regiments and leading them forward in the fray, or helping calm the fears of a Tennessee regiment by riding down its lines and touching the points of bayonets while remarking, "These will do the work . . . ." Another impression was of Johnston the concerned soldier who dispatched his own surgeon to help Confederate and Federal wounded alike. Others would always remember General Johnston on his horse Fire-Eater at Shiloh.

Then a single minie ball ended the vision, the reality, the life, and the career. To Colonel William Preston, Johnston had once remarked, "When I die, I want a handful of Texas earth on my breast."[4]

On January 23, 1867, a committee from Texas arrived in New Orleans and exhumed the body. Because of Reconstruction, no formal ceremony was planned, but that did not stop hundreds of people from silently gathering at the grave. Former Confederate Generals Beauregard, who had assumed command of the army at Shiloh after Johnston's death, and Simon Buckner, who had

4   The often quoted remark by Johnston to Preston can be found in Johnston, *The Life of A. S. Johnston*, p. 699.

commanded ill-fated Fort Donelson, were present, as was John Bell Hood, Richard Taylor, and Braxton Bragg, all of whom had commanded the Army of Tennessee. James Longstreet, Lee's old warrior was also in attendance. The body was transported by railroad to Brasher City and from there, via steamer, to Galveston, Texas.

The citizens of Galveston were planning a very public ceremony to meet the remains. This included a procession up the Strand to the Presbyterian church. City bells were to be tolled and it was requested that church bells also join in the salute with all stores closed during the service.

Before Johnston's remains arrived home, however, the Federal authorities stepped in. General Charles Griffin, commanding the headquarters district of Galveston, issued orders on January 24 to Mayor Charles Leonards that, owing to the deceased's "position" toward the U.S. Government in "the latter part of his life," the planned funeral procession was forbidden. There was to be no outward sign of public affection or popular demonstration. If these conditions were met, then and only then would Johnston's remains be transported from Galveston to Houston.[5]

Needless to say, the people of Galveston were enraged. To a city who had buried Federal naval officers with full military honors after the battle of Galveston, the idea of being ordered not to hold a funeral for a Texas public servant was, at best, an insult. "Now, in a time of profound peace" wrote the *New Orleans Crescent*, "when it has been promulgated by the highest authority in the land that civil law prevails throughout its length and breadth, a mandate has gone forth at Galveston, from a subordinate military commander, that the house of God shall be closed against the bones of Albert Sidney Johnston, and that no processions of his countrymen, whom he served so long and so faithfully, shall follow his remains to their last resting-place."[6] Despite the protests, Federal authorities were adamant on their position. Even General Phillip Sheridan refused permission, noting that he had too much "regard for the memory of the brave men who died to

---

5   Charles Griffin, Brevet Major-General commanding, District of Texas to C. H. Leonard, Mayor of Galveston, January 24, 1866. Reprinted in whole in Johnston, *The Life of A. S. Johnston*, p. 703.
6   *New Orleans Crescent*, January 27, 1867.

preserve our Government" to allow "Confederate demonstration over the remains of anyone who attempted to destroy it."[7]

Galveston was forced to accept the order. Once the body was forwarded to Houston on January 26, a second order was published by the Federal commander there which followed the same hard line as the Galveston order. This time it was not, however, enforced. "Every house was draped in mourning from turret to foundation, with long streamers of crepe and illusion; each store waved its dark plumage; no business was done, and the city presented the appearance of a vast sepulchre. On the arrival of the train from Galveston, the citizens rushed to the depot and the remains were carried to the Academy, while placards were on the street, 'Our honored dead must and shall be respected.' The remains lay in state until to-day on the rostrum in the Academy . . . Bells were rung, and if Texas were an independent power they could not have carried matters to a greater extent."[8]

Texans were still enraged with Sheridan and Griffin when Johnston's remains returned to the city where he had once served as secretary of war. After an impressive service at the capitol, officiated by Governor Throckmorton, the body, accompanied by a procession reported to be at least a half mile long, was taken to its final resting place at the State Cemetery. Rev. J. W. Philips, chaplain of the senate, preformed the Episcopal burial service. There was no bell tolling, again because of Federal orders, but it was observed, "Silence is sometimes more eloquent than words"[9] The *Austin State Gazette* reported, "the final funeral rites over the remains of General Albert Sidney Johnston were performed on last Saturday at the Capitol. All that was mortal of him now rests in the State Cemetery. There his honored dust must remain in a humble tomb, without monument or inscription, until the time shall come when it will be no crime to erect memorials, or to speak well of the illustrious dead. That it cannot now be safely done, we know, nor is it worth while, perhaps to speak of . . . these things must be left for posterity."[10]

---

7 Johnston, *The Life of A. S. Johnston*, p. 703.
8 Letter dated January 28, 1867. Full text in Johnston, *The Life of A. S. Johnston*, p. 708.
9 Johnston, *The Life of A. S. Johnston*, p. 714.
10 Entire *Austin Gazette* article is quoted in Johnston, *The Life of A. S. Johnston*, pp. 713-714.

The story did not end there. For it was another twenty-five years before the Texas Legislature, under urging from the *Austin Daily Statesman*, began plans to honor Johnston. After nine more years, the legislature appropriated funds to have a suitable monument erected on Johnston's grave.

Elisabet Ney, an eccentric sculptor, was selected to come up with a design for this monument. From the moment she entered the project, Ney had a singular vision. The monument would, in fact, be a combination of a recumbent figure and mausoleum. The open-air mausoleum would consist of a Gothic canopy supported by wrought iron bars. This design would allow visitors to view the statuary from all sides without actually entering. The statue itself would be of Johnston as he would have appeared just after being carried off the battlefield (or at least Ney's vision of this scene). A Confederate flag would cover his body while a Texas flag would serve as a pillow. Individual five-pointed stars would be added for that "Texas" touch to the canopy.

Ney's design was accepted, but one of the committee members, Adelia Dunovant, representing the United Daughters of the Confederacy, wanted some additions. She felt that since, in her opinion, Johnston had died for his Constitutional rights, a copy of the U.S. Constitution should be placed in the statue's hands. Ney did not agree but did offer to put a scroll version of the Constitution on the base. Dunovant objected.

The battle of artistic opinions raged for some time, but Ney finally won out. The final design, despite some artistic changes at the insistence of the committee, still followed Ney's original concept. In 1903 the model was sent to Seravejga, Italy, where the Italian cutters "stood in deepest admiration before ASJ."[11]

The sculpture was displayed at the 1904 St. Louis World's Fair, where it won a bronze medal. But before it got to Austin, yet another debate was raised. Ney wanted the monument placed somewhere other than the cemetery where it would be "forever hidden."[12] Despite much "feeling stewed up against Miss Ney," the completed statue arrived in Austin.[13] In June 1906, it was at

---

11 For more on the life and career of Elisabet Ney and her role in designing the present monument see, Cutrer, Emily, *The Art of the Woman: The Life and Work of Elisabet Ney,* (Lincoln: University of Nebraska Press, 1988), p. 209.
12 Cutrer, *Elisabet Ney,* p. 203.
13 Cutrer, *Elisabet Ney,* p. 209.

last placed over the grave. Nearly 44 years after his death at Shiloh, Albert Sidney Johnston not only had a handful of Texas soil on his breast, but an impressive monument as well.

Today, the statue of Stephen Austin, with arms outstretched, gazes down from the slight hill upon the reclining likeness of Johnston. That is appropriate indeed, since it was Austin's speech in 1836 which inspired Johnston to come to Texas. The graves of dozens of Confederate veterans surround him, including Generals John Wharton and Ben McCulloch. The passage of time has not diminished Elisabet Ney's artistic tribute; nor has it diminished Johnston's greatest love. For despite separation, controversy, death, Reconstruction, and changing attitudes, Albert Sidney Johnston's great wish was obtained.

CHAPTER NINE

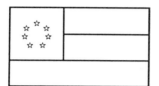

Texas'
Bloodiest Day

The 1st Texas Infantry at Sharpsburg
September 17, 1862

There seems to be some debate on just what day should be considered the saddest day in Texas history. Many incidents in the history of our Lone Star State naturally, and sadly, come to mind. Foremost among these in recent memory would certainly have to be the 1947 Texas City disaster which resulted when a freighter exploded, destroying hundreds of acres of property, wiping out the entire community fire department, and killing or wounding hundreds of factory works, volunteers, and townspeople. Another contender is the Galveston hurricane and flood of 1900 in which over 6000 souls were lost. Others will remind you of the infamous Goliad Massacre, when the defeated and unsuspecting command of Colonel James Fannin was executed by orders of Santa Anna during the Texas Revolution. Nearly 320 Texian and

American volunteers were killed that bloody day. Still others may speak of the explosion in 1937 which destroyed the New London Consolidated School, taking with it an entire generation (some 293) of innocent children and teachers.

If you want to look at this answer in terms of military combat, then perhaps you can categorize the saddest day as the bloodiest. With those clarifications, Goliad or the 1813 Battle of the Medina (and its aftermath) are still in the running. But in actuality, there is really no debate. The answer is painfully easy: September 17, 1862.

That was the day when Robert E. Lee's Army of Northern Virginia and George McClellan's Army of the Potomac slammed into each other near the town of Sharpsburg, Maryland. The Confederates, of course, took the name of the town for that of the battle while the Federals, in keeping with their tradition, used the name of the nearby creek — Antietam. The fighting started at first light and continued until dark. By the time it was over nearly 13,000 Yankees were either killed, wounded, or were missing. The Confederates had lost around 10,000. When totaled together, the casualties for the day numbered somewhere between 23,000 and 26,000 men.[1]

Keep that in mind — somewhere around 25,000 casualties in a single day's fighting in which both armies were using muzzle-loading rifles and artillery. Even after two world wars, that day's casualties has, mercifully, never been equaled by an American military force. Antietam stands out not only in 1862, but still today, as the bloodiest day in American history.

Another aspect of Antietam stands out. That conflict produced the highest percentage casualty loss in a single regiment during the entire war. That bloody honor goes to the men of the 1st Texas Infantry, whose regiment lost 82.3 percent of its men. A sister regiment, the 4th Texas, lost 53.5 percent of its men that day, while the entire Texas Brigade suffered over 548 dead, wounded, and missing. Keep in mind, being wounded in 1862 and wounded now do not have the same meanings or successful survival rates. Survival rates were hideously lower in the 1860s.

---

1   For a discussion on casualties at Antietam, see Sears, Stephen W., *Landscape Turned Red*, (New Haven: Ticknor and Fields Publishing, 1983), p. 296, and Frassanito, W. R., *America's Bloodiest Day*, (New York: Charles Scribners and Sons, 1978), p. 78.

Texas Brigade in camp in Virginia, 1862. Courtesy of the Institute of Texan Cultures, San Antonio.

The Texas Brigade — the one to whom John Bell Hood gave his name — fought at Antietam in the area occupied by the Dunker Church and later in the famous cornfield. Colonel W. T. Wofford commanded the brigade that day. Just as the sun came up, the Texans formed their line of battle with the 5th Texas on the right, the 4th Texas in the middle, and the 1st Texas on the left, followed by Hampton's South Carolina Legion and the 18th Georgia. After passing through a woods and emerging into a open field, they were hit by enemy fire. The smoke from the weapons was so thick it was almost impossible to return fire or even spot the enemy. The 5th Texas, by the end of the day, had fired all of its ammunition.

In the course of the cornfield fighting, the 1st Texas lost at least eight of its color bearers trying to keep their Lone Star flag waving. The banner had been carried through every confrontation so far and proudly bore the battle honors of Seven Pines and Gaines Mills. Privates John Hanson and John Kinsley of Company "L" along with James Day of Company "M" and "A" Company's James K. Malore were among those who fell dead or wounded trying to keep the colors flying. When the regiment retired at the end of the day, the confusion and the smoke were so intense that those trying to bear it back through the cornfield were killed and the flag was lost. Solomon Blessing, a twenty-one-year-old private in the Lone Star Rifles saw it go down. His first impulse was to pick it up, but he thought he could do more good by remaining active as a rifleman. He was soon shot in the hand and through the leg and was forced to "hobble" back to the woods where he was taken to a field hospital.[2]

A Yankee private later found the flag still lying in the cornfield, surrounded by thirteen dead Texans, one of which, Lieutenant R. H. Gaston, lay stretched across it.[3] Lieutenant Colonel P. A. Work, who commanded the 1st Texas that day, later wrote, "There was no such conduct upon their part as abandoning or deserting the colors. They fought bravely, and unflinchingly faced a terrible hail of bullets and artillery until ordered by me to retire. The colors started back with them and when they were lost, no man knew

2   Yeary Mamie, compiler, *Reminiscences of the Boys in Gray, 1861-1865*, (McGregor, Texas: Privately published, 1912), pp. 60-61, Reprint, (Dayton: Morningside House, Inc. 1986).
3   W. E. Barrey to George Brunard, December 17, 1908 in Polly, J. B., *Hood's Texas Brigade*. (Dayton: Morningside Bookstore Edition, 1976), p. 128.

Some of the casualties at Antietam. *Courtesy of the Antietam National Park.*

1st Texas Infantry colors that were lost at Sharpsburg. *Courtesy of the Texas State Library, Austin.*

The Texas monument at the Antietam National Battlefield. *Courtesy of the Antietam National Park.*

save him who had fallen with them."[4] The chaplain, Nicholas A. Davis, of the 4th Texas cynically wrote, "Well, let them [the Federals] make the most of it, for it's the first Texas flag they have got, and I guess many of them will bite the dust before they get another."[5]

Later that evening, when General Lee asked General Hood, "Where is the splendid division you had this morning?" all Hood could say was, "They are lying on the field where you have sent them."[6] One member of the 4th Texas noted, "I doubt if the dead and wounded ever lay thicker upon any field than was seen from the old Dunkard [sic] church north, for more than half a mile."[7]

The Texas Brigade of the Army of Northern Virginia was broken and bloodied as it joined the rest of Lee's army in their retreat southward from Sharpsburg. But they were far from finished. Fredericksburg, Gettysburg, Chickamauga, The Wilderness, Cold Harbor, Petersburg, and Appomattox all still lay before them. By the time Appomattox came around, out of the nearly 4,000 men who had served in the three Texas regiments since 1861, only 427 officers and privates where left to surrender that April day.[8]

The fighting around Sharpsburg and Antietam Creek had illustrated a great chapter in history. Because of Lee's lack of success, Abraham Lincoln felt the climate right to issue his Emancipation order, which changed the direction and the goals of the conflict. The savage day's fighting also illustrated just how murderous this type of warfare could be. Nothing before or nothing after it would equal its grisly cost. But even after the guns had been silenced there, two nations still resolved to hammer the issues out on the battlefield. Chaplain Davis' comments were ironically more than a boast. Thousands more would "bite the dust."

---

4   Polly, *Hood's Texas Brigade*, pp. 126-127.
5   Davis, Nicholas A., *The Campaign From Texas To Maryland*, (Richmond: Privately published, 1863) Reprint, (Austin: Steck Company, 1961), p. 100.
6   Polly, *Hood's Texas Brigade*, p. 134.
7   Polly, *Hood's Texas Brigade*, p. 133.
8   For the list of brigade members who surrendered at Appomattox with the Army of Northern Virginia see Polly, *Hood's Texas Brigade*, pp. 296-297.

CHAPTER TEN

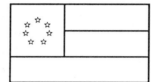

"Oh! We were butchered like dogs!"

William P. Rogers and the 2nd Texas Infantry at the Battle of Corinth, Mississippi 1862

The battle of Corinth, fought on October 3, 1862, at the important railroad crossroads in northeastern Mississippi, is a little known chapter in the public's popular history of the War Between the States. Like many other battlefields located in close association with communities, the battleground of Corinth has been swallowed up by urban growth since 1862. A small public park is preserved at the site of some of the most serious fighting

— the Federal Battery Robinette. Amidst the small cluster of monuments honoring the participants, a large, single shaft stands looming over the rest.

That particular monument is in memory of Colonel William P. Rogers who died leading his regiment into the Yankee works. A Mississippian by birth, Rogers rests in his native soil, but far away from the state he had adopted and fought for — Texas. For William Rogers died commanding the 2nd Regiment of Texas Infantry, also known as the "Texas Sharpshooters." They were a hard fighting regiment who saw their baptism of fire at Shiloh (just 20 miles up the road) and, as part of the Army of Mississippi, served at Iuka and Farmington. Later the regiment proudly and stubbornly defended the 2nd Texas' lunette at Vicksburg. Following the surrender of that city on July 4, 1863, the regiment, despite orders to reform east of the Mississippi, gathered back in Texas to finish the war defending Galveston and the surrounding coastline. While Shiloh and Vicksburg mark the beginning and end of the regiment, it is for the fight at Corinth that the 2nd Texas is really remembered.[1]

The regiment was the pride of Harris, Jackson, Galveston, Gonzales, Brazos, Burleson, and Robertson counties. The regiment, in fact, was the first infantry regiment commissioned for Confederate service from Texas. But thanks to politics, the regimental number was exchanged with a Texas regiment being formed from independent companies in Richmond by Senator Louis Wigfall. That unit became the 1st Texas Infantry in Hood's Brigade.

So the ten companies which formed the backbone of the Texas regiment became the 2nd Texas. Four of these companies, "A" through "D," were raised in Harris County. The rest came from various locations and brought with them colorful designations. It was a prestigious outfit, having in its ranks the cream of Texas manhood. A number of veterans of the Texas Republic and the Mexican War filled its ranks, joining with the more aggressive of the younger generation. The sons of two former presidents of the Texas Republic, Sam Houston and Anson Jones, served in the regiment.

---

1   For the most current overall history of the 2nd Texas Infantry, see Chance, Joseph E., *From Shiloh To Vicksburg*, (Austin: Eakin Press, 1984).

The officer core was especially impressive. The commander of Company "C," the Bayland Guards, was the stern-faced Ashbel Smith. A Yankee-born graduate of Yale University, Smith had spent most of his life in the service of his adopted Texas. This included the post of surgeon general of the army of the Texas Republic and the Lone Star Republic's chargé d'affaires to Great Britain and France, not to mention secretary of state under Texas president Anson Jones. Eventually, Smith would command the regiment at Vicksburg.[2]

John Creed Moore, a Tennessee native and graduate of the U.S. Military Academy (class of 1849) was commissioned the regiment's colonel. His previous military experience, with the 2nd Artillery, included stints in the Seminole War and garrison duty in Santa Fe and Baton Rouge. Moore resigned his commission in 1855 and became a college teacher.[3]

And then there was William P. Rogers. The Mississippi native had been educated in both medicine and the law. When the call for volunteers came during the Mexican War, he quickly organized Company "K" of the Mississippi Rifles. Rogers distinguished himself at Buena Vista on the day his commanding officer, Jefferson Davis, ordered the Rifles to form an unorthodox V formation to repel Mexican cavalry. It worked. After the war, Rogers moved to Texas and taught law in Washington County. He was a prominent member of the secession movement and, despite this, maintained a deep personal relationship with Sam Houston. When the 2nd Texas was formed, Rogers was elected its lieutenant colonel.

The regiment trained at Galveston, where Sam Houston often paid a visit and inspected the progress of his son's regiment. As the war progressed east of the Mississippi, the regiment soon received its marching orders and joined Albert Sidney Johnston's army in time to fight the battle of Shiloh. "No other regiment," Colonel Moore later wrote, "entered a fight that day under more unfavorable circumstances. Not having received the provisions

---

2   For more on the life of Ashbel Smith see Silverthorne, Elizabeth, *Ashbel Smith of Texas*, (College Station: Texas A & M University Press, 1982).

3   Warner, Ezra J., *Generals in Gray*, (Baton Rouge: Louisiana State University Press, 1964), p. 219.

ordered for the regiment, we left with a short two and a half day's rations. By Saturday morning our provisions were all exhausted.[4]

In addition, many of the men had left camp with shoes already so worn that many finished the fight barefooted. Prior to the battle, the regiment was resupplied with ill fitting, undyed wool uniforms. A Federal prisoner was reported later to have inquired, "Who were them hell cats that went into battle dressed in their grave coats?"[5]

William Rogers almost missed his regiment's baptism of fire. Traveling to the battle lines separately from the regiment, he was unable to locate the 2nd Texas and ended up, at least temporarily, on General Breckenridge's staff. When he was finally able to locate the regiment, he had been with them only ten minutes when the regiment was ordered forward. As part of Jackson Brigade, the Texas men were one of the first regiments into the battle which, on April 6, 1862, was a basic surprise attack against U. S. Grant's Federals clustered near Pittsburgh Landing on the Tennessee River.

The regiment fought well that day but the men also suffered. Company "E" watched in silence as their commanding officer, Captain Belvedere Brooks, was carried off the field mortally wounded. Ashbel Smith was severally wounded in the arm. Lieutenant Daniel Gallahar was dispatched to find more ammunition and he never returned. Grant's massing of artillery and siege guns late in the day stopped the Confederate advance. The 2nd Texas spent its first night after combat without tents, in a heavy rain, with intervals of heavy shells fired from Federal gunboats throughout the miserable night.

The second day's fighting found changes, primarily because Federal reinforcements arrived during the night. Colonel Moore found himself in command of a hastily assembled brigade and Rogers assumed command of the regiment.

The second day at Shiloh proved controversial for the regiment — a fact that was to hang over them and John Moore for the rest of the war. Moore had taken the field with his new brigade, under orders from General Jones Mitchel Withers, when an officer of higher rank and his staff arrived, asked for Withers, and upon finding him absent, ordered Moore to throw two companies of the

---

4   Moore, April 19, 1862. OR, Series 1, Volume 10, Part 1, pp. 560-563.
5   *Confederate Veteran*, 12:116.

2nd Texas forward as skirmishers. When Moore asked who had issued these orders, the reply was, "General William Hardee."

Moore hardly had time to execute this order when the same authority countermanded it. Moore's temporary brigade now moved forward under Hardee's personal direction. A warning was issued to the troops to be on watch for friendly troops who were supposed to be in front fighting the Yankees.

After advancing some two hundred yards, a large force was sighted to the front and to the right. It was assumed that this was the friendly force but that assumption proved to be wrong. As the 2nd Texas continued forward through a thicket, it suddenly became apparent that the supposed "friendly troops" were, in fact, Federals. A cross fire developed, catching the left wing of Moore's exposed brigade in the open. "So sudden was the shock and so unexpected was the character of our supposed friends," he wrote, "that the whole line soon gave way from left to right in utter confusion. The regiment became so scattered and mixed that all efforts to reform them became fruitless." A good number of the officers, however, succeeded in gathering squads and joined other regiments during the unsuccessful Confederate attack. The second day at Shiloh was lost to the Federals, and the army fell back to Corinth.[6]

William Hardee, in his report, singled out the 2nd Texas. "In one instance, that of the Second Texas Regiment, commanded by Colonel Moore, the men seemed appalled, fled from the field without apparent cause, and were so dismayed that my efforts to rally them were unavailing."[7] It is rather interesting that Hardee failed to mention any other regiments in Moore's Brigade. Moore was quite clear in his tone when he fired off a letter to General S. Cooper (adjutant and inspector-general) challenging Hardee. He reminded Cooper that Hardee had, in fact, taken personal charge of the brigade and that "I saw enough on that morning to satisfy me that the advance and the attack of our Brigade was a bungling, ill-fated affair." Moore also pointed out that William Rogers and not Cooper was the regimental commander.[8]

Rogers himself wrote a letter to his wife about the entire affair. "Facts speak for themselves," he said. "The regiment did not run,

---

6   Moore, April 27, 1862. OR, p. 564.
7   Hardee's report can be found in OR, pp. 566-571.
8   Rogers Papers, April 24, 1862.

it fell back 2 or 3 hundred yards. I, with others of my officers, led it again to the fight and for its conspicuous gallantry I have been authorized to inscribe Shiloh on my flag. Second Texas run — My God — It has been bad at every field. 250 of our bravest are now in their graves. The Second Texas has been made an independent regiment of Sharpshooters — This is a high honor for in the attack we are in the advance and in the retreat we are in the rear. Now if all that does not give lie to our enemies we can say no more."[9]

Historians, for the most part, have sided with Hardee, primarily because of his reputation as a fine officer (he translated the manual of arms used by both armies in the war). Those who side with Moore and the 2nd Texas make the argument that it is only his fame as a general which makes his credit good. It is highly possible that Hardee was using Moore and the regiment as a scapegoat for his own military blundering.

Seven months later, this regiment that Hardee had expended his wrath at (and was still bad-mouthing) stood before Corinth. In the passing months, the whole of northern Mississippi had been lost to the Confederacy. A Federal army estimated to be 15,000 troops strong was holding the rail terminal at Corinth. The Army of Mississippi, under Generals Sterling Price and Earl Van Doren, boasted 22,000 men. The odds were in favor of a brilliant Confederate victory that would drive the Yankees out of Mississippi and open Tennessee for liberation.

The 2nd Texas had added the battles of Iuka and Farmington to their honors. Rogers, still in command of the unit (but hoping for a brigadier-general's position) remarked in a letter home, "In all of their engagements the Regiment displayed the cool, obstinate, and determined bravery of veterans and the counties of Burleson, Robertson, Galveston, Gonzales, and Jackson may well be proud of them. The hardships to which they are subjected are indeed great, for many of them are without blankets, tents or shoes."[10]

The pain of command was wearing on Rogers. Ashbel Smith, recovered from his Shiloh wounds and promoted to second officer, had been dispatched to Texas to secure conscripts to fill the depleted ranks. The prospects of having such men in the regiment was not pleasing to the high-minded lawyer. He felt that would

---

9   Rogers Papers, April 24, 1862.
10 Rogers Papers, April 24, 1862.

discredit the regiment. He warned that he would fire off a formal protest to General Price in order not to have them.

The usual lack of supplies also plagued the colonel. The regiment had not been properly equipped since Shiloh. Rogers begged in vain for blankets, tents, and shoes. In disgust, Rogers wrote his wife that his men "then must supply them or there will be trouble."[11]

Rogers, in reality, had little time to press the issue further, for the army moved from Pocahontas towards Corinth. Rogers himself felt that they were heading for Jackson, Tennessee, and from there on into Kentucky. But soon it became apparent that Van Doren's target was the rail head at Corinth. As usual, the "Texas Sharpshooters" marched in the advance. As they headed down the railroad lines, an unexpected Union cavalry patrol crossed their path. A quick, hot skirmish followed with little result save warning the Yankees that Van Doren was marching on Corinth. As it turned out, the Federal commander, William S. Rosecrans, had actually suspected a Confederate advance and had greatly reinforced the area around the town. The confident Confederate victory as envisioned by Van Doren now seemed to grow distant.

The old Confederate entrenchments constructed following Shiloh now served as the chief line of defense for the Yankees. Corinth was completely encircled by a series of earthen fortifications. Batteries Tannrat and Lothrop protected the southern approach and the Mobile and Ohio Railroad running in that direction; Battery Madison watched the west, guarding the Memphis and Charleston line. Battery Powell, to the north, covered Purdy Road. The heart of the defenses were three batteries running from the north of Boneyard Road to both flanks of the Charleston and Ohio line running west; Battery Williams on the south side of the rail, Battery Robinette on the north, and Battery Phillips covering Boneyard Road.

The Confederates commenced their general attack against these works on October 3. Three divisions formed an arch to the northwest of the city, which increased in size as the attack pressed closer. The 2nd Texas, still part of John Moore's brigade, formed to the right of General Dabney H. Maury's division near the Memphis and Charleston Railroad line. The fighting on the third

---

11 Rogers Papers, April 24, 1862.

had been fairly successful, as the Confederates had pushed well beyond their old positions. Most spent a rather sleepless night, within range of the Federals, among the bodies of both armies' dead. By daylight, the Yankees had fallen back and tightened their lines.

Fighting commenced early on the fourth. As Maury's division moved out, its right line of march committed them straight for Battery Robinette. Before they could even get near the Federal position, they had to first cross a line of fallen trees and ditches. But nothing seemed to stop them. Officers in both armies watched in awe as the unrelenting line of Moore's brigade pushed forward, sighting on the guns of Robinette and the huge American flag floating over the works. A lieutenant in the 42nd Alabama left a vivid remembrance of the drama around them: "The regiment with the brigade rose unmindful of the shot or shell and moved forward marching about 250 yards to the rising crest of the hill. The whole of Corinth with its enormous fortifications burst upon our view. The United States flag was floating over the forts and in the town."[12]

Moore stopped his brigade of combined Mississippi, Arkansas, Alabama, and Texas infantry only briefly before continuing forward. The Alabama lieutenant, caught in the sweep of the events around him, recalled, "We were met by a perfect storm of grape, canister, cannon balls and minie balls. Oh God! I have never seen the like. The men fell like grass even here."[13] Colonel Rogers leading the pack of howling soldiers, charged forward, his horse having been shot out from underneath him. "At a given signal, they [Rogers and the 2nd Texas] moved forward rapidly under a heavy fire of grape and cannister from our artillery," remembered an Iowa private. "The battery on the left, followed at supporting distance by their reserves . . . they crossed with difficulty the abatis of trees just outside the town, and gaining a position where there were no obstructions, they came gallantly forward at a charge, sweeping everything before them."[14]

Also watching this spectacle was a young Illinois lad, William Paul, a private in Company "E," 64th Illinois Volunteer Infantry.

---

12 Jackson, Oscar L. *Colonel's Diary*, pp. 86-87. Quoted in Hartje, *Van Doren*, p. 231.
13 Jackson, *Colonel's Diary*, p. 86.
14 *Memphis Bulletine*, October 14, 1862.

The remains of
the 2nd Texas
Infantry before
Battery Robinette,
October, 1862.
Colonel Rogers is
on the left.
*Courtesy of the
Alabama State
Archives.*

Paul later wrote to his parents, "The enemy they came on to the edge of the bank in solid column five brigades deep mostly Arkansas troops. We filled the gully full of the dirty devils . . ."[15]

One of these devils agreed with Paul, as the Alabama lieutenant recalled, "Giving one tremendous cheer we dashed to the brow of the hill on which the fortifications were situated and here we found every foot of the ground covered with large trees and brush cut down to impede our progress. Looking to the right and left I saw several brigades charging at the same time . . . I seemed to be moving right into the mouth of a cannon, for the air was filled with grape and canister. I rushed to a ditch of the fort right between some larger cannons. Gradually, I managed to get halfway up the sloping wall, but didn't shoot for fear of having their heads blown off. Our men were in the same predicament. Five or six were on the wall and thirty or forty in the ditch and several were killed on top of another and rolled down the embankment in ghastly heaps. Oh! We were butchered like dogs."[16]

In the 125 years since that day, there has been much confusion and debate on what actually took place once Moore's brigade and the 2nd Texas hit Battery Robinette. Apparently, the 2nd Texas pushed over the battery and smashed head on against the line of the 63rd Ohio Infantry. The Ohio regiment, with half of its men dead or wounded, retreated. Rogers then turned his attention on the 43rd Ohio, which attempted to rally, but instead were caught in a Confederate volley. Their commander, Colonel Joseph Kirby, fell dead.

The 9th Texas, supported from the dismounted Texas and Arkansas Cavalry, launched their attack against the 27th Ohio. Again, the Ohio men made a desperate stand in an attempt to hold their right flank, but soon, under an avalanche of screaming Confederates, were forced back. For a brief moment, the Confederates held the much sought after battery. Then, Federal troops took the field, and the Ohio regiments, joined by other infantry, pushed forward against them. The devastation from combined musket and cannon fire took its toll, and soon the Confederates were thrown back. One Yankee remembered, "The

---

15 Paul, William, "Letters of William Paul, Company "E," 64th Illinois Volunteer Infantry." *Camp Chase Gazette* May 1975, p. 4.
16 Jackson, *Colonel's Diary*, pp. 86-87.

Battery Robinette Park as it appears today. The tall monument marks Colonel Rogers' grave. *Courtesy of Luanne Parish.*

rebels melted like snow and most of them stood their ground and died in and around the little fort."[17] Captain Oscar Jackson wrote, "It reminded me of a man cutting heavy grain, striking at a thick place."[18] Private Paul watched, in awe, "one 64lb ball go through a solid body of the Second Texas killing almost one company . . . ."[19]

Captain Edward Daly of Company "D" went down with a bullet in the groin and another in the leg. Captain Timmons had been hit with grape shot and was being carried off the field. Colonel William Rogers himself had also fallen — apparently as he planted the Texas flag on the battery. General Rosecrans would state that Rogers had been brought down by a pistol shot from a Union drummer boy. Others claimed he had attempted to surrender and was shot anyway. The evidence seems to support the popular image of Rogers dying while attempting to cross the

---

17 Hartje, *Van Doren*, p. 231.
18 Jackson, *Colonel's Diary*, p. 74.
19 "Letters of William Paul," *Camp Chase Gazette*, p. 4.

battery. It is doubtful that a pistol ball could have been the fatal shot, for Rogers was wearing body armor under his uniform. The armor, a genuine prize of the war, now rests in the collection of the Wisconsin Historical Society. The hole in the thick plate could only have been made by a well-charged minie ball or grape shot. The photograph taken of the 2nd Texas dead piled before Robinette after the battle shows Rogers, stripped of uniform, and his under garments opened at the chest showing a large hole in his person. Some accounts state that he was shot by no less than five rounds.

And so, amid the carnage and destruction, a popular image arose. William P. Rogers, leading the 2nd Texas, with a Confederate flag in one hand, a revolver in the other, leaping the ditch, scaling the parapet, and, with his companions, being gunned down at the height of the battle.

The battle of Corinth was soon concluded. Van Doren ordered a general retreat. General Price wept as the remains of the army limped out of the city. Moore's brigade had lost nearly 1300 men, including 166 from the 2nd Texas. The Federal commander ordered Rogers buried with full military honors.

The private war between William Hardee and John Moore would continue. Vicksburg still lay ahead. But the regiment Hardee had called cowards at Shiloh had, on that October day at Corinth, illustrated their determination and bravery. Before Battery Robinette, the men of the 2nd Texas proved themselves beyond measure.

CHAPTER ELEVEN

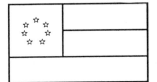

Yankees, Gunboats, and Yellow Fever

The Defense of Port Lavaca
October 31, 1862

While Van Doren's army made its futile attempt to liberate Northern Mississippi and Southern Tennessee, the war had become a reality on the Texas coast.

The Federal navy elected to flex its muscles and show the residents of this region that its blockade was to be taken seriously. Rear Admiral David G. Farragutt, commanding the Western Blockade Squadron, ordered Commodore W. B. Renshaw to make demonstrations along the Texas coast with the intent of disrupting blockade running and trade. On October 4, 1862, Renshaw commenced his attack on Galveston. After some confusion as to terms, the Confederates agreed to a four-day truce, during which time their commander, Colonel Joseph J. Cook, withdrew his defenders. Outgunned by the Yankees, who had vowed "to hoist the United States flag over the city or over its ashes,"[1] the Confederates had little choice.

Having secured Texas' largest eastern port, Renshaw's success continued with considerable ease. Corpus Christi, Sabine City, and, on the 25th, the western port of Indianola were all occupied. The Federal officers' policy of offering surrender or "ashes" was having its effect.

Up Matagorda Bay, the citizens of Port Lavaca were having problems of their own. Yellow fever, the curse of the coast, had made a dreadful appearance, striking men, women, and children with equal vigor. Several of Major Daniel Shea's Van Horn Guards who, with the Indianola Guards, made up the community's garrison, were also down with the fever. While the women of the community served as nurses in an effort to help fight the epidemic, Shea's men were alarmed when, on the morning of October 31, two Federal steamers, *Clifton* and *Westfield*, appeared in sight, steering for the city. By 11:00 A.M. the two warships had anchored, and at 1:00 P.M. a longboat under a flag of truce arrived at the shore.[2]

Shea, with four townspeople, met the Federals at the beach. The terms from Renshaw were the same — surrender or be destroyed. Shea's options were extremely limited. He commanded two artillery batteries in a community that was racked with yellow fever. Not only did he have women, children, and male civilians to consider, he had sick civilians to worry about. The Federals certainly had him outgunned. The side-wheeler *Clifton* boasted no less than eight cannons, including a Parrot rifle which threw a 30-pound shell over a mile. *Westfield* commanded six pieces, including a 100-pound Parrot rifle and a 9-inch Dahlgren.[3]

---

1   Brigadier General P. O. Herbert to Colonel James Deshler, October 15, 1862. *Official Records of the Union and Confederate Navies in the War of the Rebellion* (Washington, D.C.: Government Printing Office, 1903). Series 1, Volume 17, p. 790.
2   For the official Confederate account of the bombardment, see Lieutenant George E. Conklin to Major E. F. Gray, November 1, 1862 in OR, Series 1, Volume 15, pp. 182-183. Conklin was the Post Adjutant for Port Lavaca.
3   Armament of *Clifton* and *Westfield* is cited in Gibbons, Tony, *Warships and Naval Battles of the Civil War*, (New York: Gallery Books, 1989), pp. 78, 161, 169. *Westfield* was destroyed during the Confederate recapture of Galveston while *Clifton* ran aground during the battle of Sabine Pass.

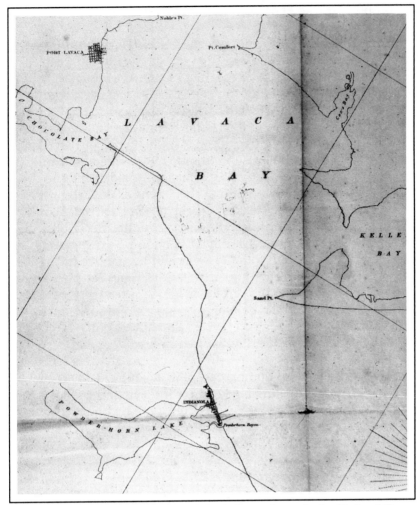

Map of Lavaca Bay. *Courtesy of Ford Green, from the Institute of Texan Cultures, San Antonio.*

Daniel Shea was not in a mood to have terms dictated to him by the Federals. He informed the officer that he was at Port Lavaca to defend it, and defend it he would. However, remembering his civilians, he requested time to evacuate the women and children. Renshaw agreed and gave orders that only one hour should be allowed for this activity, but, out of consideration for the yellow fever victims, the deadline was extend by thirty minutes. Negotiations ended as the Federals returned to their gunboats and Shea to his batteries.

Even in the time allowed, which General Hamilton Bee (commanding the subdistrict of the Rio Grande) would later cite as an example of "the barbarous conduct of the Abolitionists,"[4] Shea was unable to evacuate all the civilians. As the appointed hour arrived, the soldiers at the two batteries, commanded by Captains John A. Veron of the Van Horn Guards and Joseph Reuess of the Indianola Guards, prepared to receive the brunt of the Federal attack. They were not disappointed, for the Federals quickly opened fire. "Both officers and men performed their duty," Lt. George Conklin wrote, "working their guns as coolly as though on inspection, while a perfect storm of shot and shell rained around them; and this, although yellow fever had decimated their ranks, and that many of the men who manned the batteries had but partially recovered from the fever, entitles them to the highest praise."[5] Amidst the shot and shell, a Mrs. Chesley, Mrs. Dunn, and her two daughters braved the fire and "acted the part of true Southern heroines,"[6] to deliver coffee, bread, and meat to the artillerymen, while ordnance officer Captain H. Wilke labored to keep the batteries supplied with ammunition.

Remarkably, the stubborn Confederate defenders not only withstood the Federal bombardment of nearly 174 shells lobbed into the city, but also managed to hit the Federal gunboats and partially disabled one of the ships. Renshaw had no intention of losing any of his ships. The two gunboats were ordered to retire outside of the range of Shea's guns. From a safer distance, they resumed firing until the sun went down.

Shea and his command took a breath. Despite the bombardment and considerable damage to the town, they and the citizens of Port Lavaca still held out. And they had not lost a single man, women, or child. Up the coast at the town of Texana, on the Navidad, some twenty miles away, Mrs. Maurice Simons noted: "heard heavy firing in direction of Lavaca."[7]

---

4   Brigadier General Hamilton Bee, OR, p. 181.
5   Conklin to Gray, OR, pp. 182-183.
6   Conklin to Gray, OR, pp. 182-183.
7   Malsch, Brownson, *Indianola — The Mother of Western Texas*, (Austin: State House Press, 1988), p. 169.

The next day, All Saints Day, Mrs. Simons again noted: "Heavy firing again this morning; all anxious to hear the fate of Lavaca."[8] As the sun rose that morning, Port Lavaca once again was subjected to bombardment. Because of the range, Shea's batteries were unable to fire back. But after a morning of heavy fire, which sent another 78 shells into the already blasted city, the Federals quit and sailed away. General Bee at San Antonio was ecstatic: "It gives me great satisfaction to call the attention of the general commanding to the gallantry of Major Shea and his command. Although his ranks had been decimated by the yellow fever, his means of defense limited, and the force of the enemy far superior in guns and caliber, yet, sustained by patriotism and courage, he compelled the enemy to retire. The patriotism and love of country displayed by the citizens of Lavaca, who willingly gave up their homes to destruction rather than that the enemy should land, is worthy of all praise, and will serve as a bright example to their fellow-countrymen . . . The Abolition fleet has retired from the waters of Lavaca Bay, the objects of their visit being entirely frustrated."[9]

Apparently, Commodore Renshaw had been satisfied by his bombardment of Port Lavaca. It demonstrated to the people of the Gulf Coast that the war was very real and just a cannon shot away. It also sent a message to the Confederate military that the Federal army and navy had intentions of keeping Texas at bay. While the citizens of Indianola and Corpus Christi reoccupied their homes and the Confederates strengthened their defenses at Fort Esperanza on Matagorda Island, Galveston still remained in Yankee hands.

But the defenders of Port Lavaca had also sent a message, one the Federals seemed to ignore. Even the easiest of targets could represent a strong defense which could not only stall the Yankees, but possibly defeat them.

---

8   Malsch, *Indianola*, p. 169.
9   Bee, OR, p. 181.

PART THREE

1863

1863

January 1	Confederates recapture Galveston on the day the Emancipation Proclamation takes effect.
January 11	C.S.S. *Alabama* sinks U.S.S. *Hatteras* off Galveston Island.
May 1-3	The battle of Chancellorsville, Virginia.
May 16	Confederates try to stop Grant at the battle of Champion's Hill, Mississippi.
May 19	Siege of Vicksburg commences as Grant surrounds city.
May 21	The siege at Port Hudson, Louisiana begins.
May 22	General U. S. Grant assaults Vicksburg.
June 16-26	Confederate calvary under John Hunt Morgan begins raids in Ohio and Indiana.
July 1-3	The battle of Gettysburg.
July 4	The city of Vicksburg surrenders.
July 8	The city of Port Hudson surrenders.
July 18	The 54 Massachusetts (colored) leads unsuccessful assault against Charleston's Battery Wagner.
July 30	Confederate guerrillas under Quantrill sack Lawrence, Kansas.
September 8	**The battle of Sabine Pass, Texas.**
September 19-20	The battle of Chickamauga, Georgia.
November	**Pendleton Murrah elected governor of Texas.**
November 22-30	Fort Esperanza on Matagorda Island captured.

CHAPTER TWELVE

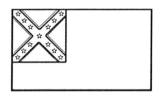

"My father is here"

The Battle of Galveston
January 1, 1863

The year 1863 started out with a literal bang throughout the United States and the Confederacy. In a year destined to hold two of the most critical battles of the conflict — Gettysburg and Vicksburg — New Year's Day set the tone. This was the day that Lincoln signed the Emancipation Proclamation. It was also the day that the Confederate forces in Texas actually got together and did something constructive — they recaptured Galveston.

The battle of Galveston is a shining moment for Texan-Confederates. Yankee troops would never again occupy the city until after the surrender in May of 1865. It was truly a moment of glory for the career of "Prince" John Magruder.

Magruder already had a reputation as a dandy when the war broke out. A native Virginian and graduate of West Point (class of 1830), he resigned his United States commission in April 1860. By October he had risen to the rank of major general and commanded part of the Confederate army in Virginia during the stalemated

131

Peninsular Campaign. His lack of military success compelled his transfer to Texas where, in October 1862, he assumed command of the military district of Texas.[1]

"Prince John" arrived in the wake of Renshaw's expedition against the Texas coast. His presence alarmed the new commander considerably. Magruder felt that if the Federals were to be successful in establishing a base on the Texas Gulf, then they could very easily move inland. It was bad enough they had actually secured Galveston. With its railroad link to Houston and Harrisburg, the city was a threat in Federal hands. Magruder had no intention of repeating this problem. He ordered the San Antonio and Mexican Gulf Railroad linking Indianola to Port Lavaca and Victoria destroyed, as well as the lighthouses at Saluria and Pass Cavallo. Only the lighthouse at Aransas was spared — it was made of brick.

"God protect us from our 'friends,'" a citizen of Victoria moaned.[2] Magruder's orders did not meet with approval from the citizens of these communities who had labored long to build the rail links. They saw their future commercial routes being destroyed.

While most of Texas was of the opinion that their new commander was doing more harm than the Federals, Magruder himself was devising a plan to neutralize the Yankee occupation of Galveston. "Prince John" was certainly one to never shrink from a fight, his record in the Mexican War had proven that. This time, there would be no destruction of rail lines or bridges; Magruder intended to capture the city. What was to occur would restore morale in Texas and make Magruder a hero.

Magruder's plans were two-fold. He intended to launch a joint naval and land attack against the Federals. The aspects of the land attack were not so complicated, for the causeway railroad bridge which linked Galveston to the mainland was not only still standing, but was clear of any obstacle. Confederate scouts had been using it to make visits to the city for weeks, and Magruder himself crossed over on it to check enemy positions prior to the battle.

---

1   For a more complete biographical outline of Magruder's career, see Warner, Ezra J., *Generals In Gray*, (Baton Rouge: Louisiana State University Press, 1964).

2   Malsch, Brownson, *Indianola — The Mother of Western Texas*, (Austin: State House Press, 1988), p. 171.

John B. Magruder, the hero of Galveston. *Courtesy of the Eugene C. Barker Research Center, University of Texas at Austin.*

The real problem was the second phase of the attack. Commodore Renshaw, who commanded the city, could count on heavy support from his flagship *Westfield*, the side-wheel steamers *Harriet Lane, Clifton, Owasco, Sachemn,* and schooner *Coryphous.* In addition, he had at least two transports and two coal tenders. On shore, three companies of the 42nd Massachusetts Infantry stood ready. The Federal fleet represented the major obstacle to the Confederate attack. Magruder, on December 25, issued instruction that two medium river steamers, *Bayou City* and *Neptune,* be taken to the dock at Harrisburg and converted into warships.

Major Leon Smith was given the job of converting the steamers. Magruder's suggestion was to use cotton bales for protection. *Neptune* was armed with two 24-pound howitzers while *Bayou City* was given a six-inch heavy rifle. The cotton bales were used liberally around the steamers, in some cases three bales high. Smith called his "fleet" "The Cotton Clad Squadron."

The Federals had received word that an attack was in the making, but Renshaw hoped that if it occurred it would be after the remainder of the 42nd Massachusetts arrived. Additionally, elements of the 1st Texas U.S. Cavalry, made up of Unionist Texans (which had been formed at New Orleans) were also promised.

Magruder had taken more time than planned to get his forces together. Almost every available Texas soldier was used, including the remains of Sibley's force from New Mexico, under General Tom Green. Colonel Alfred Hobby's 8th Texas Infantry from South Texas was also part of the force, including two companies of Hispanics from Refugio and Goliad. Cavalry, infantry, and artillery all mixed together for the attack.

Magruder's hopes were high when he issued his orders: "I will attack from the City about one o'clock; take the boats as near as you can to the enemy's vessels, without risk of discovery, and attack when signal gun is fired from the City. The Rangers of the Prairie send greeting to the Rangers of the Sea."[3]

Aboard *Bayou City,* "Commodore" Smith's mood was less cheerful. When asked by the cavalry and infantry officers aboard if the cotton bales would really protect the men and the ships, he responded, "None whatever, not even against grape shot."[4] The

---

3   Franklin, Robert M., *Battle of Galveston,* (Galveston: Privately published, 1911), p. 6.
4   Franklin, *Battle of Galveston,* p. 6.

The capture of *Harriet Lane* at the battle of Galveston. Courtesy of the Institute of Texas Cultures, San Antonio.

only chance they had, Smith added, was to get alongside the Federal gunboats before they could rank the Confederates with broadsides. General Green, in a somber mood, remarked that he had volunteered for this attack only because he did not want his men to go where he would not go himself.

Smith and his Cotton-Clads took up their position while Magruder and his land troops, with six pieces of artillery, crossed the two-mile railroad bridge and made their way overland some four miles into Galveston. There were additional delays as the land troops deployed. Smith and his men impatiently waited for the signal gun, which was now some two hours late, when the Federal ships apparently noticed the Cotton-Clads and commenced signal lights. Renshaw immediately started to move his flagship to a better position, only to have *Westfield* run aground on the Pelican Slit. At this point, at 3 A.M. on New Year's morning, Magruder fired his opening cannon shot. The battle of Galveston was on.

What followed illustrated how much could go wrong in a battle. With *Westfield* aground, Renshaw was trying to direct his defenses and get his side-wheeler moving. Colonel J. Cook of Magruder's forces launched his assault against the 42nd Massachusetts which was barricaded at Kuhn's Wharf on 18th Street. Unfortunately, the men discovered that the scaling ladders they had been issued were too short. As the sun came up, Smith's Cotton-Clads came into play, heading right for *Harriet Lane*. *Lane* opened fire and missed *Bayou City*, which returned fire and also missed the target. The gun crew on *Bayou City* under a Captain Weir became excited and failed to ram their third round properly. The barrel exploded, killing Weir and two of his men.

The contest to get to *Harriet Lane* was aided by the fact that the Federals did not have enough room to turn for a broadside. The Confederates actually got under her port bow, but were unable to secure a boarding. The water shifted, and the two vessels struck. The result was the partial destruction of *Bayou City*'s wheel house, and the steamer drifted away. Before the Federals could recover, *Neptune* hit the other side and proceeded to clear the decks of *Harriet Lane* with small arms fire. But the stress was too much for the converted riverboat; it began to take water. *Neptune* now broke away and was grounded.

Smith had recovered control of *Bayou City* and once again went after *Harriet Lane*. This time, he was successful and personally led the boarding party onto the vessel. Within a few moments, *Harriet Lane* was Confederate property.

Someone forgot to mention that to the land troops. Smith and his victorious crew suddenly found themselves being fired on not only by the Federals, but by Magruder's men as well. Smith suggested that his men raise a rebel yell to signal their fellows on the shore; someone else, who was probably a bit more practical, suggested using a white flag. Both ideas were employed, and the cross fire ceased.

Flags of truce went up all over the place as Smith and Magruder tried to meet with the Federals. Smith sent a captain over to *Owasco*, whose captain informed him that since he was not in command, he could not parley. So the Confederate was passed over to the nearby *Clifton*, whose officer asked for a three-hour truce in order to consult with Renshaw, still aboard the stricken *Westfield*.

On land, a parley with the Federal infantry went much easier. They surrendered. Aboard *Westfield*, Renshaw was informed that the Confederates had demanded the surrender of all Federal ships (save one), and if this was complied to, all Federal prisoners would be paroled and allowed to leave via the one vessel. Magruder apparently gave Renshaw a taste of his own medicine, when he added that if the Federals did not surrender, they would be destroyed.

The Federal commander elected to take advantage of the truce. In the time allowed he gave orders for *Westfield* to be abandoned and the remaining ships to set sail and evacuate the harbor. The Confederates, in good faith, had no idea of what was transpiring. Having evacuated his crew, Renshaw, accompanied by three of his officers and a small crew to man his personal gig, commenced setting fire to the stricken *Westfield*. The fires set, Renshaw started down a ladder to join the 12 men in the gig when the magazine on board prematurely exploded. Thus ended the career of Commodore Renshaw.

Command now fell on *Clifton*'s Lieutenant Commander P. L. Law. He elected to carry out Renshaw's final orders and commenced the evacuation of the fleet. Magruder was enraged. "The *Owasco*, the *Clifton*, and the *Sachem* escaped under a flag of truce, so that the harbor of Galveston was entered under a flag of truce and left by the same flagrant violation of military propriety."[5] Nevertheless, Magruder had regained Galveston with a loss of 26 killed and 117 wounded. The Federals had lost an equal number. The sisters of the Ursuline Convent, who had been offered a chance to evacuate during the fighting, had elected to remain in order to care for the wounded.

It was a shining moment for Magruder. But the victory at Galveston was also to be a rather bittersweet moment as well, for it provided yet another example of how ideologies, sectional loyalties, and devotions to country divided families.

Albert Lea — the same Lea who, along with his brother Pryor, had been involved with the Knights of the Golden Circle activities in Goliad and Refugio — had followed a true course and volunteered for service in the Confederate army. Lea had been employed as an engineer with the Aransas Railroad project. As a matter of fact, his entire prewar career had been in engineering, including such jobs as being the chief engineer of Tennessee, the locating engineer of the Baltimore and Ohio Railroad, and a professorship at Knoxville University. As a graduate of West Point (class of 1831, fifth in his class) he had served briefly in the artillery at Fort Gibson and then on various projects involving surveying and engineering improvements. Lea had left the army in 1856 to enter the private sector, but did work a stint as chief clerk of the War Department under President Harrison and was actually the acting secretary of war for six weeks.[6]

Jeff Davis had a good engineering officer in Lea, who by 1863 had risen to the rank of major. Apparently though, there was some problem with a superior officer, and Lea finally accepted a chance to return to Texas and serve there. He was on his way to report to San Antonio for duty when he learned of the expedition against Galveston. Like every other Confederate, he quickly volunteered to serve on the expedition.

---

5   For a complete account of the battle of Galveston, see Franklin, *Battle of Galveston*, or Cumberland, Charles C., "The Confederate Loss and Recapture of Galveston, 1862-1863," *Southwestern Historical Quarterly*, Volume 51. Magruder's report of the battle is in OR, Series 1, Volume 15, p. 219.

6   Twenty-Second Annual Reunion of the Association of Graduates of the United States Military Academy at West Point, New York, June 12, 1891, p. 59.

Lea was among those with Tom Green's command on *Neptune* when it came alongside *Harriet Lane*. What Major Albert Lea, CSA, didn't know was that the second in command of *Harriet Lane* was Lieutenant Edward Lea, USA. In a few short, bloody minutes, father was about to meet son.

According to one source, Tom Green, upon boarding the *Lane,* spied young Lieutenant Lea and shot him.[7] Here, his father found him. After a brief conversation in which the son confirmed the seriousness of his wounds, Major Lea went for a litter. He returned too late; the surgeon informed him that Lieutenant Lea's last words were, "My father is here."[8]

The Houston *Tri-Weekly News* ran a full account of the incident six days later. It is full of sentiment that both father and son realized they had done their duty and felt secure in their convictions.

Magruder ordered that both Lea and his commanding officer Wainright be allowed burial in the Episcopal Cemetery. Full military honors were rendered the fallen Federals. Albert Lea is said to have commented, "We defend our rights with strong arms and honest hearts, that those we meet in battle may also have hearts brave and honest as our own."[9]

---

7   *Tri-Weekly News,* Houston, Texas, Saturday, January 10, 1863.
8   *Tri-Weekly News,* Houston, Texas, Tuesday, January 6, 1863.
9   *Tri-Weekly News,* Houston, Texas, January 6, 1863.

CHAPTER THIRTEEN

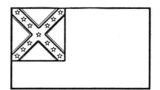

"We are the Confederate steamer, Alabama"

January 11, 1863

The Confederate victory at Galveston was barely two weeks old when the Federal navy decided to test the defenders resolve with a naval attack. A powerful naval squadron was dispatched to bombard and, if need be, generally reduce Galveston to ashes.

The Yankee fleet was in the process of blasting the city when someone on their flagship, *Brooklyn*, spotted a sail just on the horizon to the southeast. Lieutenant H. C. Blake of U.S.S. *Hatteras* received a signal at two-thirty which ordered him to set sail and investigate. *Hatteras* was an old side-wheel steamer converted in 1861 for military service. With a crew of 126 sailors and armed with four 32-pound and one 20-pound cannon, *Hatteras* could make 8 knots at top speed.[1]

The mystery ship in the distance continued away from the *Hatteras*. Blake became concerned and ordered his ship cleared for action. At about twenty miles out, with darkness already set in, the mystery ship turned. It was just 7 P.M. when Blake hailed the ship for identification. "Her Britannic Majesty's ship *Vixen*" came the response. Then came a request of identification from the hailing ship. Someone on board called back "The U.S.S. *Hatteras*."[2]

There followed what one participant called, "an awkward pause." Blake informed the *Vixen* that he was lowering a boat to board them to confirm their British registry. The boat, containing acting master L. H. Partridge and five crewmen, had just broken the water when Blake heard someone yell, "We are the Confederate steamer, *Alabama*." The announcement was followed instantaneously with a broadside.[3]

The Federal lieutenant had the unfortunate honor of having run into the newest scourge of the seas — C.S.S. *Alabama*. Other than the ironclad *Virginia*, *Alabama* was destined to become the most famous Confederate naval vessel afloat during the war. In her brief 21-month career, *Alabama* was to carry the Stars and Bars to ports as far away as Cape Town and Singapore. She would be responsible for the destruction or capture of at least 64 Union vessels valued at six million dollars.

Blake and *Hatteras* were outclassed from the start of their night's adventure, for *Alabama* was constructed for the sole purpose of disrupting Northern shipping. Construction was instituted at the Laird Brothers dock in Birkenhead, England, during the summer of 1862. The use of British shipyards, even though they were private contractors, by the Confederate government had already brought numerous protests from the United States. Because of this, *Alabama* was built under an assumed name and, when launched on July 29, 1862, it was reported that the new ship was merely going on her trials. Instead, she was sailed to the

---

1   For details on *Hatteras*, see Gibbons, Tony, *Warships and Naval Battles of the Civil War*, (New York: Gallery Books, 1989).

2   Blake's report, dated January 21, 1863, can be found in OR Navies, Series 1, Volume 2, pp. 18-21 and in Semmes, Raphael, *Service Afloat During the War Between The States*, (Baltimore: privately published, 1887), p. 545.

3   Semmes, *Service Afloat*, p. 543.

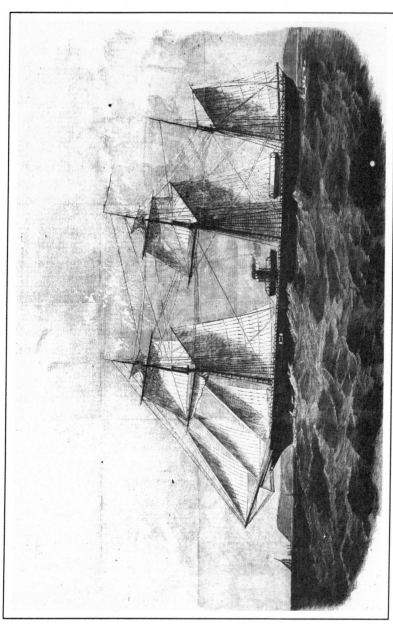

C.S.S. Alabama. Courtesy of the Institute of Texas Cultures, San Antonio.

Azores where she was fitted out, a crew (mostly English) was enlisted, and then she was commissioned as *Alabama*.

The newest addition to the Confederate navy boasted the best of two worlds — sails when required and a steam-engine powered screw. The propeller could be raised or lowered within ten minutes when needed. At top speed, *Alabama* could make 14 knots. Her armament consisted of six 32-pound cannons, one 110-pound cannon and one 68-pound cannon. A crew of 144 experienced sailors went with her.[4]

If *Alabama* outclassed *Hatteras*, then the two commanders were equally distanced. For *Alabama's* master was Raphael Semmes, who had enlisted in the United States Navy as a midshipman at the age of 17 and quickly rose in rank. Semmes served in the Mexican War and even wrote a book on his adventures in that conflict in 1851. A Marylander by birth, Semmes gave up his 35 years of U.S. Naval service to join the Confederacy. As the commander of the cruiser *Sumter*, he became the terror of the Gulf. *Sumter* ended its career when the Federal navy, after chasing Semmes across the Atlantic, was bottled up at Gibraltar. Semmes was forced to abandon his ship, but with the completion of *Alabama*, Semmes had a new deck from which to wage war on the North.

There was one good thing about Semmes; given the material, he could wage sea warfare better than anyone else. Many Federal captains were to discover this fact as *Alabama* broke out into the Atlantic and then southward into the Gulf.

Fate was to take the cruiser toward Galveston that January night. Semmes had no idea that the Confederates had recaptured the city or that the Federals were bombarding it. His reports indicated that a large Federal invasion force was leaving New Orleans to proceed up the Sabine and invade via land. This prompted hopes of the *Alabama* catching some of the Federal transports en route. Needless to say, Semmes and his crew were a little shocked when they sighted Federal warships off Galveston and the city under fire.

The options were few. *Alabama* could not hope to take on five warships by itself. Nor could Semmes run because he had

---

4   For more on the construction of *Alabama*, see Summersell, Charles, *CSS Alabama: Builder, Captain and Plans*, (Tuscaloosa: University of Alabama Press, 1985).

promised his men "some sport." While Semmes was weighing the issues, the Federals "happily came to my relief." By using both his sails and propeller, Semmes kept *Alabama* moving slow enough for the pursuing ship to keep up, but fast enough to keep it at a respectable distance. The plan worked, for Semmes successfully drew *Hatteras* far enough from the rest of its fleet to leave it quite alone.[5]

Blake later claimed that he suspected the ship before him was *Alabama*, but his actions certainly did not indicate that. Everything seems to suggest that he was clearly unaware that the mystery ship was the Confederate vessel until seconds after the first broadside. Well aware that he was outclassed, Blake elected to try to close on *Alabama* with the purpose of boarding the Confederate ship. The *Hatteras* steamed directly for *Alabama*, but as Blake later observed, "she was enabled by her great speed, and the foulness of the bottom of the *Hatteras*, and consequently, her diminished speed, to thwart my attempt when I had gained a distance of but thirty yards from her."[6] Semmes himself noted, "I saw no evidence of such an intention, in the handling of his ship; and Captain Blake must himself have known that, in the terribly demoralized condition of his crew, when they found that they had really fallen in with the *Alabama*, he could not have depended upon a single boarder."[7]

At the close range, both sides exchanged cannon, musket, and even pistol shots. The Federals offered irregular fire while the Confederates fired six full broadsides. One of the rounds entered *Hatteras* midships and set fire to the hold. At nearly the same instant, a second shell passed through *Hatteras'* sick bay and exploded in an adjoining compartment. *Alabama* suffered very little damage to both hull and rigging. A third shell from the Confederates hit the cylinder and filled the engine room with steam. It was the critical blow, for *Hatteras* now had no steam with which to either maneuver or to work the pumps. Within minutes, Blake's vessel lay crippled and on fire with no means to fight the fires.

Blake now hoped to keep up the fight long enough to attract help from the fleet off Galveston. His bold plan was rendered

---

5   Semmes, *Service Afloat*, p. 542.
6   OR, Series 1, Volume 2, p. 19.
7   Semmes, *Service Afloat*, p. 547.

impossible as word reached him that the hits below decks had ripped gaping holes in both his iron plating and the hull. Semmes took up a position just out of *Hatteras'* range and was preparing yet another volley when Blake elected to abandon ship. Semmes signaled he would help if assistance was required and Blake thankfully accepted the offer. With two of his crew dead and five wounded (most from the engine room), Blake had no more desire to risk the lives of his crew. The battle had lasted less than fifteen minutes. Some two minutes after the last of Blake's crew had been taken aboard, *Hatteras* sank.

The Federal fleet was more than alarmed by the sudden appearance of *Alabama*. Owing to the destruction of *Hatteras* and subsequent dispatching of another warship to warn Admiral David G. Farragut at New Orleans, the Federals no longer had sufficient force to reduce Galveston. The bombardment was called off.

Years later, when writing his memoirs, Semmes would take exception to the wording in Blake's official report. "Setting aside all the discourteous stuff and nonsense about 'a rebel steamer,' and a 'piratical craft,' of which Captain Blake, who had been bred in the old service, should have been ashamed, especially after enjoying the hospitalities of my cabin for a couple of weeks."[8] Blake and his crew were transported to Jamaica where they were released. Partridge and the party in the longboat were picked up by Brooklyn the day after the battle. Admiral Farragut reluctantly noted, "I have nothing but disaster to report to the Secretary of the Navy."[9]

C.S.S. *Alabama* passed out of the Gulf of Mexico and Texas waters forever. Semmes took his ship and crew for more "sport" halfway across the world — a cruise that would end off the coast of Cherbourg, France. Semmes, at last caught and with *Alabama* in need of repair, elected to make a final fight against U.S.S. *Kearsarge*. The ghost ship of the Confederate navy, for its first and final time, lost the fight. Semmes, who tossed his sword overboard to ensure it would not become a war trophy, was among those picked up by a neutral British ship. He escaped to England and made his way back to the Confederacy.

---

8   Semmes, *Service Afloat*, p. 547.
9   Farragot to James Alden, January 27, 1863. OR, Series 1, Volume 19, p. 584.

PART FOUR

1864

1864

February 20	The battle of Olustee, Florida stalls Federal occupation of state.
March 12	The Red River Campaign begins as Federals try to invade Texas via land through Louisiana.
March 19	**Federal troops' advance up Rio Grande is stopped at the Battle of Laredo.**
May 14-15	The battle of Resaca, Georgia.
April 8	Federals defeated at Mansfield, Louisiana.
April 9	The battle of Pleasant Hill, Louisiana.
April 30	The Red River Campaign ends at the battle of Jenkins' Ferry.
May 5-6	The battle of The Wilderness (Virginia).
May 7	The Atlanta Campaign commences.
June 1	The battle of Cold Harbor, Virginia.
June 18	The siege of Petersburg, Virginia, begins.
June 19	The C.S.S *Alabama* is sunk after engagement with U.S.S. *Kearsarge* off Cherbourg, France.
July 22	The battle of Atlanta; Confederates withdraw.
September 2	Atlanta occupied by Federals.
September 6	**The first battle of Palmetto Ranch; Federal occupation of Rio Grande Valley ended.**
November 16	Sherman commences his march to the sea.
November 30	The battle of Franklin, Tennessee.
December 15-16	Confederates defeated at the battle of Nashville.

CHAPTER FOURTEEN

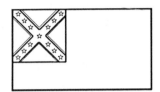

"Let their victory be a barren one!"

The Struggle for the Rio Grande Valley

The Rio Grande Valley, that almost foreign part of Texas and the Confederacy which lay between the Nueces and the Rio Grande rivers, represented much to both Washington and Richmond. Here, along the winding muddy path of the Rio Grande, in the chaparral and buffalo grass, the Confederate States shared its only international border with Mexico. Because of that, cotton could be sold or exchanged for much needed war material. Naturally, both sides saw the need to control the region.

Beyond commerce and supply, a second factor played in the importance of the Valley. Mexico, at the time of the secession crisis, was just finishing up yet another struggle between Centralist and Federalist factions. This go around had been called "The War of the Reform," and it produced not only a liberal victory, but the election of the first native Indian president of Mexico — Benito

Juarez. The 46-year-old lawyer was a visionary, whose attempts to secure and preserve Mexican civil liberties touched off a more than violent reaction from conservative forces. Juarez's policies included land reform, heavy restrictions on the church, and a proclamation informing Mexico's leading foreign creditors (Spain, France, and Great Britain) that all payments were suspended.

Juarez's timing was, perhaps, poor. His strongest ally, the United States, was in no position to support him, a fact that did not escape the notice of France's ambitious Louis Napoleon. As Emperor Napoleon III of France, this cousin of the first empire worked and dreamed for a second glorious age for the Bonapartes and France. Seeking to get a foothold in Mexico, Louis Napoleon convinced Spain and Great Britain to join France in a joint expedition and occupation of Vera Cruz to press Juarez. The plan was pretty convincing, but once it was realized that France's goals were much broader and more ambitious than just collection of foreign debts, Spain and Great Britain abandoned the project. It suited Napoleon III just as well, for Vera Cruz was under his control and afforded a base from which to strike at the interior of Mexico.

Ironically, the first French attempt to march on Mexico City was stopped cold at the city of Puebla. Juarista commander General Ignacio Zaragoza (who was, in fact, born in Goliad, Texas) became the first Mexican commander to stop an invader from marching on the Mexican capital since the days of the Aztecs. The defense of Puebla on May 5, 1862, became legendary as Cinco de Mayo. Unfortunately, the French regrouped under a new commander and returned. Puebla was taken, forcing Juarez and his government to abandon Mexico City. In June 1863 the French occupied the city.

The fall of Mexico City left two governments vying for control of the country: Juarez and his cabinet in flight in the north, and a new government made up of anti-Juarista Mexicans under French control. That coalition became the basis for the Mexican Empire, which offered its imperial crown (at Napoleon's suggestion) to the Austrian Archduke, Maximilian von Hapsburg. By 1864 the Mexican Empire under Maximilian was in place.[1]

---

1   For more on this period, see Hana, Albert J., and Katheryn A., *Napoleon and Mexico: American Triumph over Monarchy*, (Chapel Hill: University of North Carolina, 1991).

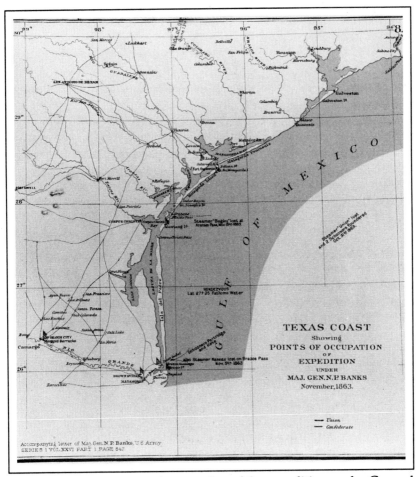

Map showing the points of occupation of the expedition under General
N. P. Banks in November 1863. *Courtesy of the Institute of Texas Cultures,
San Antonio.*

Confederate flirtations with the French did not make the
Federals take the matter of the new Mexican Empire lightly. From
the start, Lincoln refused to recognize the puppet French government and demanded French withdrawal from Mexico. But with
most of its resources committed, there was little physically the
United States could do.

The Confederate-Mexican border, however, was not a contact
point between French Imperialist forces and the Confederacy.

The current political chief of northern Mexico (and governor of Nuevo Leon and Coahuila) was Santiago Vidauri, one of those unique Latin American bosses who ruled with almost total independence. Vidauri was technically a Juarista, and therefore had no dealings with the French, who were too occupied trying to control the central states. The port of Bagdad, located on the mouth of the Rio Grande on the Mexican side, was doing a more than large business. But the Confederacy was not receiving large amounts of supplies from this quarter, nor was Southern cotton making any huge profits. Vidauri did allow trade, but drew the line on weapons. Also, he placed a high tariff on imported cotton. Texas planters, already paying high prices just to transport their bales into the valley, were now having to contend with the tax.[2]

Ironically, the Federals did not seem to grasp this fact. They viewed the valley with a great disgust, seeing only importation and a market for cotton which by-passed the blockade. They also looked at the growing power of the French and reasoned that necessity deemed it urgent to control South Texas. In the fall of 1863, the Rio Grande Valley found itself at war. A combined Federal army and navy operation succeed in capturing Brownsville and the mouth of the Rio Grande. Feeling ambitious, the Federals proceeded to move up river and secure Ringgold Barracks. In the wake of this occupation, Texan Confederates moved cotton trade operations up river to Eagle Pass, above the city of Laredo.

General Magruder had larger plans than just transferring his cotton trade. As he had exhibited at Galveston, Magruder had no intention of allowing the Yankees to occupy Texas soil. Magruder called upon Texas Ranger John Ford to once again take the field to secure South Texas. Oddly enough, Ford held no official Confederate army commission, and for some reason, President Davis would not give him one. Not to be stopped, Magruder recognized Ford as a colonel (Davis later confirmed the title) and gave him full authority to commence organization of a force to take into the Rio Grande Valley.[3]

---

2   See Irby, James A., *Backdoor to Bagdad: The Civil War on the Rio Grande,* (El Paso: University of Texas El Paso Press, 1972).

3   For a more complete look at this period, see Ford, John S., *Rip Ford's Texas,* edited by Stephen B. Oates (Austin: University of Texas Press, 1963), pp. 342-366.

Before Ford could move, the Federals became bolder. Seeking to stop the cotton trade wherever it was located, an expedition moved out of Ringgold Barracks up river towards Laredo. On March 19, 1864, word was received in the sleepy river town that the Yankee army was on its way.

One of the chief political families in the city was the Benavides. Three brothers, Santos, Refugio, and Cristobal headed it. The family was bound to the city from its birth — Santos' great-great grandfather had been the founder. Laredo had always been on the fringe of Texas — one of those places where families, not governments, control. The Tejanos of Laredo, who had already survived the rule of five countries, were an independent lot who maintained a stronger sense of home than most of their fellow Texans. It has been suggested that Mexican-Texans did not support the Confederate cause. A sampling of the delegates of the Secession Convention clearly shows that none were Tejanos, nor were most of the organizers of the Secession movement in the South Texas area. However, the generalization is clearly not the case, as the muster rolls of the 6th Texas Infantry, the 8th Texas, and other units will illustrate. While the political concepts of the Confederacy may not have been appealing, or in the case of slavery, either practical or economically possible, the concept of home was. An estimated 9,900 Hispanics served in the War Between the States.[4] The Benavides brothers were prime examples of this. Early in 1861, they clearly declared their support for the Confederate States. Santos, who had been offered a brigadier-general's commission if he joined the Union army,[5] settled for a Confederate commission and helped raise the 32nd Regiment of Texas Cavalry, which in turn his two brothers supplied companies for.

The arrival of a Federal army at their doorstep did not sway the Benavides' loyalty. News of the Federal advance caught the forty-year-old in his sick bed. Santos, who had seen his first combat in the bitter Federalist-Centralist wars between 1838-1840, realized the odds were against him. He nevertheless set into motion defense plans. Riders were sent out to bring back part of his men on grazing duties up river. Gathering his 70 odd de-

---

4   Thompson, Jerry Don, *Vaqueros in Blue and Gray*, (Austin: Presidial Press, 1987), p. 5. Thompson, a professor at Laredo College, has, to date, published the most complete works on the role of Texas Hispanics in the war.

5   Ford, *Rip Ford's Texas*, pp. 357-358.

fenders, Santos directed Captain Chapman's company to defend the main plaza of the city while Refugio was dispatched to defend the outskirts of the city.[6]

The population of the city, mostly Hispanic, now had the option of either staying or evacuating. The citizens elected not only to stay, but joined in the inner defenses with Chapman's men. The unity exhibited was most impressive; even Santos, who knew his people, was touched. Impressive also was the determination of the Tejano commander, who ordered his brother Cristobal to fire all Confederate property, including five thousand bales of cotton, should the Federals capture the city. He also directed his brother to burn his own home proclaiming, "Nothing of mine shall pass to the enemy. Let their victory be a barren one!"[7]

At around three that afternoon, the Federal troops approached the city from the south. "Yankees, consisting of about 200 men (Americans and a few Mexicans), all regular soldiers and superiorly armed, halted when about a half mile from town, formed and charged in squads, each numbering about 40 men." Benavides wasted no time in meeting the attack head on. "My men gave the Texas yell, commenced firing on them and compelled them to retreat to their main force."[8]

The Federals reformed, dismounted, and came again. Once more the Laredo defenders met them head on. This time some personal heroics entered into the fray. Major J. S. Swope and Juan Ibarra rode forward by themselves and personally stalled the advance of one of the Yankee squads. Both men kept firing until out of ammunition and then coolly retired. The spectacle of the lone Anglo and Hispanic standing up against the Federals impressed Benavides enough to make mention of the incident in his official report.

The fighting continued well into the late afternoon with the Federals never getting beyond the outskirts. At dark "the Yankees thought it best to skedaddle in their own peculiar style and give up their intention of walking into Laredo that day."[9]

---

6 Benavides' account of the battle can be found in OR, Series 1, Volume 34, Part 1, pp. 647-649 and in Ford, *Rip Ford's Texas*, pp. 355-357.
7 Ford, *Rip Ford's Texas*, p. 357.
8 Ford, *Rip Ford's Texas*, p. 356.
9 Ford, *Rip Ford's Texas*, p. 357.

Confederate reinforcements arrived that night, causing a spon-
taneous fiesta complete with bell ringing and trumpet blowing.
Benavides had no intention of stopping there, however. At sunup
he dispatched Refugio and 60 well-mounted men to outflank
the Federals from the rear. But the previous day's fighting had
broken more than just their spirit — the Yankees were in full
retreat. Not only had Benavides saved Laredo, but he had started
the Confederate liberation of the Rio Grande Valley. "Please send
some Mississippi yagers, shotgun, minie rifles, Belgian muskets
and navy-style six shooter cartridges if possible" he wrote.[10] For
their stubborn defense of Laredo, Santos and Refugio Benavides
were officially thanked by joint resolution of the State Legislature.

While the Federals occupied the Rio Grande, a second expedition was dispatched under General Nathaniel Banks to begin a
push up Louisiana's Red River. This too was designed to eliminate
Confederate-Mexican trade and to put pressure on the French.
Banks' army represented a serious threat to North Texas and the
Trans-Mississippi Department. Its commander, General Edmund
Kirby Smith, sounded the alarm to his subcommanders in Louisiana
and Texas. The response was impressive as Confederate com-
mands from as far as Port Lavaca raced to Western Louisiana. On
April 8 the Confederate army stalled Bank's advance at Mansfield.
Here, General Hamilton Bee finally saw combat, and the Tejanos
of Colonel Hobby's 8th Infantry contributed greatly to the rout of
the Yankee invader. The Federals regrouped at nearby Pleasant
Hill and successfully defended their position. A series of fights
continued in the region, but by May 22 the threat to northeastern
Texas was over.

Rip Ford, with the Cavalry of the West, commenced to reclaim
the valley in the months following the Laredo victory. By July 29
the Federals had evacuated Brownsville, and on the next day the
Cavalry of the West entered the city. The Federals retired to the
island of Brazos de Santiago off Boco Chico. Here, they dug in,
determined to remain on at least one piece of Texas soil. Ford,
more concerned with reopening the trade market with Mexico,
simply put up with them. The old Ranger went to work trying to
reestablish Confederate ties with Mexico. The situation was deli-
cate, as his old enemy from before the war, Juan Cortina,

---

10 Ford, *Rip Ford's Texas*, p. 357.

now represented the Juarista government in Matamoros. Ford attempted to open friendly relations by informing Cortina that "the forces of Mr. Lincoln's government had retired from the mainland." He stated further that in "renewing official relations with the Mexican authorities, I take pleasure in reassuring them of my sincere desire to cultivate friendly relations, and to do all in my power to render our intercourse officially, commercially, and otherwise, pleasant and mutually advantageous."[11]

But while the American Civil War was settling down in the valley, the Mexican Civil War was escalating. An expedition of French naval and marine forces under Commodore A. Veron landed at Bagdad on August 22, 1864. The thriving port was now under Maximilian's control. Everyone assumed that Cortina would abandon Matamoros, but the old bandit remained steadfast. Ford, seeing the handwriting on the wall, approached Veron to determine what his attitude was towards Confederate trade. The French responded that "If the exigencies of war should take me to Matamoros, you may rest assured that I shall see that all persons and property covered by the flag of your nation are duly respected."[12]

Oddly enough, relations with Cortina now began to sour. The Juarista colonel commenced dealings with the Union army, who apparently offered him a commission in the United States Army. Incidents between Juaristas and Confederates became regular and Cortina stopped trade between Matamoros and Brownsville. A major skirmish erupted at Palmito (or Palmetto) Ranch between Brownsville and Boco Chico as Cortina's men opened fire from the Mexican side of the Rio Grande on some Confederates stationed at the ranch. The Confederate commander retreated back to Brownsville, some eight miles to the west.

It became apparent to Ford that the Federals were about to make a push inland. Equally apparent was that Cortina had agreed to help them capture Brownsville. The night of September 6, 1864, was an uneasy one for Ford and his men, who expected an immediate attack. Fortunately, it rained, causing the roads to wash out. The next day, Confederate spirits were high.

---

11 Ford, *Rip Ford's Texas*, p. 369.
12 Ford, *Rip Ford's Texas*, p. 370.

Texans in gray — the Benavedies brothers of Laredo. *Courtesy of the Institute of Texas Cultures, San Antonio.*

Ford realized that Cortina probably was holding off his attack from the Mexican side until the Federals, advancing from the coast, had pulled Ford and his command toward them. Ford would not allow this to happen. He sent one part of his command to meet the Federals while he remained at Brownsville. The plan worked. On September 9 the Federal force was defeated at Palmetto Ranch. They retired back to Brazos Santiago on the 12th. Cortina never crossed the river. Two weeks later, General Tomas Mejia of the Imperial Mexican Army marched on Matamoros. Cortina conveniently switched sides. Many of his officers refused to turn traitor and fled into the United States, where Ford treated them with all kindness. From them, the Confederates learned that Cortina had planned to transfer his entire command into the Federal army — an act most resisted.

While Ford, Benavides, and their men enjoyed a highly successful campaign in South Texas, events further east were taking a turn for the worse. On May 7, 1864, the Federals under General William Sherman commenced their drive out of Tennessee and, in a series of successful flanking moves, moved on the important railroad terminal of Atlanta. Despite repeated attempts by the Army of Tennessee under General Joe Johnston and, later, John Bell Hood, the Confederates were forced to abandon Atlanta on September 1. In Virginia, the ring grew tighter around the Confederate capital as Lee's Army of Northern Virginia dug in at Petersburg. By the end of the year, Phil Sheridan's Yankees would destroy the Shenandoah Valley and Sherman would cut the back off Atlanta and march to the sea. Christmas of 1864 would be a bitter one for the Confederacy.

But in Texas, there would be no such destruction. For as the winter of 1864 settled into South Texas, the Confederate flag floated over the Rio Grande Valley, the French-Mexican Imperialist banner over Matamoros and Bagdad, and the Stars and Stripes over Brazos Santiago. The fighting in the valley had temporarily stopped. Most, by this time, would be content to let the fate of the Union or the Confederacy be decided on distant battlefields.

CHAPTER FIFTEEN

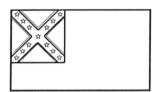

"Cold-blooded murder"

Granbury's Texas Brigade
at Franklin, Tennessee
1864

To the majority of Americans and Texans, the most famous moment of the war is the charge of Confederate General George Pickett's Division at Gettysburg on July 3, 1863. Historians still debate the real impact of Gettysburg on the outcome of the war. Their academic debate does not, however, diminish the popularity of this historic battlefield, which is now a national park. Gettysburg is alive today with a sea of preserved fields, split rail fences, markers, monuments, and visitors. Texans visiting the Gettysburg National Park may have to look high and low for the small granite marker honoring Texas' participation in the battle. It is there, though, at the south end of the park. Near its location, the famous Hood's Texas Brigade, by then under the command of Felix

Robertson, fought valiantly and stubbornly on July 2. In the rocks of Devil's Den and up the steep slopes of Little Round Top, Texans waged their fight at Gettysburg. Some Texans feel slighted, in a macabre sort of way, that on the next day, when Pickett's men made their famous charge, no units of the Lone Star State were present.[1]

Anyone who does feel cheated should not, for Pickett's charge was pale when compared with the charge of the Army of Tennessee at Franklin, Tennessee, almost a year and a half later. If Pickett's charge was slaughter, then the one at Franklin was murder. Nearly 16,000 Confederates, forming a line of battle over two miles long, marched against and then charged 32,000 Federals entrenched behind strong earthworks. Even though repulsed, the veterans of the Army of Tennessee renewed their attacks again and again. For five bloody hours the murderous contest was waged in stubborn brutality. When it was at last over, more than 6,000 dead and wounded Confederates lay before and in the Yankee works. Thirteen regimental commanders lay dead along with six generals.

After Gettysburg, the Army of Northern Virginia was able to fight again. In the summer of 1863 there were still enough reserves of supplies and manpower for the Confederates to recuperate from such a loss. Not so for the Army of Tennessee after Franklin.

John Bell Hood was in command of the Army of Tennessee that fall. Hood had once served in Texas as a young cavalry officer before the war and had commanded the legendary Texas Brigade in Lee's army. He had been given command of the Army of Tennessee in the wake of the Atlanta campaign. Following the fall of Atlanta to Sherman, Hood marched his army north. With the hated Yankees preparing to drive across Georgia toward the sea, Hood intentionally made plans to hit Sherman's communication lines and threaten his rear. Or at least that was the original plan. But as the campaign progressed during that fall, Hood dramatically altered his original objectives. He advanced into occupied

---

1   For an account of the Texas Brigade (Hood's) at Gettysburg, see Simpson, Harold B., *Hood's Texas Brigade—Lee's Grenadier Guards*, (Hillsboro, Texas: Hill Junior College Press, 1970). The Texas monument at Gettysburg was dedicated during the Civil War Centennial and was rededicated in 1988 during the 125th anniversary celebrations by members of the 1st Confederate (King's) Brigade Reenactment group who were representing Hood's Brigade.

John Bell Hood. *Courtesy of the National Archives; Jeff Hunt.*

Tennessee, determined to drive up the center of the state and perhaps into Kentucky. The plan was daring and bold.

At first the Federals offered little resistance. Then, in an unexpected move at Spring Hill, Tennessee, an entire Federal army marched past Hood's men in the dark of night, escaping to fortified positions at the town of Franklin, some fifteen miles south of Nashville.

Union General J. M. Schofield now had the advantage. With the center of his defenses located around the Carter farm on the southern edge of town, the Federals blocked the Columbia-Nashville Pike. No one — not the Yankees, the townspeople, or even Hood's own officers — expected what was to follow.

Hood wanted to show the South, the North, and perhaps even the world, that his Army of Tennessee was better than the Army of Northern Virginia. He yearned to emulate the greatness of Jackson and Lee. Despite several suggestions that an attack on their flanks might turn the Yankees, Hood instead announced that his command would launch a massive frontal assault in the grandest style possible.

Many claim that Hood was too ill to command. He had lost the use of an arm at Gettysburg and had a leg amputated at Chickamauga. As historians James Lee McDonough and Thomas L. Connelly observed, he was a broken soul, old before his time in spirit and flesh.[2] Years later, he would justify his plans to take Franklin quickly before Schofield could strengthen his position further or fall back to join Thomas at Nashville.

Generals Cheatham and Cleburne tried to persuade him not to attack; Nathan Bedford Forest begged to test the flanks. But Hood only thought of attack. Grady McWhiney and Perry Jamison suggested that perhaps Hood's strong Celtic-Southern heritage drove him to employ tactics typical of ancient Scotland — the Highland charge. Connelly and McDonough noted a pattern of reckless behavior throughout his career. On November 30, whatever passions guided him, Hood ordered the Army of Tennessee into a line of battle south of Franklin.

The Texas Brigade formed ranks at Franklin, but not the celebrated unit to which volumes have been devoted. This was Granbury's Texas Brigade. It derived its name from Hiram

---

2   McDonough, James Lee, and Connelly, Thomas L., *Five Tragic Hours—The Battle of Franklin*, (Knoxville: University of Tennessee Press, 1983), p. 24.

Bronson Granbury, a Missouri native who had established a law office in Waco during the 1850s. When war came, Granbury organized the Waco Guards and served as its captain until promoted to major and later colonel of the 7th Texas Infantry. In 1862 he and his regiment were among those captured when Fort Donelson surrendered. Paroled, the wild-eyed Granbury was, by the time of the Tennessee campaign, a brigadier general.

In November 1863, when his brigade was formed, it consisted of the 6th, 7th, 10th, and 15th Texas Infantry along with the dismounted 17th, 18th, 24th, and 25th Texas Cavalry. There was also a Tennessee regiment, the old 35th. His men hailed from almost every part of Texas — and they had experienced hard luck. All of the Texas regiments, save the 7th, had been at Arkansas Post where they were captured. The 6th Texas lost the colors presented to them by the ladies of Victoria. Typical of the officers in the brigade was 35-year-old Samuel T. Foster, the former chief justice

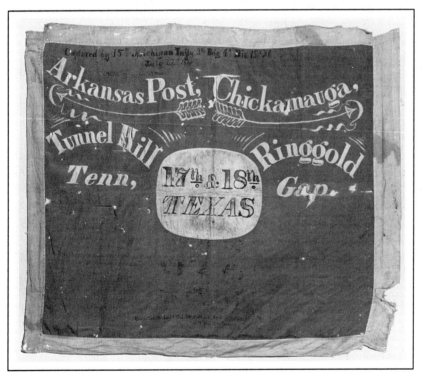

The flag of the 17th and 18th Texas Infantry. *Courtesy of the Texas State Archives in Austin.*

of Live Oak County. Foster had enlisted in Company "H," 24th Texas Cavalry only to suffer the shame of having the regiment's horses taken away in Arkansas during the summer of 1862. Foster was among those captured at Arkansas Post. He spent time in a Yankee prison camp before being paroled and returned to his old company.[3]

Another member of the brigade was Jim Turner, who traveled from his farm in Travis County to enlist in Captain Rhoades Fisher's Travis Rifles. The company received orders to proceed to Victoria for military instruction. The various units which were to become the 6th Texas assembled at Camp McCulloch, north of town. There the men from Calhoun, Gonzales, Matagorda, Hays, Travis, Guadalupe, Bell, De Witt, Bexar, La Vaca, and Victoria counties learned the art of soldiering. Turner and his fellows were soon equipped with smooth bore Springfield muskets, belts, cartridge boxes, and light brown colored uniforms and then proceeded to Arkansas and the disaster at Arkansas Post. Turner found himself being transported north in bitter cold weather for a brief stay as a prisoner at Camp Butler near Springfield, Illinois. Despite an outbreak of smallpox, Turner noted that he and his comrades were well treated by the Federals. Paroled, they joined the consolidated brigade. Turner particularly liked being in the division commanded by General Patrick Cleburne — "Old Pat" as he called him. Much to the men's delight, the Irishman occasionally sent a drink of whiskey to his veterans.

By the time of the Tennessee invasion, Foster and the rest of these men were all seasoned veterans of Missionary Ridge and the Atlanta campaign. Granbury's Texas Brigade had already established a reputation for its "stark fighting ability."[4] This included not only fights against the Yankees, but each other, as was evident in the great snowball fight at Dalton, Georgia, which Granbury's men apparently won and were rewarded with a ration of whiskey from "Old Pat."

If one believes in divine warnings, then Granbury's Brigade certainly received a frightful omen at the start of the Tennessee

---

3   The memories of this officer can be found in Foster, Samuel T., *One of Cleburne's Command*, edited by Norman D. Brown (Austin: University of Texas Press, 1980).

4   Henderson, Harry McCorry, *Texas in the Confederacy*, (San Antonio: Naylor Press, 1955), p. 82.

campaign. Just after the men had stacked their rifles one evening, a small thunderhead appeared and the next instant, a bolt of lightning hit the rifles. The effect was more than dramatic; at least two soldiers were killed. One of the officers, standing ten feet away, was thrown five feet. Nearly every man in the 24th Texas was shocked — "some are lame, some sore and some are not exactly of sound mind." The weapons were broken, bent and others just thrown to the ground unhurt.[5]

If the lightning incident wasn't enough, perhaps the snow-storm that hit the advancing Confederates as they crossed into Tennessee added to the drama. A few miles into the occupied Confederate state, the brigade marched under a large white flag bearing the motto: "A Grave or a Home." Unaware of what laid ahead of them, the Confederates cheered.[6]

On the 21st of November, the regimental commanders called their men together and informed them that Hood was going to take the army into Tennessee. They were told to expect hard marching and some fighting, but not to worry, for Hood would not risk a chance for a defeat in Tennessee. Hood would not fight unless he had an equal number of men and the choice of the ground. Or so everyone believed.

Nine days later they stood before Franklin. The numbers were far from equal and the Yankees had the choice of ground. The regimental bands played the familiar strains of "The Bonnie Blue Flag" and the Army of Tennessee moved forward toward the Federal lines. As part of General Patrick Cleburne's division, the Texans marched to the east of the Columbia Pike. Their target was the gap in the Federal lines where the road passed between the Carter House and the cotton gin. The advance, over rolling terrain, was over a mile and a half. With their blue and white battle flags floating over a sea of gleaming bayonets, the Confederates presented a mighty sight. A Union division posted to the front of the works was quickly swept away, and as its broken soldiers raced for the cover of the works, the Confederates pushed quickly forward.

One hundred paces from their target, the Confederates were hit with the full force of Yankee rifle and cannon fire. Cleburne's

---

5   Foster, *One of Cleburne's Command*, pp. 136-137.
6   Captain W. G. Post to editor, December 15, 1864, Houston *Tri-Weekly Telegraph*, March 1, 1865.

division charged the works. Federal artillery crews resorted to using axes, picks, and rams to fight. The nearly exhausted Confederates now faced fire from reserve Union troops, who drew forward to plug the gap. In a war in which the bayonet was put to very little combat use, Franklin stands out as a dramatic departure. In the yards of the Carter House, men fought like devils as the hand to hand combat was savage. One survivor recalled that they passed into the "veritable jaws of death and destruction."[7]

The carnage went on for some forty minutes around the Carter House until the Confederates were, at last, forced back. But they came forward again. Once more, they were pushed back. Others were caught in a terrible storm of cross fire between flanking Federal positions. For five hours it went on; some of the Confederates threw clods of dirt or even sticks at the Federals. At around nine that evening, the exhausted Army of Tennessee quit and, in the cover of darkness, fell back. Later that night, the Yankees did the same, preferring the safety of Nashville to another day at Franklin.[8]

Over 7,000 Confederates were either dead, wounded, or missing. Out of 90 men on the field, only 14 members of the 10th Texas were able to report. One third of Hood's infantry was gone. There were no replacements. Directly south of the cotton gin, some 60 yards away, burial details found the beloved Irishman Pat Cleburne, the "Stonewall of the West," shot dead in the chest. A few hundred yards away from him lay General John Adams. General Otho Strahl lay dead west of the Pike. They found Hiram Granbury in one of the ditches east of the Pike, a bullet through his brain. Their bodies were taken to the McGavoch home, "Carnton," where they lay on the gallery as surgeons inside desperately tried to save the hundreds of wounded. Also dead was the South Carolinian General "States' Rights" Gist. General John C. Carter was wounded and later died. The legendary status of the Franklin Six was born.

Others died besides the generals. Thomas Stokes, from Johnson City, serving as brigade adjutant, was last seen marching down

---

7 Yeary, Mamie, compiler, *Reminiscences of the Boys in Gray, 1861-1865,* (McGregor, Texas: Privately published, 1912), Reprint, (Dayton: Morningside House, Inc., 1986), p. 623.
8 For the best overall account of the battle, see McDonough and Connelly, *Five Tragic Hours.*

The Carnton Confederate Cemetery in Franklin, Tennessee. *Courtesy of the Carter House, Franklin, Tennessee.*

The Carter House Museum, Franklin, Tennessee. *Courtesy of the Carter House, Franklin, Tennessee.*

the Pike with his old 10th Texas. William Chase, the impatient Goliad schoolteacher, would never have to worry again about which sister would return his affections; he lay dead near Hughes Ford on the Harpeth River. In one of life's bitter ironies, CSA Captain Todd Carter fell mortally wounded in the yard of his boyhood home. He died later that night in his own bed. Of the eleven men who went into battle representing Company "B," 7th Texas Infantry, five were killed, three wounded, one captured, and two escaped.[9] Men from the north prairies, the central farmlands, and the coastal bend of Texas — Sgt. William Driscoll, James Brook, T. J. Lewis, Lieutenant P. W. Perry, Adam Braden — lay dead and dying. Nor are the Texian names restricted to the Anglo-Celtics. Lieutenant Eugeno Navarro was missing, Simon Garza was wounded in the right foot, and Andrew San Miguel was shot in the head. Where their remains rest today, no one can be certain. At least 89 of them are at Carnton.[10]

Two years later the owner of Carnton became alarmed when the Confederates' wooden grave markers were being stolen for firewood. He donated two acres of his own land for a cemetery and, with his own funds, had the remains of nearly 1,481 soldiers moved and reburied, by state, in sections. Granbury himself was the first buried at Ashwood Cemetery at Columbia. He was moved, in November 1893, to the city of Granbury, Texas, which was named in his honor. The irony is that the town is the county seat for Hood County, named for John B. Hood.

Hood himself was not satisfied with the bloodletting at Franklin. He pressed on to Nashville with the remains of his army. The effort was in vain. In the end, the remains of the Army of Tennessee, many without shoes or proper clothing, retreated southward in the ice and snow. As they went, some of the men commenced singing a new verse for the popular "Yellow Rose of Texas." This one, however, was neither kind nor romantic:

> I am heading back southward,
> My heart is full of woe.
> I'm going back to Georgia,

---

9 Yeary, *Reminiscences*, p. 797.
10 Casualty lists for Granbury's Brigade are incomplete, but Sergeant-Major M. O'Donoghue of the Sixth Texas Infantry did supply a partial list which was printed in the Houston *Tri-Weekly Telegraph* on March 3, 1865.

To find my Uncle Joe.
You may talk about your Beauregard
And sing of General Lee,
But the Gallant Hood of Texas,
Played hell in Tennessee!

There was no vast population to refill the decimated ranks, no experienced cadre to replace the lost officers. While the Army of Tennessee would remain together (at least in part) and fight on to the end, its effectiveness was destroyed that cold winter in Tennessee. One officer in Granbury's Brigade bitterly recorded, "... the wails and cries of widows and orphans made at Franklin will heat up the fire of the bottomless pit to burn the soul of General J. B. Hood for murdering their husbands and fathers at that place that day. It can't be called anything else but cold-blooded murder."[11]

Unlike Gettysburg, there are no impressive monuments or preserved fields at Franklin today. The war ended too soon for the battle's name to be etched into the minds of the population. The Texas newspapers did not start receiving news of the battle until February 1865, and the casualty lists did not arrive until mid-March. The Carter House stands delicately and lovingly preserved but surrounded by urban developments that include a Pizza Hut. Unlike Gettysburg, you can no longer stand in the Carter yard and gaze into the open valley to imagine the sight of the masses of men, battle flags, and bayonets. You can still walk on the gallery at Carnton where Granbury and his fellows lay dead. The two-acre cemetery is also preserved, within hitting distance of some tennis courts. The people of Franklin, past and present, should be thanked for what they have managed to preserve. For with the exception of Mississippi, Louisiana, Missouri, and South Carolina (who responded to a plea for financial aide in 1915), the preservation of these sites has been all their responsibility.[12]

But nothing can diminish the drama of Franklin. If you walk the Confederate cemetery just before dusk in the fading light, you can still feel the power and the anguish of that terrible

---

11 Foster, *One of Cleburne's Command*, p. 151
12 For a history of the cemetery, see *McGavock Confederate Cemetery*, (Franklin Chapter No. 14, United Daughters of the Confederacy, 1989).

winter's day in 1864 when the Army of Tennessee and Granbury's Texans marched to glory and found hell. No Texan ever need feel cheated because of Pickett's charge, for Texan courage abounded at Franklin.

CHAPTER SIXTEEN

Prairie Forts and Rockets

1864

Albert Lea had sufficiently recovered from his son's death at Galveston by the summer of 1864 to return to his duties as an engineer. One of the projects given to him perhaps seemed a little odd. It was to erect a fortification at Gonzales, Texas. Not on the coast mind you, but inland several hundred miles at a town extremely landlocked.

Gonzales is located approximately 70 miles east of San Antonio and some hundred miles west of Houston. As one of the original Anglo-Celtic settlements established before the 1836 war for independence, the tiny community grew to almost legendary importance during that struggle. The first shot of the Texas revolution was fired here, and the community was the only town to send reinforcements to the besieged Alamo. The original settlement was burned by Sam Houston's order in the wake of the Mexican army's push across Texas. After San Jacinto, its settlers returned to start anew. By 1860 the community had grown into a major cotton/agricultural supplier.

Like most of Texas, the citizens of Gonzales supported secession and the war effort. The area had been one of the prime recruiting centers for the Knights of the Golden Circle and, subsequently, supplied many companies of infantry and cavalry to the Confederate cause. But the community itself was never to see a Yankee soldier until well after the war. Yet in the fall of 1864, General Hamilton Bee became worried that the Federals might try to push up the Guadalupe River and strike at the center of the state. Gonzales sat not only at the junction of the San Marcos and Guadalupe rivers, but also on the main road between Houston and San Antonio. One critical local landmark was the impressive covered bridge over the San Marcos just east of town.

Records concerning the activities of Lea and his subordinate, Captain H. Wickland, are far from complete, but work may have commenced on an earthen fort just north of town as early as December 1863. During a scare that the Federals might have started to advance from the Matagorda Peninsula, General Magruder ordered General Hamilton Bee to direct Lea, with the engineers, implements, and "all the Negroes he has," to proceed, "as rapidly as possible to the confluence of the San Marcos and Guadalupe, near Gonzales."[1] A second order informed the planters of Gonzales, De Witt, Victoria, Calhoun, Jackson, Lavaca, Wharton, Colorado, and Austin counties, west of the Brazos, to send their slaves to Gonzales. Lea was cited as the contact officer. The planters were ordered to provide all "able-bodied male slaves between the ages of sixteen and fifty years" and that the owners were to the "extent of their ability, furnish their slaves with intrenching tools, such as axes, spades, shovels, hoes, picks, grubbing hoes, & c."[2] In the following weeks, Colonel James Duff was ordered to send two of his companies under his personal command to Gonzales and "report to the engineer officer at that place."[3]

The site selected was a good-size hill which commanded not only the town, but the road, the rivers, and the bridge. Under-

---

1   OR, Series 1, Volume 26, Part 2, pp. 490-491.
2   OR, p. 839.
3   OR, pp. 512-513.

Brigadier General Hamilton B. Bee. *Courtesy of the DRT Library at the Alamo.*

standing local politics, Wickland and Lea named the fortification after General Waul, who had come from this community.

What developed on the hilltop was a fortification some 250 feet by 750 feet long. What is illustrated on Wickland's map is a typical field fortification, with four corner bastions and two side redans.[4] The measurements that Wickland gives for superior slopes, interior slopes, etc. conforms to Mahan's "Field Fortifications." The thickness of the parapet of Fort Waul indicated that Lea had designed the works to be able to withstand fire from not only small arms fire, but shot from artillery as heavy as twelve pounders.[5]

According to local tradition (which is supported by Magruder's orders), work was carried out by slaves under the direction of Home Guard troops. It is probable that as matters turned for the worse outside of the state, construction on the fort slowed down. While it appears that the exterior works were, in part, finished, the fort was far from completed by the end of the war. Visitors to the fort today are less than excited, since the remaining lower earthen walls do not meet the image of the typical stone forts. And needless to say, no Federal gunboats ever got up the Guadalupe to test the thickness of the walls.

Despite its remote location, Texas did make efforts to supply the Confederate war machine with goods. Jean cloth was produced at the state's prison facility in Huntsville. There was an experimental torpedo works at Port Lavaca. Marshall, toward the end of the war, became an ordnance center. But wartime production reached its zenith in northeast Texas' piney woods. Trans-Mississippian officials had established a series of military depots at Tyler, including a pharmaceutical laboratory and commissary/quartermaster's department. Three area merchants, J. C. Short, William S. Biscoe, and George Yarborough established a small arms factory and armory. The merchants were slow in implementing production, however, causing Confederate officials to purchase the facility under the Ordnance Bureau. The ordnance at Little Rock, Arkansas, was moved to Tyler because of Federal

---

4   A redan is a small work with two faces terminating in a salient angle used to cover a camp. Scott, Henry L., *Military Dictionary*, (New York: D. Van Nostrand, 1864).

5   Post of Gonzales, February 22, 1864, Record Group 109, War Department Collection of Confederate Records, National Archives.

threats against the Arkansas capital. By the end of the war, over 2,223 Tyler rifled muskets complete with cartridges had been produced.

Tyler was also the site of the only prisoner of war facility to be located within Texas. Commencing in 1863, Camp Ford, a former Confederate camp of instruction, was redesignated as a holding facility for Yankee prisoners. The site boasted a magnificent spring, which afforded plenty of fresh and safe drinking water. However, there were no actual barracks or buildings to shelter the prisoners, many of whom dug small caves in the sand or built arbors called "shebangs" for protection from the elements.

The failure of the 1864 Red River campaign sent large numbers of Federals into the camp, overcrowding it. But Camp Ford never became the hell hole that Andersonville, Libby Prison, or Camp Douglas, a Federal prison camp in Chicago, became. Out of the 5,300 men held, only 286 died. That is more than a good track record, considering 15 percent of the prisoners held in other Southern camps died, as did 12 percent in Federal camps.[6]

Down on the coast, Dance and Brothers of Columbia (now West Columbia) had commenced producing a fine grade of pistols for the Confederate cause as early as 1862. There were to be five types of Dance revolvers, all based on Samuel Colt's designs. The threat of Federal occupation of the coast finally caused the Dances to give up their Brazoria County location and head for Anderson in Grimes County. Despite wartime shortages, the Dances were still manufacturing pistols when the war ended.[7]

Because of its strategic location, San Antonio had become a center of activity for the all important cotton trade. A tannery had also been started close to the headwaters of the San Antonio River near the site of the present San Antonio Zoo. Large amounts of saltpeter were also accumulated to assist the Confederate war effort. In the summer of 1864, the Alamo City became the center of yet another wartime project — the development of military rockets.

---

6   For more on Tyler's wartime production, see Betts, Vicki, *Smith County, Texas, in the Civil War*, (Tyler, Texas: Smith County Historical Society, 1978), pp. 35-45.

7   For more information, see Wiggins, Gary, *Dance and Brothers: Texas Gunmakers of the Confederacy*, (Orange, Virginia: Moss Publications, 1980).

As strange of this may seem, the use of exploding rockets by the military could be traced back as far as the War of 1812 when the British employed them against the Americans. When Texas was a republic, George Hockley, ordnance officer, recommend that the Texian military consider using similar rockets as part of their military armament. "The congreve rocket," he wrote, "which can be thrown immediately amongst them [Indians] if formed in a body — excite terror and probable confusion if within their vision."[8] The Confederates in Virginia had also experimented with rockets, including a rumored two-stage machine.

The San Antonio experiments were triggered by a German mechanic named Schroder in the CSA engineer corps. Schroder claimed to have been a lieutenant in a rocket battery in the Austrian-Hungarian army. Because of this, he professed a great knowledge of the construction and arming of military rockets. His superior officer, Lieutenant Getulius Kellersberger, had been director of the iron works at Wiener-Neustadt and had attended the annual imperial rocket maneuvers.

Early tests by the two produced several small rockets loaded with six-pound grenades on the front of one three-foot rocket. One of the problems was a lack of proper chemicals. The abundance of saltpeter in San Antonio quickly transferred the project to this location. While the lieutenant worked in earnest, his superior began to have doubts about the entire project. That did not stop the senior officers or the public from becoming excited by the project. Soon a thousand rockets had been constructed.

At last, as his confidence wore thin, the senior officer demanded a test of the existing rockets, and a proper site was selected. The first rocket fired correctly, hit the ground, and then ricocheted. It returned to the ground directly behind the senior officer's horse. The horse was neither impressed nor amused by the rocket or its trajectory. A second rocket was fired and it hit the ground almost at once, sputtered across the sod, and sent several of the enlisted men into flight.

Kellersberger's worst fears had been realized. However, the commanding general, Hamilton Bee, had already scheduled a public test of the rockets. Kellersberger's protests to delay this exhibition went unheeded. When the day rolled around, the

---

8   George Hockley to Albert S. Johnston, March 28, 1839. See Kourey, Michael J., *Arms for Texas* (Boulder, Colorado: Old Army Press, 1973), p. 80.

engineer developed a headache and was unable to attend. His fears, however, once again proved well founded.

The first rocket exploded in its firing stand and a second tore the stand down, causing a massive chain reaction. Horses bolted and the festive picnic atmosphere turned into a general rout as soldiers and civilians ran for cover. That night, Kellersberger received orders from Bee stating that the rocket battery was dissolved. Kellersberger took the rest of the nearly 1,200 rockets and tossed them into the deepest part of the San Antonio River. San Antonio's days as a rocket center were over.[9]

---

9   Kellersberger, Getulius, *Memories of an Engineer in the Confederate Army in Texas*, Translated by Helen S. Sundstrom, (Austin: University of Texas Press, no date), pp. 46-47.

PART FIVE

1865

1865

January 19	Sherman commences campaign in the Carolinas.
March 4	Lincoln inaugurated for second term.
March 19-21	The battle of Bentonville, North Carolina.
April 1	The battle of Five Forks (Virginia).
April 3	Richmond occupied by Union troops.
April 9	Robert E. Lee surrenders the Army of Northern Virginia at Appomattox Court House (Virginia).
April 14	Abraham Lincoln assassinated.
April 26	Surrender of the Army of Tennessee at Bennett House near Durham, North Carolina.
May 12-13	**The battle of Palmetto Ranch.**
June 2	**Kirby Smith surrenders Trans-Mississippi Department.**

CHAPTER SEVENTEEN

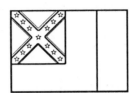

Gloomy Days and Feuding Generals

The End of the Trans-Mississippi Department 1865

As the new year settled in on Texas and the Trans-Mississippi South, the world for Southerners was quickly coming to an end. Grant's armies pushed on Petersburg with designs on Richmond . . . the remains of the Army of the Tennessee retreated into the Carolinas as Sherman's invaders cut the back out of Atlanta and pressed to the sea. More than half of the Confederacy was now occupied territory.

Texas remained free but isolated. The Trans-Mississippi Department was now headquartered in Shreveport, Louisiana, and Texas Departmental Headquarters under Magruder remained at Houston. Federal troops still occupied the tiny island of Brazos Santiago, but these troops were apparently no real threat.

Confederate commander John S. Ford and Union commander
General Lew Wallace had developed an unofficial understanding.
In their minds, the outcome of the war was being decided in
Virginia. So why should more bloodshed be spilled in South
Texas? For a while, at least, a truce of sorts kept peace in the valley.[1]

Although militarily Texas seemed secure, its economy was near
chaos. Cotton had soared to $9 a pound and essentials such as
bacon, tallow, sugar, and lard were well over the $2 mark. Flour
was near $50 and potatoes were $20. Cotton sales were still weak
and were not helped when John Williams, acting agent for the
State Cotton Agency was robbed of $5,200 of state money and
$2,000 of his own outside of Clinton while returning from the
valley.[2] The first week of March brought news of the fall of
Richmond, Charleston, and Columbia. These conditions made life
disagreeable for civilian and soldiers alike. So did lack of pay for
the troops guarding the coast. One soldier complained of his wife
not being allowed passage across a river to see him because she
could not produce the hard currency for the ferry passage.[3] The
papers became full of desertion notices. Magruder and Ashbel
Smith both realized that the troops at Galveston were near mutiny.

Tempers flared on and off the battlefield. One of the most
remarkable and most tragic examples of this occurred on April 6
at Houston. In the wake of the Red River campaign and reorganization of Texas troops, Colonel George W. Baylor found himself
in the awkward position of having to place himself and his troops
under an officer he considered less than superior. The idea, which
came down from General John A. Wharton, was insulting to the
headstrong Baylor.

Wharton was an experienced soldier, and his father had been
one of the prominent motivators of Texas independence in 1836.
A lawyer, Wharton gave up his practice in Brazoria to serve as a
member of the Texas Secession Convention. When Benjamin Terry
organized his famous Terry's Texas Rangers, Wharton was elected
captain of one of its companies. The battlefield deaths of Terry and
second in command Thomas Lubbock elevated Wharton to command of the regiment until his promotion to brigadier general in

1   For more details on this period, see Ford, John S., *Rip Ford's Texas*, edited by
    Stephen B. Oates (Austin: University of Texas Press, 1963).
2   *Galveston Daily News*, April 13, 1865.
3   *Galveston Daily News*, April 1, 1865.

November 1862. After winning laurels at both Murfreesboro and Chickamauga, Wharton was elevated to major-general in 1863. Transferred to Dick Taylor's command in Louisiana, Wharton furthered his career with his distinguished service in the Louisiana Red River campaign.

John A. Wharton. *Courtesy of the DRT Library at the Alamo.*

The major-general was on his way from headquarters to inspect troops gathering at Hempstead when he encountered Baylor in the company of Major Sorell. Both were apparently in no mood to meet each other, so the resulting exchange of words was far from friendly. Wharton demanded to know the location of Baylor's command. Baylor informed him that they were in Hempstead. Wharton then told Baylor that he "had better be with it." The conversation went from bad to worse when Wharton asked if there had been any desertions. It was Baylor's turn to become cutting. He told Wharton that there had been no desertions but warned, "there would be a damn sight of them if they were ordered to report " and if "justice was not done to him."[4]

General James Edward Harrison, who was with Wharton in his buggy, and Major Sorell with Baylor were quickly becoming alarmed at the escalating situation. Wharton demanded to know who had done Baylor any injustice. Baylor retorted that Wharton himself had. More excited words followed before Wharton ordered Baylor to report to Magruder's headquarters in Houston under arrest. Baylor did not take the order lightly. He impolitely informed Wharton that he would see Magruder and have justice done. Wharton repeated his verbal order; Baylor responded, calling Magruder a "demagogue," and informed him that there would be a day when he would meet Wharton on equal ground.[5]

At that point Wharton apparently called Baylor a liar. The old Ranger colonel took a swing at Wharton, but General Harrison quickly moved the buggy. Wharton, in a parting shot, repeated the arrest order.

Baylor obeyed the order rather quickly. Dragging Sowell with him, he angrily appeared at Magruder's headquarters only to find the general out. Heading to Magruder's private quarters at the Fannin House Hotel, Baylor found the general at breakfast. According to Magruder, Baylor was so upset that he was actually weeping. Between the sobs, he told his commander that Wharton had insulted him. Apparently, Baylor was making such a scene that Magruder took him upstairs. Finding his own room locked, he found Captain Turner's room open, took Baylor inside, and left him on the bed, ordering him to compose himself. Magruder assured him that he would return after breakfast.

---

4   *Houston Weekly Telegraph*, April 10, 1865.
5   *Houston Weekly Telegraph*, April 10, 1865.

Wharton, in the meantime, had no idea that he would run into Baylor again when he elected to postpone the trip to Hempstead and proceeded to see Magruder. He too found the general out and elected to go to the Fannin House. Finding the general's personal rooms locked, Wharton, with Harris at his side, happened into Turner's room. There sat the weeping Baylor.

Wharton went right for the confrontation. Waving his fist at Baylor, the general screamed, "Colonel Baylor, you have insulted me most grossly this morning." Apparently Wharton took a swing at Baylor. Harrison tried to get between the two and, in horror, observed Baylor pull a pistol. Harrison grabbed the gun hand while trying to push Wharton back. The pistol fired. The ball tore into Wharton's left side under the short rib. The general crumbled to the ground, dead.[6]

Magruder's breakfast was interrupted a second time when a servant raced into the room with news that Baylor had just shot Wharton. An inquest was held, but Baylor was never tried for any capital crime. There were, perhaps, too many important matters happening that week outside of Texas for anyone to worry about a supposed affair of honor.

Those outside events were crucial. On April 22 word of Robert E. Lee's surrender of the Army of Northern Virginia to U. S. Grant at Appomattox Court House was published. Three days later, details of Lincoln's assassination were learned. Within weeks, Joe Johnston was entering into surrender negotiations with Sherman concerning the fate of the Army of Tennessee. Foreseeing the crises, Kirby Smith called the governors of the Trans-Mississippi Department together for a meeting at Marshall, Texas, on May 10.[7] In the meantime, Smith issued a circular to his men stating, "Great disasters have overtaken us. The army of Northern Virginia and our Commander-in-Chief are prisoners of war. With you rests the hopes of our nation, and upon your action depends the fate of our people . . . Stand by your colors — maintain your discipline. The great resources of this department, its vast extent, the numbers, the discipline, and the efficiency of the army, will secure to our country terms that a proud people can with honor accept, and may,

---

6   *Houston Weekly Telegraph*, April 10, 1865.
7   Smith to Governor P. Murrah, April 19, 1865, Governor's Papers, Texas State Archives.

under Providence of God, be the means of checking the triumph of our enemy and of securing the final success of our cause."[8]

Despite his pleas, the commander of the Trans-Mississippi Department found himself standing alone. Although mass meetings at various communities produced resolutions that were passed to carry on the fight, the growing doom was breaking the weakening spirits of civilians and soldiers alike. On May 8 a representative of the Union army, under a flag of truce, arrived at Shreveport to deliver what amounted to terms of surrender.

The Marshall conference was held, and the governors present recommended that since resistance was futile, a plan should be agreed upon with which to disband the army, guarantee no prosecution of Confederate officials or soldiers, unrestricted immigration to foreign countries by ex-Confederates, continuation of existing state governments until conventions could be called, and the states be allowed to continue to guard the rights and property of its people. Apparently, while this was going on, the diehards in the army were meeting with the intention of replacing the current administrative bodies and producing something more constructive. Smith was not supportive of either policy. In the end, the Federal surrender demands were rejected. "I cannot accept terms which will purchase a certain degree of immunity from devastation at the expense of the honor of its army," he wrote General John Pope.[9] The world was closing in on Kirby Smith, but he desperately tried to hold on.

Smith was not encouraged by reports he was receiving from Magruder at Galveston. "Prince John" was having a devil of a time trying to keep his troops in line. In an effort to help consolidate their position, Smith elected to move his headquarters to Houston. This would leave General Buckner at Shreveport with the Louisiana section of the army still intact. Smith's arrival at Houston was to no purpose, for the garrison at Galveston had mutinied, divisions and brigades were disbanding, and soldiers were seizing public stores and transportation. Then came news that Buckner, along with Generals Sterling Price and Joseph Brent, had met with General E. R. S. Canby of the Federal army. The result of that meeting was the surrender of their commands on May 26.

---

8   OR, Series 1, Volume 48, Part 2, p. 1284.
9   Smith to John Pope, May 9, 1865, OR, Series 1, Volume 48, Part 1, p. 189.

Smith had no choice. The Trans-Mississippi Department was falling apart around him and now his own officers were negotiating surrenders with the Federals. Seeing that the end was so very near, Smith wrote his last communication to the soldiers of his department. Unlike Lee and Johnston, Smith's farewell was bitter and cutting, lashing out at his command. He stated that he had hoped to concentrate the strength of the department while awaiting negotiations from which to secure terms acceptable to both his soldiers and civilian populations. He continued:

"Failing in this, I intended to struggle to the last; and with an army united in purpose, firm in resolve, and battling for the right, I believed God would yet give us victory. I reached here to find the Texas troops disbanded and hastening to their homes. They had forsaken their colors and their commanders; had abandoned the cause for which we were struggling, and appropriated the public property to their personal use . . . I am left a commander without an army — a General without troops. You have made your choice. It was unwise and unpatriotic, but it is final . . . The enemy will now possess your country, and dictate his own laws. You have voluntarily destroyed your organizations, and thrown away all means of resistance . . . Your present duty is plain. Return to your families. Resume the occupations of peace. Yield obedience to the laws. Labor to restore order . . . may God, in his mercy, direct you aright, and heal the wounds of our distracted country."[10]

Three days later, on June 2, Smith, accompanied by Magruder, surrendered the Trans-Mississippi Department. Out of some 60,000 soldiers within the department, less than 18,000 were left to be paroled. In rapid succession, the now almost legendary units who had served Texas had stacked their arms and cased the colors for the last time: the Texas Brigade with Lee at Appomattox; what was left of Granbury's men and Terry's Rangers with Johnston in North Carolina; and the Second Texas with Magruder at Galveston. Yet one force of Texans was still left in the field and they were not quite ready to surrender.

---

10 Smith, May 30, 1863, Galveston *Tri-Weekly News,* June 5, 1865.

CHAPTER EIGHTEEN

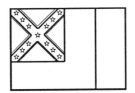

The Last Shots

1865

Nearly one month after Lee's surrender, the Confederates and Yankees in the Rio Grande Valley were preparing to fight what was destined to become the last land action of the war. It was to happen about as far south as one could go in the Confederacy and would involve a marvelous cross section of participants. On the Federal side, there would be Midwestern Hoosiers, African-American troops, and Unionist Texan Cavalry. On the Confederate side, there would be Anglos, Tejanos, Germans, Irish, Militia, Home Guards, and Rangers. And just to make things interesting, a few French and Imperial Mexican troops were involved as well.

The final clash would occur just east of Brownsville, around a ranch and hill named Palmetto.[1] In the years following the battle,

---

1 The site is also referred to as Palmito Hill. The State of Texas Historical Marker placed there during the Civil War Centennial used this name (the marker has since been stolen). However, Ford and most of the other participants use the name Palmetto.

the usual amount of folklore and misconception concerning this event would multiply. Reality, however, does not diminish the irony of the moment.

One will recall that General John S. Slaughter had been appointed as the senior officer in command of the Confederate forces in the Rio Grande Valley. However, John S. "Rip" Ford, who held a state's commission, had actually organized the military force stationed there. It had been Ford's "Cavalry of the West" who had helped clear the valley of Federal occupation in 1864. Neither officer cared for the other, yet they had realized that there was no need for further bloodshed in South Texas. General Lew Wallace, commanding officer of the Federal forces locked up on Brazos Santiago Island, apparently agreed and an unofficial truce developed. But the Federals' understanding of the truce was not quite the same as the Texan's. Wallace felt it was all dependent on the actual surrender of the Trans-Mississippian Department, which, by early May, had not yet happened. To confuse the issue further, apparently Wallace only shared his truce concept with General U. S. Grant. So when commanders changed at Brazos Santiago, so did the actual reality of the agreement.[2]

Colonel Theodore H. Barrett, a political appointee, was made the new commander of Brazos Santiago. When Barrett received word of the surrender of the Army of Northern Virginia, he felt it was his duty to form an expedition and secure Brownsville. It may be very possible that Barrett was seeking a little bit of glory for himself. After all, the war was nearly over and political careers inspired by battlefield success would soon be finished. So, with the image of being labeled "The Victor of Brownsville" as a possible inspiration, Barrett ordered on May 11, 1865, an expedition be formed to move inland and capture Brownsville.

His plans did not meet with immediate success. The original expedition couldn't even get off the island, thanks to bad weather and an ill-tempered steamer. His second attempt later that day did get off the island, and the force of nearly 300 Federals moved inland. After pausing the night for some rest, the Yankees were spotted on the morning of May 12. The force nevertheless con-

---

2   For a detailed look at the often confusing negotiations between the Confederates and the Federals in the Rio Grande Valley, see Ford, John S., *Rip Ford's Texas*, edited by Stephen B. Oates (Austin: University of Texas Press, 1963), pp. 388-398.

tinued on its way and came to Palmetto Ranch, a small station east of Brownsville on the Rio Grande. The garrison of less than 200 Confederate cavalry retired without a major fight and the Federals took possession. At around three in the afternoon, the Confederates returned. This time a skirmish erupted. The Yankees retreated eastward to White's Ranch. In the late afternoon, both sides called for help.

Barrett dispatched an additional 200 men to the mainland. In the meantime, news arrived in Brownsville that the Yankees had attacked and were pressing the valley. Ford sent the word out to gather his disbursed men. But apparently General Slaughter had intentions to abandon Brownsville and retreat. Ford would have none of it. Despite the fact that he and most of his men knew that Lee had surrendered, that Lincoln had been assassinated, that the Army of Tennessee was preparing to surrender, and the political situation of the Trans-Mississippi Department,[3] Ford's resolve was certain. "You can retreat and go to hell if you wish," he is reported to have told his superior. "These are my men, and I am going to fight."[4] Slaughter reluctantly agreed. With a force of mixed home guards, state troops, and CSA cavalry, including Refugio Benavides's company, Ford prepared to take the Cavalry of the West out for one last fight. He had no infantry, but he did have six 12-pounder cannons.

Opposing him was an interesting cross section of Federal troops. There was the 34th Indiana volunteers under Colonel Robert G. Morrison. Also known as the Morton Rifles, this unit had seen service in Grant's army at Port Gibson and Vicksburg. Of the three units comprising Barrett's command, the ranks of the 34th were full of hard core veterans.

There was also the 2nd Texas U.S. Cavalry. This unit had been originally raised in the valley with Tejano soldiers and officers. The desertion rate and its transfer to Louisiana compelled its

---

3   W. H. D. Carrington, in his account of the battle for John Henry Brown's *History of Texas From 1685 to 1892* (St. Louis: Becktold and Company, 1893), states that the men actually knew about the surrender of Lee and Johnston. However, this account was actually written in August 1883. Jeffrey Hunt, in his excellent study of the battle, has produced period source documentation confirming Carrington's statements.

4   Ford, *Rip Ford's Texas*, pp. 389-90.

reorganization. The new regiment had a much higher Anglo element. It had not yet seen actual combat.[5]

The third unit was the old 1st Missouri Colored Infantry, organized in April 1863. In 1864 it was redesignated the 62nd U.S. Colored Infantry. The use of African-Americans as soldiers had been a controversial issue since the opening days of the war. However, several Federal departmental commanders did exercise local authority and raised, either from liberated slaves or freemen, regiments. Most were not convinced that blacks could fight, but they did, as was exhibited by the 1st Louisiana Colored Infantry at Port Hudson. In 1863 the State of Massachusetts organized its first black regiment — made up primarily of freemen. This became the 54th Infantry. Its moment of glory came in the assaults against Battery Wagner, near Charleston, South Carolina, in July 1863. In a bloody, bitter contest, the 54th and supportive white troops were unable to secure the Confederate works. But it did help break the image that Negro troops could not or would not fight.

The 62nd had only seen combat once, a skirmish in Missouri. But that did not stop them from understanding the realities of what enlistment required for black men. They were aware of proclamations from the Confederates which stated blacks would be considered runaway slaves if captured. There were also images of the Fort Pillow Massacre, where Confederate troops reportedly had gunned down surrendering black soldiers. Regardless of the truth about this incident, most of the men in the 62nd felt that they could expect little comfort if captured yet they were eager to prove themselves. It was probably little consolation for them to realize that Ford's men probably hated the Unionists in the 2nd Texas Cavalry more than they did black troops.[6]

As the events of May 13th progressed, the Union reinforcements arrived at White's Ranch. The advance was sounded and, despite constant harassment by the Confederates, the Federals reoccupied Palmetto Ranch. Skirmishing continued throughout

---

5   For a history of the Second Texas U.S. Cavalry, see Thompson, Jerry Don, *Mexican Texans in the Union Army*, Southwestern Studies Series, Number 78, (El Paso: University of Texas El Paso Press, 1986).

6   For additional information on the often overlooked contributions African-Americans made in winning the war, see Hargrove, Hondon B., *Black Union Soldiers in the Civil War*, (Jefferson, North Carolina: McFarland and Company, 1988) and Cornish, Dudley T., *The Stable Arm: Negro Troops in the Union Army, 1861-1865*, (New York: Longmans, Green and Co., 1956).

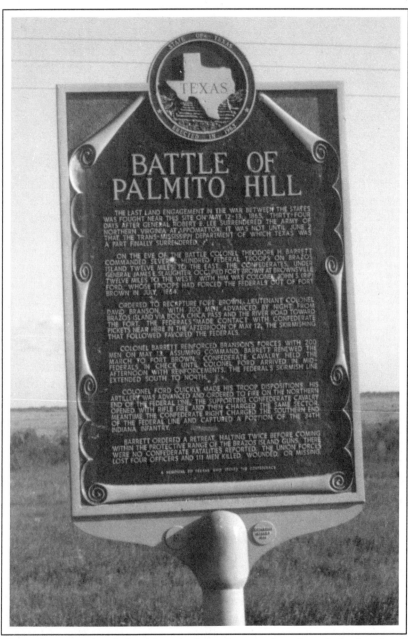

This photograph of the historical marker at the site of the battle of Palmito Hill was taken in May of 1990. The marker has since been stolen. *From the author's collection.*

the day. The 2nd Texas U.S. Calvary and a company of the 34th Indiana were engaging the Confederates when Ford arrived at the site. Appraising the size and position of his enemy, Ford felt that he was going to lose this battle. But he was still determined to carry it on. In his favor was the fact that he did have artillery and the Federals did not.

Oddly enough, one of the Confederate artillery crews were not Confederates. A company of French-Mexican Imperial artillery from Matamoros had made their services available to artillery commander Captain O. G. Jones. Needing some experienced hands, Jones took them up on the offer. Ford didn't even realize they were with his command until he rode up to the cannon and ordered it advanced. When his commands were not carried out, it was pointed out to him that the gunners were French. Ford quickly shifted to his limited French vocabulary.[7]

Just to add one last touch of international flavor, an Englishman named Anslow arrived on the field and volunteered to fight for the Confederates. And so there were all the players: French and Mexican Imperialists, one Englishman, Black Troops, Texan Unionists, Hoosiers, Tejanos, and a mixed assortment of Texans.

Despite the fact that he thought he was about to be beaten, Ford elected not to stand on the defensive. He resolved to follow the lesson of his old Ranger colonel, Jack Hays, and take the fight to the enemy. "Men," he called out, "we have whipped the enemy in all our previous fights. We can do it again."[8]

The ambiguous, if not boastful, call rallied his men. And then the incredible happened. The Confederates succeeded in turning the Federals' flank. The Federals became confused, and in their indecision, the Confederates charged. The Federals began to retreat. Ford would later claim they ran, but others stated that they retired in order. But one thing was apparent — the experienced Morton Rifles retreated with greater speed than the 62nd Colored, who, as the rear guard, would pause and fire an orderly volley or two during the retreat. The Hoosiers were in such a hurry that their entire skirmish line of 48 men was captured, en masse. The actions of the 2nd Texas U.S. Calvary are in doubt. At least 25 of its men were captured hiding in the chaparral, including their two commanding officers. Despite their and the black troop's fears of

---

7   Brown, *History of Texas*, p. 436.
8   Brown, *History of Texas*, p. 436.

execution, the Confederates did not injure a single prisoner and later paroled all of them at Brownsville. Even in the dying moments of the South, honor was held high.

The retreat continued all the way back to Boco Chico, where the Federals retired across the water to Brazos Santiago. Firing continued. General Slaughter, who had been conveniently absent at the main fight, arrived in the final moments and emptied his pistol (with no effect) toward the Yankee lines. The 62nd U.S. fired what was probably the last full musket volley of the war, while the 34th Indiana realized they had just won the dubious honor of having their regimental colors become the last captured by the Confederates. Two members of that regiment also vied for honors — Privates John J. Williams and Daniel Lee may have been the last men to die in combat.

In the fading light of May 13, a Federal gunboat fired a shell which landed with a terrible roar into the sands of Boco Chico. It had little effect but might have well been the last shot fired in anger had it not been for a young Texan. Cursing the noise of the explosion, the young soldier became so full of vigor that he aimed his Enfield musket at the shell hole and fired. His .58 caliber ball hit the sand with the same lack of effect as the Yankee parrot shell.[9] But it signaled the end of hostilities in Texas.[10]

Like the Cavalry of the West, other elements in the Trans-Mississippi Department simply began to break up on their own. By the end of May, General Kirby-Smith was unable to hold on to his own resolve. The surrender of the last Confederate department was agreed on May 26 and was signed into effect on June 2.

Smith himself headed for San Antonio with plans for Mexico. He was not to be alone. In the first weeks of June, dozens of Confederate soldiers arrived in the Alamo City, including the Missouri Cavalry of Joe Shelby. With Shelby's arrival, law and order returned briefly to the city, which had attracted all sorts of desperados in the dying months of the Confederacy. The tough

---

9 Brown, *History of Texas*, p. 434.
10 For accounts of the battle, see Brown, John Henry, *History of Texas From 1685-1892*, (St. Louis: Becktold and Company, 1893), Volume 2, pp. 431-436; Ford, *Rip Ford's Texas*, which contains Ford's account of the battle; and *San Antonio Express*, October 10, 1890 which has another of Ford's accounts). The best researched overall history of the battle is Jeffrey W. Hunt's "There is Nothing Left to Us But to Fight: The Battle of Palmetto Ranch." (Unpublished, 1990).

Missouri veterans divided the city in two military commands and commenced rounding up the "villains" between them. "Some men are born to be shot, some to be hung, and some to be drowned" observed one of Shelby's men.[11] Within a matter of a few days, San Antonio was once again a safe city.

The Missouri general set himself up in the Menger Hotel on Alamo Plaza. As mid-June came, the Menger became the unofficial headquarters for the last of the Confederates yet to surrender. Henry Watkins Allen, the last Confederate governor of Louisiana, arrived with five companions and two servants. John Perkins, former Louisiana representative to the Confederate Congress, also arrived. Perkins had personally burned his own property before fleeing the Yankees. Missouri's Governor Thomas Reynolds arrived as did the oceanographer from Virginia, Commodore Matthew Maury. Generals Sterling Price and Cadmus Wilcox, one of Lee's lieutenants, also joined the survivors at the Menger.

The Menger Hotel, San Antonio. *Courtesy of the DRT Library at the Alamo.*

---

11 Edwards, John N., *Shelby's Expedition to Mexico*, (Kansas City: Privately published, 1872), Reprint, (Austin: Steck and Co., 1964), p. 17.

The last players in the Trans-Mississippian Department soon checked into the Menger as well: John B. Magruder and Kirby-Smith. Smith was apparently still bitter about the desertion of his command. He registered under the name William Thompson, but Shelby realized who he was. The Missourians showed Smith their respect by assembling themselves and their band underneath the Menger's balcony. The band played "Hail to the Chief" but Smith did not respond. The next selection, "Dixie," did not get a response either. So Shelby and his men commenced a cheer which at last brought the depressed general out. He acknowledged their ovation with a short speech and then found solace in their continued "hurrahs." It was perhaps fitting that on Alamo Plaza, where McCulloch's men had rallied to secure the Federal property in 1861, the last acclaim was to be given to the last Confederate general.[12]

Those were the last days of the Confederate States in San Antonio. None forgot the purpose of their mission. Mexico still lay ahead. On July 4 Shelby's Brigade with Magruder, Governors Allen and Reynolds, and Kirby-Smith arrived at Eagle Pass on the Rio Grande. Negotiations had been made with the Juarista commander across the river. (Shelby's command would later, however, volunteer for service to the Imperialists.) The allegiance between these men and the Confederate States was now over. They would cross into Mexico.

Before they did, five of the brigade's colonels rode into the Rio Grande with the old tattered battle flag of the division. As one observer later wrote, "it was brought from its resting-place and given once more to the winds. Bent and bruised, and crimson with the blood of heroes — it has never been dishonored."

Attaching weights to the bunting, the colonels lowered their honored colors into the muddy Rio Grande. This was one Confederate flag which would never fall into enemy hands. Shelby took the black plume from his own hat and cast it into the water.[13]

With tears on their cheeks, the last organized force of the Confederacy rode across the river. They closed a chapter on their Civil War as they marched straight into the middle of someone else's fight.

---

12 Edwards, *Shelby's Expedition*, pp. 17-18.
13 Edwards, John N., *Shelby and his Men*, (Cincinnati: Privately published, 1867), p. 547.

Nearly two weeks before their passing, a thousand miles away in Virginia, one of the most noted Southern Nationalists came to terms with defeat. Edmund Ruffin, the prophet of secession, had lost much since he pulled the lanyard which sent the shell screaming toward Fort Sumter. His homes had been wrecked, his lands ravaged, his sons killed in battle. Old age was taking its toll as the depression of defeat surrounded him. Monuments to the Union's victory had already been erected in Virginia . . . Union troops were marching in victorious parades through Washington . . . Reconstruction was beginning.

Edmund Ruffin had seen everything he believed in and loved destroyed before him. He was, perhaps, not enough of a visionary to understand that part of his Southern nationalistic pride and arrogance had contributed to the completeness of this defeat. His fellows all sought different ways of dealing with it. Like Shelby, many would place themselves in exile. Mexico and Brazil were destined to have Confederate colonies.[14] Others sought political means; still others education. Some were unable to break away from the routines of war. Defeat brought Reconstruction, which was filled with injustice. That produced hatred, which gave us such men as John Wesley Hardin, Frank and Jesse James, and the Younger brothers. It gave us the Klan. It mingled with the beautiful fancy of the "Lost Cause" and produced a lingering attitude that carried on into our generations. We, as supposedly united Americans, have fought two World Wars but were still fighting the issues of our Civil War well into the 1970s.

Edmund Ruffin had no more desire to see the future. In his mind, so scientific and developed, Ruffin had reasoned that if the Confederacy was dying, he would die with it. "I hereby repeat & would willingly proclaim my unmitigated hatred to Yankee rule" he wrote in June 1865, "to all political, social & business connection with Yanks, & to the perfidious, malignant, & vile Yankee race."[15]

---

14 For more on the Confederate exiles, see Griggs, William Clark, *The Elusive Eden: Frank McMullans' Confederate Colony in Brazil*, (Austin: University of Texas Press, 1987).

15 See Craven, Avery O., *Edmund Ruffin — Southerner*, (Baton Rouge: Louisiana State University Press, 1976), p. 259.

These were more than just words. For before the ink had dried, Ruffin sat himself in a chair, took up a rifle, rested the butt, put the barrel in his mouth and, using a stick, pulled the trigger. Defeat seemed to haunt him, for the cap fired, but the primary charge failed.

Ruffin reprimed and tried again. This time he won.[16] The last shot had been fired.

---

16 For more on the final moments of Ruffin, see Allmendinger, David F., Jr., *Ruffin — Family and Reform in the Old South*, (New York: Oxford University Press, 1990), and Mitchell, Betty L., *Edmund Ruffin*, (Bloomington: Indiana University Press, 1981).

CHAPTER NINETEEN

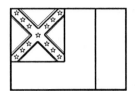

History Versus Bulldozers

Anyone who thinks the battlefields of 1861-1865 are quiet and peaceful today should take a second look around.

In 1988 the battle for Manassas Junction raged again. This time a handful of preservationists were the beleaguered army fixing bayonets and preparing to withstand the overwhelming combined forces of Big Business and the Prince William County Board of Supervisors. In the balance were 540 acres of land where a major portion of the 1862 Battle of Second Manassas was fought. There was no Robert E. Lee, or Stonewall Jackson, or even McClellan to command the forces — only an ex-Marine named Anne Snyder. She, leading a coalition of groups and individuals, stood squarely against the plans to commercially develop the entire area.

How this endangerment transpired reads like an episode of "L. A. Law." It seems that a large area of the Manassas battlefield had not been included in the creation of the existing national park back in 1940. One of the areas that slipped into the crack was the Brawner Farm. On that particular piece of real estate, Robert E. Lee had established his headquarters during the battle and James Longstreet launched his successful counter-attack. By 1988, with eastern real estate booming, the property had become more than commercially viable. At one point, the owners of the property planned to build a theme park on the site, which is across from the existing national park. That drew local opposition.

Then the Hazel-Peterson Corporation elected to build a "campus style" office park. Looking at a considerably larger tax base, the Prince William County Supervisors approved an open ended zoning permit for the 600-acre track. After all, the folks at Hazel-Peterson did stress how unobtrusive the complex would be and even suggested that they would erect a screen of trees to hide the complex from visitors at the nearby national park.

And with the blessings of the supervisors and with the non-residential zoning permit in hand, the good folks at Hazel-Peterson changed their minds. Joining with independent developer Edward DeBartolo, Sr., they announced they had scrapped the "campus style" office park and were instead going to build a shopping mall.

Yes — a shopping mall — complete with street to street parking lots, lights, and traffic. It was promoted as the second largest retail complex in northern Virginia.

These then would be the modern tributes to the soldiers of 1862; the new permanent markers for the site of Lee's headquarters and Longstreet's advance. Incidentally, part of Longstreet's command at this battle was Hood's Texas Brigade. So, Texans had a stake in this saga as well.

Naturally, those who understood the impact of this development rallied. They requested a hearing — it was denied. After all, the supervisors had given DeBartolo and Hazel-Petersen a blanket approval. One county supervisor was quoted as saying "the handful of local activists" were "against growth" and that they were probably against "motherhood and apple pie too." The developers added that the site had little historical significance.

Representatives Robert Mrazek of New York and Michael Andrews of Texas did not agree. They started the campaign in the House to "Stonewall the Mall." Former White House aide Jody Powell joined in, as did the Department of the Interior. Rallies were held; letter writing campaigns were instituted. A "Save the Battlefield Coalition" was formed. More and more, the momentum grew. But the developers arrogantly went on — the land was cleared, pipelines were laid. The situation looked bad.

But in the end, the federal government, combined with the people who fought to save Manassas, won. It cost a considerable amount of money to save Manassas, probably over 50 million dollars, most of which the developers received as payment for the property. But it did happen.

Unfortunately, the recent battle of Manassas is only a brief victory, for many Civil War sites are endangered. Preservation is slow and an uphill battle. Only a few Civil War sites are national parks. Of the 128 sites listed in a recent comprehensive list, only 34 are national parks. Another 19 are state or city parks. Only 72 are listed as either National Historic Landmarks or are on the national register.

Starting in 1890, the combined Chickamauga / Chattanooga battlefield became the first "military park." Others followed, including Antietam and Gettysburg. But even that is misleading, for only sections of the battlefields were to become parks. The famous cornfield at Antietam, where Hood's Texas Brigade fought, was not included . . . the cavalry battlefield where Custer became a national hero at Gettysburg was excluded . . . the abovementioned portion of Second Manassas and dozens more were excluded. Hundreds of others have never been made parks, either state or national.

The Manassas battle, however, has helped the cause of preservation. As volunteers try to repair the damage done by developers, the Department of the Interior announced plans for a private / public program designed to help save 25 Civil War battle sites currently threatened by developers. The American Battlefield Protection Program has the mandate to help save such sites as Perryville, Kentucky, Glorieta Pass, Fort Fisher, Brandy Station, and Franklin, as well as help secure additional historic lands around Prairie Grove, New Market, Richmond, The Wilderness, Gettysburg, Antietam, Kennesaw Mountain, and Port Hudson. Franklin and Corinth are also targeted.

Spurring everything along was the Richard King Mellon Foundation which purchased or has purchase agreements for such sites as 920 acres of land at Five Forks; 226 acres of the cavalry field at Gettysburg; 5,556 acres of the Forked Lightning Ranch at Glorieta

Pass; 135 acres at The Wilderness, and the historic cornfield at Antietam. No shopping malls are planned for these sites, for the Mellon Foundation handed all the property over to the Department of the Interior.

The only preserved battlefield in Texas is Sabine Pass. To call it preserved is stretching it, for nothing remains of the actual fort or site. Cattle still graze around the ranch house at Palmetto Ranch . . . coastal and urban development have rendered the battle sites at Port Lavaca, Corpus Christi, and Galveston invisible. The camps where the 2nd Texas or the 4th Texas were formed are forgotten fields.

Perhaps it is sad enough that the numerous sites in our own state have fallen between the cracks. Maybe we should pay attention to our own problems. Perhaps the Prince William County supervisor who said "we should mind our own business" was correct. But Texans fought on the endangered ground at Manassas: just as they did at Corinth, at the cornfield, in the rocks of Devils Den, along the waters of Wilson's Creek, in the fields near Shiloh, in the yard of the Carter House at Franklin. They fought at these far away places just as hard, just as determined, and as stubbornly as they did at Galveston, Laredo, and Brownsville or would have on the banks of the Colorado, the Brazos, or the Sabine. Their legacy does not stop or diminish at Texas borders, it only grows. For anywhere they fought and died was baptized as part of the Lone Star State with their blood.

Civil War Battlefield Preservation Groups

For more information concerning Civil War battlefield preservation, please contact any of the following organizations:

Association for the Preservation of Civil War Sites
P. O. Box 1862
Fredericksburg, VA 22402

Gettysburg Battlefield Preservation Association
P. O. Box 1863
Gettysburg, PA 17325

Friends of the National Parks at Gettysburg, Inc.
P. O. Box 4622
Gettysburg, PA 17235-4622

Save Historic Antietam Foundation
P. O. Box 550
Sharpsburg, MD 21782

Save the Battlefield Coalition
P. O. Box 110
Catharpin, VA 22018

Shenandoah Valley Heritage Alliance
P. O. Box 1000
Harpers Ferry, WV 25425

Civil War Round Table Associates
P. O. Box 7388
Little Rock, AR 72217

The Conservation Fund
1800 N. Kent, Suite 1120
Arlington, VA 22209

Bibliography

GOVERNMENT RECORDS

The War of the Rebellion: A Compilation of the Official Records of the Union and Confederate Armies. Washington, Government Printing Office, 1880-1901.

Official Records of the Union and Confederate Navies in the War of the Rebellion. Washington, Government Printing Office, Washington, 1894-1927.

Records of the Office of the Quartermaster General, Consolidated Correspondence File 1794-1915 files on the Alamo, Edwin B. Babbit and San Antonio.

Records of the Office of Chief of Engineer (RG77), National Archives.

COLLECTIONS

Sam Houston Papers, Governor's Correspondence, Texas State Library

Thomas Lubbock Papers, Governor's Correspondence, Texas State Library

Pendleton Murrah Papers, Governor's Correspondence, Texas State Library

John S. Ford Papers, Eugene C. Barker Research Center, University of Texas at Austin

William P. Rogers Papers, Eugene C. Barker Research Center, University of Texas at Austin

Ashbel Smith Papers, Eugene C. Barker Research Center, University of Texas at Austin

George C. Bickley Papers, Texas Tech Southwestern Collection, Lubbock

BOOKS

Allmendinger, David F., Jr. *Ruffin — Family and Reform in the Old South.* New York: Oxford University Press, 1990.

Anderson, Charles. *Texas Before and on the Eve of the Rebellion.* Cincinnati: Privately published, 1884.

Anderson, John. *Campaigning With Parson's Texas Cavalry Brigade, CSA.* Hillsboro, Texas: Hill Junior College, 1967.

Bailey, Anne J. *Between The Enemy and Texas: Parson's Texas Cavalry in the Civil War.* Ft. Worth: Texas Christian University, 1989.

Betts, Vicki. *Smith County, Texas, in the Civil War.* Tyler, Texas: Smith County Historical Society, 1978.

Blessington, J. D. *The Campaign of Walker's Texas Division.* New York: Lange, Little and Company, 1875.

Bowden, J. J. *The Exodus of Federal Forces From Texas, 1861.* Austin: Eakin Press, 1986.

Brightwell, Juanita S. *Roster of the Confederate Soldier of Georgia, Index.* Spartanburg, South Carolina: Reprint Company, 1982.

Brown, Frank. *Annals of Travis County and the City of Austin.* Austin: Texas State Library, no date.

Brown, John Henry. *History of Texas From 1685-1892.* St. Louis: Becktold and Company, 1893.

Buenger, Walter L. *Secession and the Union in Texas.* Austin: University of Texas Press, 1984.

Carr, Albert Z. *The World and William Walker.* New York: Harper & Row, 1963.

Chabot, Frederick C. *With the Makers of San Antonio.* San Antonio: Privately published, 1937.

Chance, Joseph E. *The Second Texas Infantry.* Austin: Eakin Press, 1984.

_____ . *From Shiloh to Vicksburg.* Austin: Eakin Press, 1984.

Connelly, Thomas Lawrence. *Autumn of Glory — The Army of Tennessee, 1862-1865.* Baton Rouge: Louisiana State University Press, 1971.

Conner, J. E. *The Centennial Record of the San Antonio Army Service Forces Depot, 1845-1945.* San Antonio: Privately published, 1945.

Cornish, Dudley T., *The Stable Arm: Negro Troops in the Union Army, 1861-1865.* New York: Longmans, Green and Co., 1956.

Craven, Avery O. *Edmund Ruffin — Southerner.* Baton Rouge: Louisiana State University Press, 1976.

Cutrer, Emily. *The Art of the Woman — The Life and Work of Elisabet Ney.* Lincoln: University of Nebraska Press, 1988.

Darrow, Caroline. "Recollections of the Twiggs Surrender." *Battles and Leaders of the Civil War,* Vol I. New York: Thomas Yoseloff, Inc., 1956.

Davis, Edwin Adams. *Fallen Guidons.* Santa Fe: Stagecoach Press, 1962.

Davis, Nicholas A. *The Campaign From Texas to Maryland.* Richmond, 1863. Reprint. Austin: Steck Company, 1961.

Douglas, L. R. *Douglas' Texas Battery, CSA*. Tyler, Texas: Smith County Historical Society, 1966.

Duaine, Carl L. *The Dead Men Wore Boots — The 32nd Texas Cavalry*. Austin: San Felipe Press, 1966.

Edwards, John N. *Shelby's Expedition to Mexico*. Kansas City: Privately published, 1872. Reprint, Austin: Steck and Co., 1964.

_____ . *Shelby and His Men*. Cincinnati: Privately published, 1867.

Everett, Donald, ed. *Chaplain Davis and Hood's Texas Brigade*. San Antonio: Trinity University, 1962.

Faulkner, William. *Intruder in the Dust*. New York: Random House, 1948. Vintage Book Edition, 1972.

Ford, John S. *Rip Ford's Texas*. Edited by Stephen B. Oates. Austin: University of Texas Press, 1963.

Fornel, Earl Wesley. *The Galveston Era: The Texas Crescent on the Eve of Secession*. Austin: University of Texas Press, 1961.

Foster, Samuel T. *One of Cleburne's Command*. Edited by Norman D. Brown. Austin: University of Texas Press, 1980.

Franklin, Robert M. *Battle of Galveston*. Galveston: Privately published, 1911.

Frassanito, W. R. *America's Bloodiest Day*. New York: Charles Schribner and Sons, 1978.

Fremantle, Arthur James Lyon. *The Fremantle Diary*. Edited by Walter Lord. Boston: Little, Brown and Company, 1954.

Friend, Llerena. *Sam Houston: The Great Designer*. Austin: University of Texas Press, 1954.

Gibbons, Tony. *Warships and Naval Battles of the Civil War*. New York: Gallery Books, 1989.

Glatthaar, Joseph T. *Forged In Battle — Civil War Alliance of Black Soldiers and White Officers*. New York: Free Press, 1990.

Graber, H. W. *A Terry Texas Ranger*. Austin: State House Press, 1987.

Greer, Jack Thorndyke. *Leaves From A Family Album*. Edited by James Judge Greer. Waco: Texian Press, 1975.

Griggs, William Clark. *The Elusive Eden: Frank McMullans' Confederate Colony in Brazil*. Austin: University of Texas Press, 1987.

Hana, Albert J. and Katheryn A. *Napoleon and Mexico: American Triumph Over Monarchy*. Chapel Hill: University of North Carolina, 1991.

Hargrove, Hondon B. *Black Union Soldiers In the Civil War*. Jefferson, North Carolina: McFarland and Company, 1988.

Hartje, Robert G. *Van Doren — Life & Times of a Confederate General.* Nashville: Vanderbilt University Press, 1967.

Hartman, Francis B. *Historical Record and Dictionary of the United States Army, 1789-1903.* Urbana: University of Illinois Press, 1965.

Heartsill, W. W. *Fourteen Hundred and 91 Days in the Confederate Army.* Edited by Bell Irwin Wiley. Jackson, Tennessee: McCowat and Mercer Press, Inc., 1953.

Henderson, Harry McCorry. *Texas in the Confederacy.* San Antonio: Naylor Press, 1955.

Hood, John B. *Advance and Retreat.* New Orleans: Privately published, 1880.

Hughes, W. J. *Rebellious Ranger: Rip Ford and the Old Southwest.* Norman: University of Oklahoma Press, 1964.

Irby, James A. *Backdoor to Bagdad: The Civil War on the Rio Grande.* El Paso: University of Texas El Paso Press, 1972.

James, Marquis. *The Raven: A Biography of Sam Houston.* Indianapolis: Robbs and Merrill Company, 1929.

Johnson, Sidney Smith. *Texans Who Wore the Gray.* Tyler, Texas: Privately published, 1907.

Johnston, William Preston. *The Life of Albert Sidney Johnston.* New York: D. Appleton and Company, 1880.

Kellersberger, Getulius. *Memories of an Engineer in the Confederate Army in Texas.* Translated by Helen S. Sundstrom. Austin: University of Texas Press, no date.

Kennedy, Frances H., ed. *The Civil War Battlefield Guide.* Boston: Houghton Mifflin Company, 1990.

Kerby, Robert L. *Kirby Smith's Confederacy.* New York: Columbia University Press, 1972.

Kourey, Michael J. *Arms for Texas.* Boulder: Old Army Press, 1973.

Lane, Walter P. *Adventures and Recollections of General Walter P. Lane.* Austin: Jenkins Publishing Company, 1970.

Larson, Christopher. *Tennessee's Forgotten Warriors.* Knoxville: University of Tennessee Press, 1989.

Laurence, F. Lee and Glover, Robert W. *Camp Ford, CSA.* Austin: Texas Civil War Centennial Anniversary Commission, 1964.

Lubbock, Francis Richard. *Six Decades In Texas.* Edited by C. W. Raines. Austin: Ben C. Jones and Company, 1900.

Madus, Howard M. and Needham, Robert D. *The Battle Flags of the Confederate Army of Tennessee.* Milwaukee: Milwaukee Public Museum, 1976.

Mahan, Dennis Hart. *A Complete Treatise on Field Fortifications*. Unknown: Wiley & Long, 1836.

Malsch, Brownson. *Indianola — The Mother of Western Texas*. Austin: State House Press, 1988.

Marks, Paula Mitchell. *Turn Your Eyes Toward Texas: Pioneers Sam and Mary Maverick*. College Station: Texas A & M Press, 1989.

Maverick, Mary. *Memories*. Edited by Rena Maverick Green. Lincoln: University of Nebraska Press, 1989.

May, Robert E. *The Southern Dream of a Caribbean Empire, 1854-1861*. Baton Rouge: Louisiana State University Press, 1973.

McCaffrey, James M. *This Band of Heroes — Granbury's Texas Brigade, CSA*. Austin: Eakin Press, 1985.

McDonough, James Lee and Connelly, Thomas L. *Five Tragic Hours — The Battle of Franklin*. Knoxville: University of Tennessee Press, 1983.

McGavock Confederate Cemetery. Franklin Chapter No. 14, United Daughters of the Confederacy, 1989.

McMurry, Richard M. *Two Great Rebel Armies*. Charlotte: University of North Carolina Press, 1989.

McWhiney, Grady. *Cracker Culture — Celtic Ways in the Old South*. Tuscaloosa: University of Alabama Press, 1988.

McWhiney, Grady and Jamison, Perry P. *Attack and Die: Civil War Tactics and the Southern Heritage*. Tuscaloosa: University of Alabama Press, 1982.

Mitchell, Betty L. *Edmund Ruffin*. Bloomington: Indiana University Press, 1981.

Nofi, Albert A. *The Gettysburg Campaign*. Conshohcken, Pennsylvania: Combined Books, 1986.

Nunn, W. C. ed., *Ten Texans In Gray*. Hillsboro, Texas: Hill Junior College Press, 1968.

Oates, Stephen. *Confederate Cavalry West of the River*. Austin: University of Texas Press, 1961.

Parks, Joseph Howard. *General Edmund Kirby Smith, CSA*. Baton Rouge: Louisiana State University Press, 1954.

Petty, Elijah P. *Journey to Pleasant Hill*. Edited by Norman D. Brown. San Antonio: Institute of Texan Cultures, 1982.

Polly, J. B. *Hood's Texas Brigade*. Dayton: Morningside Bookstore Edition, 1976.

Pomfrey, J. W. *A True Disclosure and Exposition of the Knights of the Golden Circle*. Cincinnati, Privately published, 1864.

Reagan, John H. *Memories*. Austin: Pemberton Press, 1968.

Regulations for the Army of the Confederate States, 1863. Richmond: J. W. Randolph, 1863.

Revised Regulations for the Army of the United States, 1861. Philadelphia: J. G. L. Brown, 1861.

Rister, Carl Cook. *Robert E. Lee in Texas*. Norman: University of Oklahoma Press, 1946.

Roberts, O. M. *Confederate Military History, Volume XI: Texas*. Atlanta: Confederate Publishing Company, 1899.

Roland, James P. *Albert Sidney Johnston*. Austin: University of Texas Press, 1964.

Rose, Victor M. *The Life and Services of General Ben McCulloch*. Philadelphia: Pictorial Bureau of the Press, 1888.

Rugeley, H. J. H. *Batchelor-Turner Letters, 1861-1864*. Austin: Steck Company, 1961.

Rules, Regulations & Principles of the KGC. New York: Benjamin Urner Printers, 1859.

Scott, Henry L. *Military Dictionary*. New York: D. Van Nostrand, 1864.

Sears, Stephen W. *Landscape Turned Red*. New Haven: Ticknor and Fields Publishing, 1983.

Semmes, Raphael. *Service Afloat During the War Between The States*. Baltimore, Privately published, 1887.

Silverthorne, Elizabeth. *Ashbel Smith of Texas*. College Station: Texas A & M University Press, 1982.

Simpson, Harold B. *Hood's Texas Brigade — Lee's Grenadier Guards*. Hillsboro, Texas: Hill Junior College Press, 1970.

_____ . *Hood's Texas Brigade in Poetry and Song*. Hillsboro, Texas: Hill Junior College Press, 1968.

_____ . *Gaines' Mill to Appomattox — Waco and McLennan County in Hood's Texas Brigade*. Waco: Texian Press, 1963.

_____ . *Cry Comanche — The Second U.S. Cavalry in Texas, 1855-1861*. Hillsboro, Texas: Hill Junior College Press, 1979.

Sinclair, Arthur. *Two Years on the Alabama*. Boston: Lee and Shepherd, 1895.

Smith, Page. *The Nation Comes of Age*. New York: McGraw-Hill, 1981.

Sprague, J. T. *The Treachery In Texas*. New York: Press of the Rebellion Record, 1862.

Spurlin, Charles. *West of the Mississippi with Wallers' 13th Texas Cavalry Battalion, CSA*. Hillsboro, Texas: Hill Junior College, 1971.

Summersell, Charles. *CSS Alabama: Builder, Captain and Plans*. Tuscaloosa: University of Alabama Press, 1985.

Swanberg, W. A. *First Blood — The Story of Fort Sumter*. New York: Charles Scribner and Sons, 1957.

Thompson, Jerry Don. *Mexican Texans In the Union Army*. Southwestern Studies Series, Number 78. El Paso: University of Texas El Paso Press, 1986.

_____ . *Vaqueros In Blue and Gray*. Austin: Presidial Press, 1987.

Twenty-Second Annual Reunion of the Association of Graduates of the United States Military Academy at West Point, June 12, 1891.

Viele, Egbert L. *Handbook for Active Service*. New York: D. Van Nostrand, 1861.

Warner, Ezra J. *Generals In Blue*. Baton Rouge: Louisiana State University Press, 1964.

_____ . *Generals In Gray*. Baton Rouge: Louisiana State University Press, 1964.

Webb, Walter Prescott, ed. *Handbook of Texas*. Austin: Texas State Historical Association, 1952.

West, John C. *A Texian in Search of a Fight*. Hillsboro, Texas: Hill Junior College, 1969.

Wiggins, Gary. *Dance and Brothers: Texas Gunmakers of the Confederacy*. Orange, Virginia: Moss Publications, 1986.

Wiley, Bell Irwin. *The Life of Johnny Reb*. Indianapolis: Bobbs-Merrill Company, 1943.

Williams, E. W. *With the Border Ruffians*. New York: E. P. Duntton Company, 1907.

Williams, R. H. and Sansom, John W. *The Massacre on the Nueces River*. Grand Prairie, Texas: Frontier Times Publishing House, no date.

Wilson, Francis W. *The Hardeman Impact on Early Texas History*. Privately published, 1986.

Winkler, E. W., ed. *Journal of the Secession Convention of Texas, 1861*. Austin: Austin Printing Company, 1912.

Woodworth, Steven G. *Jefferson Davis and his Generals*. Lawrence: University of Kansas Press, 1990.

Wright, Marcus J. *Texas in the War, 1861-1865*. Edited by Harold Simpson. Hillsboro, Texas: Hill Junior College Press, 1965.

Years, W. Buck, ed. *The Confederate Governors*. Athens: University of Georgia Press, 1985.

Yeary, Mamie, compiler. *Reminiscences of the Boys in Gray, 1861-1865.* McGregor, Texas: Privately published, 1912. Reprint, Dayton: Morningside House, Inc., 1986.

Zuber, William P. *My Eighty Years In Texas.* Edited by Janis Boyle Mayfield. Austin: University of Texas Press, 1971.

ARTICLES

Barr, Alwyn. "Records of the Confederate Military Commission in San Antonio — July 2-October 10, 1862." *Southwestern Historical Quarterly*, Volume 70.

_____ . "The Making of a Secessionist: The Antebellum Career of Roger Q. Mills." *Southwestern Historical Quarterly*. Volume 77.

Betts, Vicki. "Private and Amateur Hangings: The Lynching of W. W. Montgomery, March 15, 1863." *Southwestern Historical Quarterly*. Volume 87.

Bridges, C. A. "The Knights of the Golden Circle: A Filibustering Fantasy." *Southwestern Historical Quarterly*, Volume 44.

Crenshaw, Ollinger. "The Knights of the Golden Circle: The Career of George Bickley." *American Historical Review*, Volume 47.

Crimmins, M. L. "Colonel J. K. F. Mansfield's Report of the Inspection of the Department of Texas in 1856." *Southwestern Historical Quarterly*, Volume 42.

_____ . "Colonel Charles Anderson Opposed Secession in San Antonio." *West Texas Historical Association Year Book*, Volume 29.

Crownover, Sims. "The Battle of Franklin." *Tennessee Historical Quarterly*, Volume 14.

Cumberland, Charles C. "The Confederate Loss and Recapture of Galveston, 1862-1863." *Southwestern Historical Quarterly*, Volume 51.

Dobney, Frederick J. "From Denomenationalism to Nationalism in the Civil War: A Case Study." *Texana*, Volume 9.

Dunn, Roy Sylvan. "The KGC In Texas, 1860-1861." *Southwestern Historical Quarterly*, Volume 70.

Duty, Tony E. "The Home Front: McLennan County in the Civil War." *Texana*, Volume 12.

Elliot, Claude. "Union Sentiment in Texas, 1861-1865." *Southwestern Historical Quarterly*, Volume 50.

Fornell, Earl W. "Texans and Filibusters in the 1850s." *Southwestern Historical Quarterly*, Volume 59.

Garner, Bob. "Let Us Be Patriots and Texans — A Content Analysis of the Secession Rhetoric of Sam Houston, 1854-1861." *Texana*, Volume 12.

Hicks, Jimmie. "Some Letters Concerning the Knights of the Golden Circle in Texas, 1860-1861. *Southwest Historical Quarterly*. Volume 65.

Jager, Ronald B. "Houston, Texas Fights the Civil War." *Texana*, Volume 11.

Kelly, Dayton. "The Texas Brigade at the Wilderness." *Texana*, Volume 11.

Ledbetter, Bill. "Slave Unrest and White Panic: The Impact of Black Republicanism in Antebellum Texas." *Texana*, Volume 10.

Lowe, Richard and Campbell, Randolph. "Wealtholding & Political Power in Antebellum Texas." *Southwestern Historical Quarterly*, Volume 79.

McDonough, James Lee. "The Battle of Franklin." *Blue and Gray Magazine*, Volume II.

McWhiney, Grady. "Historians as Southerners." *Continuity*. Volume 9 (1984).

Orlins, Dr. Alan to editor. *Civil War Magazine*. Volume 8, Number 6, (November-December, 1990).

Paul, William. "Letters of William Paul, Company "E," 64th Illinois Volunteer Infantry." *Camp Chase Gazette*, May, 1975.

"Revisiting the Civil War." *Newsweek*, October 8, 1990.

Rippy, James Ford. "Border Troubles Along the Rio Grande, 1848-1860." *Southwestern Historical Quarterly*, Volume 70.

Roth, David E. "The Mysteries of Spring Hill, Tennessee." *Blue and Gray Magazine*, Volume II.

Sandbo, Anna Irene. "Beginnings of the Secession Movement of Texas." *Southwestern Historical Quarterly*, Volume 17.

_____ . "The First Session of the Secession Convention of Texas." *Southwestern Historical Quarterly*, Volume 18.

Simmons, Laura. "Waul's Legion From Texas to Mississippi." *Texana*, Volume 7.

Smith, David P. "Civil War Letters of Sam Houston." *Southwestern Historical Quarterly*, Volume 81.

Smyrl, Frank H. "Texans in the Union Army." *Southwestern Historical Quarterly*, Volume 75.

Thompson, Jerry Don. "Mexican-Americans in the Civil War: The Battle of Val Verde." *Texana*, Volume 10.

Ticknor, Philip C. "The United States Gunboat Harriet Lane." *Southwestern Historical Quarterly*, Volume 21.

Turner, Jim. "Jim Turner, Company G, 6th Texas Infantry, CSA." *Texana*, Volume 7.

Weinert, Richard P., Jr. "The Confederate Regular Cavalry." *Texana*, Volume 10.

Williams, Robert W. & Wooster, Ralph A. "Life In Civil War Central Texas." *Texana*, Volume 7.

Young, Kevin R., "Major Babbit and the Alamo Hump." *Military Images*, Number 6 (July-August, 1984).

NEWSPAPERS

Houston Tri-Weekly News,	January 6, 1863
Houston Tri-Weekly News,	January 10, 1863
Houston Tri-Weekly Telegraph,	February 1, 1865
Houston Tri-Weekly Telegraph,	March 1, 1865
Houston Tri-Weekly Telegraph,	April 10, 1865
Indianola Courier,	November 24, 1860
Memphis Bulletine,	October 14, 1862
New Orleans Crescent,	January 27, 1867
San Antonio Alamo Express,	August 18,1860
San Antonio Alamo Express,	August 25, 1860
San Antonio Alamo Express,	February 19, 1861
San Antonio Alamo Express,	February 23, 1861
San Antonio Alamo Express,	February 25, 1861
San Antonio Alamo Express,	March 4, 1861
San Antonio Alamo Express,	May 13, 1861
San Antonio Express,	October 10, 1890.
San Antonio Citizen League,	July 9, 1914.
Seguin Southern Confederacy,	February 22, 1861

UNPUBLISHED

Hunt, Jeffrey W. "There Is Nothing Left to us But to Fight: The Battle of Palmetto Ranch."

Index